THE FIRE OF HEAVEN

A Jack Dantzler Mystery

TOM WALLACE

Hydra
Publications

CRITICS PRAISE FOR THE JACK DANTZLER MYSTERIES

Critics praise for

Jack Dantzler mysteries

THE FIRE OF HEAVEN

The Fire of Heaven pulls you in right from the very first paragraph . . . Tom Wallace also created an entire cast of memorable characters without taking the focus off (Jack) Dantzler . . . the author fantastically weaves several murders together in a way that keeps you guessing who the real killer is and what his or her motives could be . . . I can't wait to see who Dantzler tangles with next.

   —Natasha Jackson (Readers' Favorite)

THE LIST

"*The List* contains all the must-haves of the thriller genre—danger, intrigue and suspense. Powerful villains. Exciting action scenes. Anticipation. . . Tom Wallace excels is in his ability to make his characters come alive. As with Wallace's previous thriller, *Gnosis*, I ended up finishing this book in less than two days. This book makes for an absorbing and enjoyable read, the kind that had me incessantly turning the pages.

--Mary Fan

"*The List* is a fast-paced, thrilling read. It takes the reader on a journey of intrigue immersed in political and corporate greed. Detective Jack Dantzler's quest to solve the mystery behind his parent's deaths thrusts him into a world of international crime. It has graphic detail but it is perfectly balanced as the story of death, fear and reprisal unfolds. Not a book for the faint of heart."

--Patricia Day (Readers Favorites)

GNOSIS

"A page-turner. *Gnosis* is a book that's virtually impossible to walk away from."

--Mary Fan

"The book features cerebral challenges for readers who like their murder mysteries served Kentucky-style."

--Kentucky Monthly Magazine

THE DEVIL'S RACKET

"BRAVO!! By far the best book ever. Jack Dantzler is a complicated man and a unique detective with a long shelf life, reminiscent of Michael Connelly's Harry Bosch. *The Devil's Racket* grabbed me from the beginning and it held me to the end. This is a book that you will want to read and pass on to your friends and family. What we have here is a winner."

--MyShelf.com

"Central Kentucky's stunningly beautiful horse farms are the picture of serenity and refinement, but who knows what evil lurks beyond those four-board fences? Enjoy the ride, although it's bumpy and bloody. It just might give you a shiver as you drive past the next pretty horse farm—so pretty, it's, well, scary."

--Lexington Herald-Leader

WHAT MATTERS BLOOD

"A masterpiece of murder. Jack Dantzler is a complicated man and a unique detective with a long shelf life, reminiscent of Michael Connelly's Harry Bosch. I suspect Dantzler will be around for quite a while. HIGHEST RECOMMENDATION."

--MyShelf.com

"Tom Wallace delivers a wallop of a thrill with *What Matters Blood*. With masterful characterization, his portrayal of the serial killer is chilling, as well as authentic, enough to elicit goose bumps. The story is fast-paced, the dialogue realistic, and the search for the killer intriguing. One galvanizing read that will hold the reader's interest throughout."

--Midwest Book Review

ALSO BY

Tom Wallace

———

COPYRIGHT

ISBN-13: 978-1-942212-86-7

Second Edition

Hydra
Publications

Goshen, KY 40026
www.hydrapublications.com

For my sister-in-law Wanda Underwood
and my brother-in-law Ed Watson

CHAPTER ONE

J ack Dantzler had no plans for going out tonight. Stay in, kick back, order a pizza, pop in a movie, maybe *Heat* for the umpteenth time, and watch *Godfather's* Pacino and De Niro give a classic acting lesson in their first-ever shared scene. A second possibility: *Miller's Crossing*, which he judged to be the eccentric Coen Brothers' greatest achievement. Either choice a winner.

With Laurie out of town—one week through a four-week training seminar at Quantico—and with no active homicide investigations to work, he was experiencing that rarest of circumstances: free time, alone.

His time.

Dantzler was seldom happier or more fulfilled than during those hours, days and weeks when matching wits with a murderer. Putting scumbags away was his calling, his duty, his responsibility. It was righteous work in every way. But this time alone, with absolute freedom to do as he wished, to come and go as he chose, this autonomy over his own life, was not something to be taken lightly or for granted.

It was a luxury and should be appreciated as such.

In the end, however, his work would eventually be an unwelcomed intruder. Work would end his quiet sabbatical. Dantzler knew this with absolute certainty. Already, somewhere in the dark corners of Lexington, the grim elixir for future homicides was surely brewing, concocted by men and women filled with anger, hate, greed, rage, jealousy and stupidity. It would all close in on him soon enough. Chew into his time, take his own life away from him, once again making him captive to circumstances, deeds and actions created by men and women he didn't know, or ever cared to know.

In short, bring him back into the real world.

But on this Saturday night his time belonged solely to him. He was going to enjoy it to the fullest.

Dantzler nixed ordering a pizza on the grounds that it was too late for food so heavy and cholesterol-rich. Tonight, he would make the healthy decision and give his arteries a break. Instead, he mixed a Pernod and orange juice (good for the arteries, maybe, but not so good for the liver), popped in a Leonard Cohen CD and flopped down on the sofa. Cohen, the brilliant Canadian poet, was Dantzler's all-time favorite singer-songwriter, and had been for more than thirty-five years. As Cohen's raspy, cigarette-ravaged voice sang *In My Secret Life*, Dantzler sipped his drink, leaned back, closed his eyes and listened.

Looked through the paper, makes you want to cry; nobody cares if the people live or die.

Can't agree with you on that one, Leonard, Dantzler thought to himself. Some of us do care. Some of us make our living by caring.

Sometimes too much, in fact.

Caring too much was both the blessing and the curse for any good homicide detective. And Dantzler was, even by his own reckoning, one of the very best.

The doorbell rang so softly Dantzler wasn't sure if the sound was real or part of the song. He raised himself to a sitting position, set his glass down and glanced at the clock above the TV. Eight forty-five. Kind of late for a visit. As a detective who had put away dozens of violent criminals, he was naturally wary of unannounced callers, especially those who showed up after dark. There was always the chance one of the bad guys he had put away, one who had sworn revenge, might be the person knocking on his door.

Striding across the room, he mentally ran through a short list of possible late-night visitors. Richard Bird, head of the Homicide Department, topped the list. This unusual lull in criminal activity had also provided Bird with more free time on his hands than normal, so perhaps he wanted to drop by for some small talk. Or maybe it was David Bloom, the psychiatrist and Dantzler's old college tennis teammate. Could be he was in search of a late-night tennis match. The third possibility was his uncle Tommy Blake. But that was unlikely. At eight forty-five on a Saturday night—on *any* night, for that matter— Tommy was well into a fifth of Jim Beam, using alcohol to fend off the legions of personal demons that haunted him twenty-four hours a day.

But Dantzler's hunches were wrong. Opening the door, he was surprised to find a tall, very pretty, dark-haired young woman standing in front of him. She was dressed in Levis, a blue University of Kentucky sweatshirt, white Nikes. A red baseball cap bearing the logo for Devonshire Farm cast a shadow over her eyes. Standing there, she shifted nervously from side to side as though she was somehow trying to balance herself, and she constantly rubbed her hands together.

Dantzler didn't recognize the woman but he did recognize the logo on her cap. Devonshire Farm was owned and operated by Amy and Nick Curtis. Amy was Milt Brewer's youngest daughter. Milt was the senior member of the Homicide squad.

"I know it's late," she said, before Dantzler had the door completely open, "but I would really like to speak with you. It's a matter of some importance. Well, it's important to me. However, I'll understand if you think it's too late. Just give the word and I'll scram."

"What do you want to talk about?"

"Please, if you don't mind." She looked over her shoulder. "I would really feel more comfortable discussing this inside rather than out here."

"Are you being followed?"

She seemed surprised by the question. "No . . . I don't think so. Why do you ask?"

"You're acting a little skittish, that's all."

"No . . . no, I'm fine. I just need to speak with you, if it's okay."

Dantzler waved her inside, closed the door and followed her into the living room. She moved quickly, with the grace of an athlete, purpose in her stride. She sat on the couch, removed her baseball cap, unleashing a mountain of piled-up brown hair, leaned back and let out a deep sigh.

"You okay?" Dantzler asked. He sat in the leather chair across from her. "You appear to be a little . . . stressed."

She let out a deeper sigh, and for an instant Dantzler was certain she was going to cry. But whatever moment of weakness she felt quickly passed, replaced by a look of steely resolve in her bright hazel eyes. After several seconds, the frown melted and her lips curved into a slight grin.

"You really must think I'm nuts, coming here this late at night." Her grin broke into a full-fledged smile. "A complete and total stranger just barging in like this."

Dantzler shrugged. What could he say? At the moment, nuts wasn't entirely out of the question.

"I suppose you're asking yourself why I'm here," she continued. "Well . . ."

"Actually, I'm asking myself who you are."

"Oh, yeah, I guess I should identify myself. It's just that, well, we met several years ago, and I thought you might remember me. But . . . that's a pretty stupid assumption on my part. We only met for a few minutes."

Dantzler pointed to the baseball cap she held in her hands. "Obviously, you know Amy and Nick Curtis," he said.

"Yes, yes, I do. And that's where we met. On their farm nine or ten years ago, while I was still in college. I spent two summers working for Amy and Nick. Doing odd jobs, feeding the horses, mucking stalls— that kind of stuff. You came to the farm for a visit. It was just after you'd cleared a big case. I remember Amy telling me you were the youngest detective to ever get a gold shield. In Lexington, I mean. Amy said you are a great cop, better even than her father."

"Prejudicial testimony, I'm afraid. You see, I'm Amy's godfather. So, anything she says about me wouldn't hold up in a court of law, Miz . . ."

"Nikki . . . with two Ks . . . Bradford."

"Okay, Nikki with two Ks, now that we've solved that mystery, let's move on to the next one. Why *are* you here?"

"Because I want you to investigate a death."

Dantzler had readied himself for a thousand possible answers to his question. Investigating a death hadn't been on his list.

Nuts was definitely the early leader in the clubhouse.

"Whose death?"

"My former partner. Danny Tucker."

Danny Tucker. The name clanged around inside Dantzler's head like a pinball. He'd heard it somewhere, recently, but . . . where, when, in what context? TV? Newspaper? The office? Bar conversation? Where? The answer was tantalizingly close, but for now he couldn't locate it.

"You and Danny Tucker were partners?"

"Yes."

"As in living together?" Dantzler said.

"Oh, no, no. Partners, as in we worked together. When he was still with the Sheriff's Department. I'm still with the Department, but . . . in fact, we joined the Sheriff's Department on the same day. Back in oh-five." Nikki looked down at the floor, then back up at Dantzler. "We weren't full-time partners, but we did work together on several occasions. Until . . ."

"Until his death?"

"No. Until he left the Sheriff's Department and went to work for the State Police."

"When was this?"

"Two years ago."

"Why the switch?"

"Purely a matter of finances. Danny made several thousand more a year working for the State Police. He got married about the same time, so he needed the extra money."

Danny Tucker. "How and when did Danny die?" Dantzler said, still trying to place the name.

"Two weeks ago. Ruled a suicide."

The pinball stopped clanging, memory cells clicked. *Danny Tucker.* Sure, the young cop who offed himself. Dantzler recalled reading about it in the papers and hearing about it on the tube. But the details of what he remembered were sketchy, fragmented. It happened in the house, Danny Tucker's body was found a day or so later by . . . who?

That particular detail Dantzler couldn't recall. He also couldn't recall the manner of death.

Dantzler said, "The way you say the word suicide, I get the distinct impression you disagree with that conclusion."

Nikki nodded quickly. "Most definitely. No way Danny took his own life."

"Cops have a high suicide rate, Nikki. It's a sad fact of life. Maybe the job got the best of Danny, drove him to the point where he felt he had no choice but to eat his gun. Unfortunately, it happens all too often in this business."

"But Danny didn't eat his gun. He didn't slash his wrists, and he didn't lock himself in the garage and leave the motor running. He . . . "

Nikki looked straight into Dantzler's eyes.

". . . died as a result of poisoning. Cyanide, to be exact."

"That's certainly not your garden variety method of suicide, that's for sure."

"Because it wasn't suicide."

"Then it's either accidental or a homicide. There's not much else left in between."

"Danny Tucker was murdered," Nikki said. "I believe it with every fiber in my being."

"What was the coroner's ruling?"

Nikki snickered and rolled her eyes, at the same time raising both hands in a they're-all-idiots gesture. "Suicide. Danny put cyanide in his coffee, drank it, died. Simple as that. And, of course, the department signed off on it. Couldn't shut it down quick enough. Unhappy, depressed young cop, stressed out, couldn't handle the pressure, checked himself out. A terrible tragedy, we offer our prayers for his family and friends, now let's move on. Pure party-line bullshit."

"Every suspicious death is considered a potential homicide until proven otherwise," Dantzler pointed out. "As such, I should have been involved in the investigation. I wasn't, and as far as I know, no one from the department was. Any reason why we weren't involved?"

"Danny and Anna lived in Lexington," Nikki answered.

"Anna is . . .?"

"Danny's wife. But Danny died at his parents' home in Versailles. I don't guess you work Woodford County."

"No, I don't. Why was he at their house? And where were they on the day Danny died?"

"They were in Florida. With them gone, and with Anna out of town, Danny was staying at his parents' farm. They have a few horses, so Danny was taking care of them."

"Do you know who did investigate?" Dantzler asked.

"A detective named Amos Garland. Do you know him?"

"We've met, but I don't know much about him."

"Will you speak with him? Get his take on what happened?"

Dantzler let out a heavy sigh. He suddenly felt the need for another drink. Maybe several more. What he didn't need was to be trapped in his living room at nine o'clock listening to a disillusioned cop regurgitate the details of a former partner's death. He wanted to tell her to hit the road, to forget about sticking her nose into dark corners, to simply leave things as they now stand. To go home and get on with her life.

But—

He wouldn't tell her to leave. Couldn't. And he knew why, too. Like it or not, he was intrigued. Cop, suicide—not exactly earth-shattering news. Happens all the time. But cyanide? That's a worm in the salad. A foul ball. He'd never heard of a law enforcement officer using any poison to check himself out, much less cyanide. Cyanide was what the Nazi thugs took rather than face a trial and execution. But a cop? Didn't figure.

There was something else, too. Nikki was so damn earnest it was virtually impossible not to fall in step with her. She believed the sermon she was preaching. Absolutely, totally believed it. And her enthusiasm made you *want* to believe it. She was like a Girl Scout hawking those damn cookies nobody really wants or needs but buys anyway. You want to say no, but you can't quite make yourself do it.

"Would you care for something to drink, Nikki?" Dantzler said, standing. "Pepsi, Ginger Ale, water? Beer, if you are brave enough to try a Guinness?"

"Are you having something?"

After giving serious consideration to a Guinness, he finally said, "Pepsi."

"Pepsi sounds good."

Dantzler went into the kitchen, filled two glasses with ice and Pepsi, came back into the living room and handed a glass to Nikki. She took it from him, said thanks, took a quick sip and held the glass in both hands.

"So . . . honestly. Do you think I'm nuts?"

Dantzler laughed. "Nuts? No. Misguided? Likely."

"I'm not nuts, and I'm not misguided. I'm right."

"Give me two solid reasons why you don't think Danny Tucker committed suicide. Something more concrete than 'no way Danny would take his own life.'"

Nikki seemed energized by the question. "One: Danny genuinely loved his job and was about to be promoted to sergeant. Two: Danny found out a week before his death that he was going to be a father for the first time. He was absolutely thrilled, overjoyed at the prospect of becoming a dad. And for a kicker, Danny recently applied for admission to graduate school. He wanted to get his master's in Criminology and then eventually go to law school. His ultimate goal was the FBI. No one with plans and dreams like those would kill himself."

"That's not necessarily true, Nikki. Depression, if it's severe enough, can easily overpower things like dreams and plans."

"Well, it's true in this instance. Danny was anything but depressed."

"When was the last time you spoke with Danny?"

"Three days before his death. We met at Wendy's for morning coffee. I've never seen Danny in a more upbeat, positive mood. He was literally on top of the world. Then—"

Nikki took another drink and looked down at the floor. Her eyes filled with tears.

"Who discovered the body?" Dantzler asked.

"When Danny failed to show up for work or answer his phone, his captain sent one of the guys over to the house. He found the body."

"Inside or outside?"

"Danny was inside. In the kitchen."

"No. The guy who found him. Did he see the body through a

window and then break down the door to gain entrance? Or was the door unlocked, he went inside and found Danny?"

"I'm not sure. Does it matter?"

"Everything matters when you're trying to uncover the truth." Dantzler finished off the last drops of Pepsi, set the glass on an end table. "Where was Danny's wife?"

"Out of town. Visiting relatives in Chicago, if I remember correctly."

"Is she from Chicago?"

"No. Anna is originally from Alabama. Her father is a minister, heads one of those big mega-churches. Birmingham, I think. But I could be wrong. Somewhere in Alabama, though."

"How well do you know her?"

Nikki shrugged. "Not very well. She's, ah, well, she's kinda distant. Not an easy person to get to know. Very serious, very reserved."

"Sounds like you don't like her."

"I really don't know her well enough to say one way or the other. What I will say is she's definitely not the type of woman I expected Danny to fall in love with."

"Why not?"

"Danny was just so . . . so damn nice. Laid-back, funny, kind, friendly to everyone. Just a sweet, down-to-earth good guy. Anna's different. She's the exact opposite in almost every respect. Cold, distant, arrogant. There's a, I don't know, an air of superiority about her. Like she's better than everyone else."

"I'm guessing you see her as a first-class bitch. Right?"

"With a capital B."

"Could she have killed him?"

"I don't think so. I mean, *why* would she want him dead? Danny didn't have any money, any property, anything of real value. He was like the rest of us—just scraping by. I don't know how much money Anna's family has, but I have to believe it's more than Danny had."

"Homicide wears a million different disguises, Nikki. It only takes one to get the job done. And money isn't always the one that rules the day."

"But," Nikki reminded, "the cyanide was in his coffee. And he made the coffee on the morning he died. Anna was in Chicago. Wouldn't that effectively rule her out as a suspect?"

"Are you positive he made the coffee that morning? Or are you assuming he did?"

"Well . . . assume, I guess."

"Was there coffee remaining in the pot?"

"I don't know. Why?"

"It would be interesting to know if all the coffee contained poison, or if the poison was only in the coffee in his cup."

"My guess would be the poison was in all the coffee."

"Facts solve homicide investigations, Nikki. Not guesses."

Nikki placed her glass on the end table, leaned forward, her hands clasped together. "Will you look into Danny's death for me? If you will, I'm positive you'll find out I'm right. Danny was murdered."

"Have you spoken with Danny's family since his death?"

"Yes. Several times."

"How do they feel about it?"

"They believe the report, that Danny took his own life. But they are in such a state of shock I don't think they have really considered other possibilities."

"What about Anna? You spoken to her?"

"Once. She's in agreement with the family. But the M.E. is wrong. Danny did not commit suicide. Will you look into it?"

"I don't know, Nikki. Medical examiners are pretty sharp people. They don't make many mistakes. When they sign off on a case, it means they are confident in their findings."

Dantzler immediately realized his ringing endorsement of the Woodford County medical examiner had been given more out of habit than fact. This was based on his long association with Mac Tinsley, the veteran Fayette County M.E., who was quite simply the best. But things had recently changed in the coroner's office, and Dantzler, like everyone else, was having a difficult time adjusting. Mac, who worked the job for almost four decades, had retired, replaced less than two months ago by a young man named Arnie Edwards. From the reports turned in by Dantzler's colleagues, and from his own admittedly brief encounters with Mac's replacement, one fact had emerged—the jury was still out on Arnie. Unlike Mac, whose word was gold, Arnie still had to prove himself before his views and opinions were accepted outright.

Dantzler considered the possibility that he was giving the Woodford County coroner more credit than he deserved based on his tremendous respect for Mac Tinsley. That could be an error in judgment. All coroners are not created equal. Dantzler wouldn't be able to judge until after meeting with the man. Only then could he make a fair and accurate assessment.

"The medical examiner is wrong," Nikki protested, "I don't care how good he is. Please, Detective Dantzler, I need you to do this for me. I need your help, your eyes. You can see through the bullshit, find the truth."

"Maybe the truth is, Danny really did kill himself. And for whatever reason you're blind to the truth."

"Then prove it to me. If you look into it, if you find that Danny really did commit suicide, then I can live with it. But until then, I can't. I won't."

"I'll think about," Dantzler said. "But no promises."

"Thanks. That's all I can ask."

"If I do decide to look into it, is there anyone with the State Police who would be willing to discuss the situation?"

Nikki answered without thinking. "Lucian White. He and Danny were pretty tight. Lucian says he agrees with the official report, but I don't think he really buys it. I think it's a matter of him being afraid to go against the party line. Like I said, they were quick to bring it to a close."

"Were Lucian and Danny partners?"

"No, Lucian was, you know, like a big brother to Danny. A mentor."

"He could be risking his job, talking to an outsider about the case without permission. He'd need to consider that before making any decisions."

"Lucian will help—I know he will. He really cared for Danny."

"Was Lucian the one who found Danny's body?"

"Keith Davis did. And I'm not sure how cooperative he'll be. Keith's . . . well, he always thinks about Keith Davis first."

Dantzler opened the door and walked Nikki to her car. When she got in, he said, "Can you think of anyone who *would* want to kill Danny? Anyone who would benefit from his death?"

Nikki shook her head as she started the car. "No, I absolutely cannot. I've racked my brain a hundred times and I can't come up with a single name. Everybody loved Danny. Everybody."

Not everybody, Dantzler thought, as he watched her drive off into the night.

CHAPTER TWO

For the next hour Dantzler sat at his computer searching through cyberspace for stories relating to Danny Tucker. He didn't expect much, and he wasn't surprised or disappointed when his prediction came true. The information highway yielded little in the way of details concerning Nikki's friend and ex-partner. Only two hits, both reprints of articles appearing in the *Herald-Leader*. Neither offered much in the way of pertinent or useful information.

The first article, which appeared in the May 4 edition, the day after Danny's death, provided a quick overview of what happened: Danny Tucker, 31, a two-year member of the Kentucky State Police, was found dead at his parents' residence in Versailles at approximately 10:30 yesterday morning. His body was discovered in the kitchen by a fellow officer sent to the house on Cedar Ridge Lane after Tucker failed to show up for work or answer his phone. Cause of death was not immediately known, but according to a KSP spokesman, "this tragedy has all the earmarks of a suicide." The spokesman went on to say there would be a full and thorough investigation, but foul play was not suspected at this time. The article listed Danny's next of kin: wife Anna, who is three months pregnant with the couple's first child, parents Wendell and Naomi Tucker, and sister, Kelly Tucker. Funeral arrangements were still pending at the time the article was written.

The second article, found in the Briefs Section four days later, was primarily limited to a quote from the coroner, Malcolm Kinnison, stating he had officially ruled Danny Tucker's death a suicide. No manner of death was given.

Cyanide.

Dantzler considered the possibility.

Then quickly dismissed it.

He wondered if Danny Tucker even knew what cyanide was. And if Danny did know, he damn sure didn't use it to commit suicide.

Had to be murder.

Dantzler shut down the computer, stood and stretched his legs. Although it was almost two in the morning, he was wired. No surprise there. Homicide investigations had a way of getting his adrenaline flowing, his blood pumping, his mind racing. It had been this way since he first joined the Homicide unit more than twenty-five years ago, and it wasn't likely to change. For him, each homicide investigation was a battle, both personal and professional, that had to be won. When you speak for the dead you simply cannot fail.

First thing Monday morning he would make a few phone calls, do some background research, and see what might be hidden under the rocks. But doing so meant looking into a case that happened in another county. A closed case, at that, and one involving a fellow law enforcement officer. He would have to dance carefully, making sure he didn't step on anyone's toes. He had to show respect, and the only way to do so was to go through proper channels. Talk to Captain Bird, have him contact his counterpart in Woodford County and, hopefully, get permission to speak with Amos Garland and the coroner.

By the book, on the up and up, professional. Exactly the way he would expect it done if an outsider wanted to look into one of his cases. Judiciously courteous.

Dantzler grabbed a bottle of water from the fridge and went out onto the deck, which overlooked the lake that bumped up against his back yard. The night was cool, the air crisp and clean. With the moon hidden behind a wall of black clouds, the water looked like black ice.

The loons and crickets, a normally rowdy lot, had tucked it in for the night. There was nothing but darkness and silence.

Falling into a recliner, Dantzler thought about his conversation with Nikki Bradford. He not only thought about what was said, but also what had gone unmentioned. Specifically, a trio of factors he had not discussed with Nikki that could be important.

First: What was Nikki's real relationship with Danny Tucker? She said they were former co-workers, and although she never specifically said they were close friends, a strong friendship had been implied. But was it more than friendship? Did Nikki feel a romantic attachment to Danny? And vice versa? Were they romantically involved? Having an affair? Could jealousy be at the heart of Nikki's obvious dislike for Anna? Especially now that Anna is carrying Danny's child?

That possibility couldn't be dismissed.

Second: What if Danny Tucker wasn't the intended target? There was every bit as much reason to think Danny wasn't the one who was supposed to swallow the deadly poison as there was reason to believe it was meant for him. To make the assumption Danny was the intended target, which the Woodford County folks and the State Police had obviously made, required a leap Dantzler wasn't ready to take. After all, the murder—if it was a homicide—happened at Danny's parents' farm. What if one or both of the elder Tuckers were the actual targets? Maybe someone had it in for them, for whatever reason. Or maybe there was no one from the outside. What if Mom, wanting to get rid of dear old Dad, made the coffee with the cyanide in it, then forgot about it when the couple left town? Or maybe Dad had grown tired of listening to Mom's incessant nagging and he doctored the coffee. Either way, Danny comes to stay, gets up in the morning, drinks the deadly potion and dies. A tragic case of being at the wrong place at the wrong time.

Third: What if Kelly Tucker wanted Mom and Pop out of the way? Having grown tired of being bossed around by the parental unit, maybe she sought to free herself from their shackles and chains. What if the Tuckers were worth more monetarily than Nikki said and Kelly wanted her share? The Tuckers did own land, and since God's not making any more of it, that could translate into serious money. What if

Kelly wanted to speed up her inheritance? What if she put the poison in the coffee?

What if? The two most prominent words at the start of any homicide investigation.

Feeling the chill begin to bite at his bones, Dantzler went into the bedroom, grabbed a sweatshirt from the back of a chair and slipped it on. He then went into the den, picked up a legal pad and pen, went back onto the deck, sat and began jotting down his thoughts on the Danny Tucker case. His three previous scenarios headed his list, followed by the names of family members and officials he would need to contact and interview.

- Malcolm Kinnison
- Amos Garland
- Anna Tucker
- Danny's parents
- Kelly Tucker
- Danny's Captain
- Lucian White
- Keith Davis

Of course, beginning an investigation was contingent upon getting Captain Bird's approval and the cooperation of Woodford County law enforcement officials. Dantzler was well aware that those two hurdles might be easier to clear than getting cooperation from the State Police. If Nikki Bradford was right, and the State Police had rushed to judgment in an attempt to quell an investigation, then getting their assistance might be problematic. But Dantzler had his doubts about this. Over the years he had interacted with the State Police on numerous occasions, and they had always been professional, helpful and cooperative. He simply couldn't imagine them *not* wanting to uncover the truth.

Dantzler had just finished writing when his cell phone chirped, startling him. He laid down the legal pad, picked up the phone and flipped it open. The caller was Captain Bird.

"Jack," Bird said, before Dantzler could speak, "sorry to wake you at this ungodly hour, but—"

"You didn't wake me, Rich. I'm sitting out on the deck."

"You just get back from some late-night tennis?"

"Nah. I'm relaxing, pondering the deep mysteries of the universe."

"At two in the morning most sane people are more than willing to let those mysteries wait. I'd wager a princely sum that Stephen Hawking is sound asleep even as we speak."

"You don't have a princely sum, Rich. Besides, this is Sunday. I can sleep in."

"Well, sorry to burst your bubble, but you ain't sleeping in today. As I'm sure you have already deduced, this isn't a casual call. Hell, I don't make casual calls at two a.m."

"I didn't think so. What's up?"

"Have you been watching TV tonight?" Bird asked. "The late news?"

"Haven't had it on. Why? What happened?"

"There was a huge explosion and massive fire out in Hamburg. Star Shoot Parkway, just off of Sir Barton Way. Happened around eleven, eleven-thirty. The Wiseman Health Clinic. Place blew up, was reduced to ashes within minutes. Firefighters had no chance of saving anything. All they could do was hope to contain the fire and keep it from spreading. Fortunately, the clinic was on a fairly large piece of property located a substantial distance away from other offices, retail stores and apartment complexes. Luckily, other damage was limited to a few windows shattered by the blast."

"What are the arson guys saying? Or is it too early to know anything?"

"According to Pug Tankersly, the device was most likely a cheap homemade bomb of some sort. Cheap, but powerful enough to get the job done. There was also a lot of accelerant involved, probably gasoline. Whoever did this was hell bent on making certain the clinic was completely destroyed."

"Sounds like they succeeded."

"Unfortunately, there's more. A body was found inside and . . ."

"Rafe?"

"Rafe? You mean Dr. Raphael Wiseman?" Bird said.

"Yeah, Rafe. Rafe Wiseman."

"How do you know him?"

"From the Center." Dantzler was referring to the Lexington Tennis Center, of which he was part owner. "He plays there quite a bit. Mostly doubles with David Bloom. Is Rafe the victim?"

"No, it wasn't Dr. Wiseman. In fact, he's already at the scene."

"Who is the victim?"

"Good question. The body was badly charred, a real crispy critter. Pug says they can't tell if it's a male or female. And Dr. Wiseman claims none of the clinic employees should have been there at such a late hour on a Saturday night or Sunday morning. He has no clue who the victim might be."

"He needs to phone his employees, get them all accounted for," Dantzler suggested.

"Yeah. And you need to give your guys a call and get them to the scene ASAP. Looks like our homicide vacation is over."

"I'll call Eric and Milt, have them meet me there. Laurie and Scott are at Quantico for another three weeks, so if this gets complicated, I may have to pull someone from Robbery to fill in. Maybe Jake Thomas. He's a sharp guy."

"I'll arrange for Jake," Bird said. "That shouldn't be a problem. But why call Milt at two a.m.? Hell, he's retiring in two weeks. Let him sleep in. He can stand to miss one homicide."

"Are you kidding? If I don't include Milt, we'll never hear the last of it. You know how he is."

Bird chuckled. "Yeah, you're right about Milt. Assemble your team and see what you can find out. You won't get Jake until Monday morning, so you can brief him when you meet with me."

"Sounds good," Dantzler said, adding, "you know, of all the different types of homicide investigations we work, the ones I hate the most are those involving burn victims. Blood, guts, shit, brains—that stuff is bad enough. But a charred body bothers me the most."

"Well, from what I'm hearing, this one isn't going to make you feel any better."

After hanging up with Bird, Dantzler ripped out the two pages of notes he'd written about Danny Tucker and placed them inside a manila folder. He went into the den and put the folder next to his computer. As he opened his phone and began punching in Eric Gamble's number, a single thought crossed his mind.

A macabre thought.

Danny Tucker's case was now on the back burner.

CHAPTER THREE

B y the time Dantzler arrived at the scene it was just past three a.m and the blaze had all but been extinguished. A few small fires smoldered beneath the rubble, and a thick wall of white smoke rose like a ghostly cloud toward the night sky, but the damage, although extensive, wasn't nearly as bad as Dantzler had expected it to be. All surrounding properties had thankfully been spared both fire and water damage. The Fire Department guys, always quick to the scene, had obviously done outstanding work containing the flames.

Dantzler parked next to one of the fire trucks, got out, put on a light windbreaker and grabbed his briefcase. Off to his right he saw Dr. Raphael Wiseman talking on his cell phone. Wiseman was in his late fifties but looked much younger. He had a slight build, deeply tanned skin, a prominent nose and jet black hair. Dressed in beige khakis, a blue button-down shirt with the collar open, brown sport coat and Italian loafers, he paced nervously, head down while punching in a new number.

Dantzler decided to hold off interviewing Wiseman until he had been given an assessment of the situation by someone from the Fire Department. Doing so would serve a two-fold purpose: Dantzler would have a better understanding of what had happened, and the more information he could gather translated into a better set of intelligent questions for Dr. Wiseman.

Looking up, Dantzler saw Frank "Pug" Tankersly, the lead arson investigator, headed in his direction. If ever there was a perfect pairing between a man's name and his physique, this was it. Pug was sixty-two, five-seven, two-hundred-ten pounds and built like a block of granite. There was not an ounce of fat on the man. A former all-star football player and wrestler, Pug, "Tank" to his co-workers, had stone pillar legs, Popeye forearms, no neck and a square head topped off by yellowish hair cut in a 1950s style flattop. An ex-Marine who served in Vietnam, he exuded strength and power and menace. Despite all outward appearances, which at first glance seemed threatening and intimidating, he was known as one of the kindest, most gentle humans you were ever likely to cross paths with. He was also highly respected for his intelligence and his ability to do his job.

"Well, well, Jack Dantzler, the ace of aces," Tank said, grinning. He removed a blue bandana from his pocket and wiped perspiration from his face, smearing streaks of gray soot on his forehead and cheeks. "Are you still crushing all challengers on the tennis court? Or has Father Time finally caught up with you and reduced you to a mere mortal like the rest of us?"

"Still the best in town, Tank," Dantzler answered. "Today, anyway. Who knows what tomorrow will bring?"

"Like the wise man said, Ace. Tomorrow is another day."

"You've seen those old Western movies, Tank. The ones where a young gunslinger is hell bent on putting the top guy away. Some hot shot looking to carve the big notch on his gun. Or in this instance, on his tennis racket. Maybe tomorrow I'll run into that guy. But I doubt it."

"Modest bastard, you are. Just shows some things never change."

"When you've got it, flaunt it. Right, Tank?"

"Wouldn't know. I never had it, whatever *it* is." Tank pointed to his left. "Is that Dr. Wiseman?"

Dantzler nodded.

"Is he trying to contact his employees?" Tank asked.

Dantzler was about to answer but hesitated when he noticed Eric

Gamble and Milt Brewer coming in his direction. The two men had arrived at the same time but in different cars. This told Dantzler that they had come straight from home without having first stopped by the police station.

Despite the late hour, Eric, as always, was dressed like he just walked out of a GQ photo shoot. Sharply creased charcoal slacks, red silk shirt, blue blazer, loafers. The ensemble, Dantzler guessed, cost more than his entire wardrobe.

Conversely, Milt looked like he tumbled out of bed and had grabbed the first pieces of clothing he could find. He wore rumpled jeans, a white long sleeve cotton shirt, a hooded sweatshirt and tennis shoes. His ensemble probably cost less than Eric's belt. Milt, the Homicide unit's senior detective, looked like a walking advertisement for the latest "blue light" special at Kmart.

"Denzel Washington and Walter Matthau have arrived," Tank said, shaking hands with the two men. "My night is now complete."

"How long have we known each other, Tank?" Milt asked.

"I dunno, what . . . thirty-five or forty years. Since we both got back from Nam."

"Sounds about right. And you want to know something, Tank? I didn't like you then, and I don't like you now."

"How could anyone *not* like me, Milt? Guy with my charm, my looks, my *panache*?"

Milt reached out and pinched Tank's cheek. "You're a real puppy dog, Tank. Just like Lassie."

"Gimme a break, Milt. If you're gonna compare me to a canine, at least make it one with some real *cojones*. Rin Tin Tin, maybe. Not Lassie."

"How about Scooby-Doo?" Eric said. "He's goofy but kinda smart. Like you."

Tank leaned back and assessed Eric from head to toe. "Judging by those threads you're wearing, Denzel, you must be raking in the bread from that book of yours. You gonna make enough moolah to quit this gig and write full-time?"

Tank was referring to Eric's detective novel that had been published five months ago.

"Quit this?" Eric said, waving toward the smoke. "And miss being called to crime scenes at three in the morning? Miss associating with a prince like you? Why would I even think of doing that?"

"I read your book, Denzel," Tank said. "Pretty damn good, too. I have to say I was impressed. Only problem, you didn't have a character based on me."

"Maybe next time, Tank."

"What actor would play me in the movie version?" Tank said.

"Danny DeVito, maybe. Ernest Borgnine would've been perfect if he hadn't upped and died on us."

"Come on, Eric. I was thinking more along the lines of Russell Crowe or Tommy Lee Jones."

"Keep dreaming, Tank."

Dantzler put a hand on Tank's shoulder. "Hate to break up this casting call, but it's three-thirty in the morning, I have a crime scene to work and my head is about to explode. So what do you say we get down to business? What can you tell me, Tank?"

"Well, right off the bat let me assure you that we aren't dealing with al-Qaida. We're still very much in the preliminary stage of the investigation, but that much I know for sure. Whoever did this was no ordnance expert. Everything about it screams amateur. My hunch is it was some type of homemade device. A relatively cheap IED someone could've made in the basement or garage. And judging by the lack of damage to surrounding buildings and vehicles, it was not a device packing much explosive force. In this regard, we're lucky. But the smell of gasoline was definitely noticeable. This tells me the doer either had a device containing plenty of gasoline, or he doused the place prior to setting off the explosive. The bomb definitely wasn't powerful enough to do this kind of damage on its own. Hence, the gasoline. The bomb was simply meant to be the match that lit the fuse. Whoever did this wanted to burn this place to the ground. And, gentlemen, as you can plainly see, he succeeded."

"How long before you can tell us more about the bomb?" Dantzler said.

"Tomorrow, maybe. Or the day after."

"Don't most guys who do this sort of thing have a signature?" Milt asked. "Something specific that identifies their work? Like a lot of serial killers have?"

Tank laughed. "Yeah, and this guy's signature would be incompetence."

"Where was the victim found?" Eric asked.

"I don't know the layout of the building, but I would guess somewhere near the front," Tank said. "An outer office, maybe. The new M.E.—what's his name, Jack?"

"Arnie Edwards."

"He might be able to give you more of a heads-up on the victim's location than I can."

"Is Edwards here?" Dantzler said.

"Yeah, he is. What's your take on him, Jack?"

"Haven't dealt with the man enough to make a judgment. But until he proves otherwise, I'm giving him the benefit of the doubt."

"He got here real prompt, I'll say that much for him," Tank said. "Went right to work."

"Did he tell you anything?"

"Only that he's one-hundred percent certain the victim is female."

"Could the victim have been the doer?" Milt asked. "You said amateur. Maybe she got nervous and tripped the switch by accident. Or she tripped it okay, but didn't allow enough time to get out before the blast went off."

Tank frowned, said, "Hell, anything's possible, Milt. But how many female bombers or arsonists have you heard of? In this country, anyway? I'm not sure I can recall one. Explosives and fires . . . hell, those are strictly a male bailiwick."

"Just tossing out possibilities, Tank," Milt said.

Tank nodded in the direction of Dr. Wiseman. "Jack, you are aware there is a built-in motive for what happened here tonight? The bombing and fire, at least. Don't know how the homicide fits into the scenario."

"Yeah, I know," Dantzler answered.

"What motive?" Eric asked.

"About a year ago the clinic was picketed for several days by pro-life supporters after Wiseman performed a couple of late-term abortions.

Some of the protesters got rowdy and vocal enough to get arrested. Even made the national news."

"I remember," Eric said, shaking his head. "Those folks, especially the religious nutcases, are capable of anything."

Milt said, "A doctor who performs late-term abortions is bound to have a lengthy enemies list."

"A *Jewish* doctor who performs late-term abortions," Dantzler added.

"Great. Now we can throw neo-Nazis, skinheads, rednecks and other assorted anti-Semitic assholes into the mix." Milt shook his head in disgust. "That should make for a fun investigation."

Dantzler was about to dispatch Eric to speak with the M.E. when he saw Dr. Wiseman close his cell phone and start walking in their direction. The doctor's skin color was ashen, his brows furrowed, his tired eyes red and puffy. He had the dazed, faraway look you see in people who have lost everything in some catastrophic event and are wandering around in a state of shock. Confused, stunned, fearful and discombobulated—uncertain what to do or say next.

Still several yards away from Tank and the three detectives, Wiseman said, "I've been able to contact all employees except one. Carly Shelton hasn't answered. I've phoned several times, but haven't reached her."

"Where does she live?" Dantzler said, taking out a pen and notepad. "I can send a patrol car to her house."

"McMeekin Place. Seven-ten McMeekin Place, to be exact."

"Is she a physician?"

"Oh, no, no. She handles billing and insurance.

Expensive digs for someone handling billing and insurance. "Is she married, or does she live alone?"

"Married. Her husband is Paul Shelton. You may have heard of him. He's an extremely successful stockbroker."

Dantzler had heard of Paul Shelton. "And he didn't answer, either?"

"No, he's in Los Angeles on a business trip. Carly told me he left town last Wednesday and isn't expected back until Tuesday." Wiseman snapped open his cell phone. "Let me try her again."

Before Wiseman began punching in numbers, Tank said, "What model vehicle does Carly Shelton drive?"

"A late-model Lexus. Why do you ask?"

"Burgundy?"

"Yes. Why?"

"There's a burgundy Lexus parked next to the building. You can't see it because it's hidden behind one of our trucks."

Wiseman's knees buckled and he pitched forward like he had been shot from behind. Eric and Milt grabbed him before he fell to the ground.

"Oh, God, oh, God, no, no, it can't be Carly," Wiseman screamed, tears filling his eyes. "It just can't be her. She would have no reason to be here this late at night. No reason at all."

Eric and Milt led Wiseman to Tank's vehicle, opened the door and helped the stricken doctor into the seat. Tank went to one of the trucks, filled a cup with water from a yellow Igloo cooler and then handed it to Wiseman. The doctor gulped it down in one long swallow, cleared his throat and stared out into space.

"I'll go check the vehicle and run the plates," Eric whispered to Dantzler. "Then we'll know for sure."

"Good. And while you're there, speak with Arnie Edwards. See if he has anything more to tell us." Dantzler waited until Eric took off before walking over to Tank's vehicle. He knelt next to Wiseman. "Rafe, I know this is a crappy time, but I really need to ask you some questions. If you don't think you're up to it, no problem. We can do it later today. But if you are up to it, I would like to get some preliminary questions out of the way. The sooner I can get started on this, the better our chances of finding out what happened, why, and who did it. You up to it?"

"Yes, yes . . . I'll do anything I can to help. What do you want to know?"

CHAPTER FOUR

D r. Wiseman asked Dantzler if he could phone his wife and bring up her to date before answering the detective's questions. Dantzler said it would be no problem. Wiseman walked a few yards away from Dantzler, and with trembling hands began punching in numbers.

Dantzler felt for the man, for what he was going through. It was obvious Wiseman was badly shaken by the fire and by the death of a co-worker. As the man in charge, the team leader, Wiseman carried an added burden, the heavy weight of responsibility for his employees, and to lose one in such a horrific manner was a shocking blow. Employees are, in many ways, an extended family. And no one wants to lose a family member. Dantzler had experienced a similar agony six years ago when veteran detective Dan Matthews was murdered while investigating the Victor Sammael case. It was a loss he still hadn't completely recovered from.

As the first glimmer of sunlight showed itself on the eastern horizon, Dantzler yawned, stretched and rubbed his throbbing temples. He was experiencing a rare headache, and the first rays of daylight were providing no relief. Although he had a great appreciation for sunrise, it was the sunset he loved most. There was something special, something mysterious, about seeing the majestic glowing orb, surrounded by a host of radiant clouds, dip into the darkness, into the infinity of space. He often wondered what it said about him that he preferred the death of a day to its beginning. The answer, he felt, had to do with his chosen occupation—homicide detective. Sunset, the end of a day, meant closure, when all that had transpired was completed, known. Conversely, sunrise, a new beginning, brought questions and mysteries yet to be answered or solved. Sunrise brought with it the potential for both good and bad, and in Dantzler's experience, bad typically won out.

Eric and Milt walked across the parking lot and down a small incline toward Dantzler. With the smoke rising behind them, they looked like a pair of ghosts silently drifting across the landscape. Or apparitions slowly moving forward in someone's darkest nightmare. And judging by the stern look on their faces, these ghosts were not bearing good news.

"It's definitely Carly Shelton," Eric announced. "The vehicle is registered to Paul Lamar Shelton. The registration and Carly's State Farm Insurance card were in the glove compartment."

Dantzler nodded. "Did either of you get a chance to speak with Edwards?"

"I did," Milt said. "Nice guy, too. Real professional. Answered all my questions."

"You asked the guy two questions, Milt," Eric said, laughing. "You didn't exactly plumb the depths of his knowledge."

"Yeah . . . and he answered both of them. I think the guy is going to be okay. That's all I'm saying."

"What did he say?" Dantzler said.

"Official identification of the deceased would have to come from dental records. He said it might not be until late Monday before he can get them."

"Any chance there's a second body in there?" Dantzler asked. "If Carly was having a tryst with someone, it would explain why she was here so late at night."

"Exactly what I was thinking," Eric said. "But Tank and Gus

Hanson both say no. They said if a second body was in there, they would have found it already."

Milt said, "Jack, someone needs to contact Paul Shelton and give him the news. Want me to do it?"

"Yeah. But he's out of town on business. L.A. I'll talk to Rafe, see if he can give me a number where we can reach Paul."

"In the meantime, what do you need us to do?" Milt asked.

"There's not much you can do until I speak with Rafe," Dantzler said. "Go catch a few hours of sleep, if you want to. Be in the office around ten. By then, I should have the names and contact information for clinic employees. I'll divide them up and we can get started on this."

"You sure you don't want us to hang around?" Eric said.

"It would only be a waste of time. Go, get some rest. You're gonna need it. We've got some long days ahead of us."

* * *

"Was it Carly's vehicle?" Dr. Wiseman said, his voice barely above a whisper. "Is she dead?"

"Yes, it was her Lexus. As for official identification of the body, it may take a couple of days." Dantzler sat next to Wiseman and removed his pen and notepad. "I'm very sorry for your loss, Rafe. It's never easy losing a colleague."

"Oh, Carly was more than a colleague," Wiseman said, fighting off tears. "She was a dear, dear friend. The first person I hired when I opened the clinic. This was in . . . let me think—nineteen ninety-eight. Almost sixteen years ago. Sixteen years? My, where does the time go? Carly was here from day one. She was instrumental in helping make the clinic a success. I've often said she was the glue that held us together."

"We'll need to contact her husband. Do you have a number where we can reach him? Maybe the name of the hotel where he is staying?"

"No, I don't have that information." Wiseman took a handkerchief out of his coat pocket and blew his nose. "But you can call Jonathan Daniels. He'll have Paul's cell number."

"Who is Jonathan Daniels?"

"Paul's business partner. He lives in Griffin Gate."

Dantzler took out his cell phone and punched in Milt's number. "Got a name for you, Milt. Jonathan Daniels. Lives in Griffin Gate. He'll know how to reach Paul Shelton." Dantzler listened a few seconds, then said, "Yeah, I know L.A.'s three hours behind us. It doesn't matter. The guy needs to know what's happened."

Dantzler punched off, closed his phone and dropped it into his coat pocket. Turning to Wiseman, he said, "How many employees do you have at the clinic?"

"We have eleven full-time staff, including me," Wiseman answered. "We also have several other physicians, specialists in various areas, who come in and perform necessary surgeries."

"So . . . you're what—an outpatient surgery center?"

"Precisely. But we also do much more than surgery. We treat illness, injuries, allergies . . . about every kind of problem an individual can have. We're more like a small hospital than your typical clinic. Naturally, there are many procedures we can't perform. Open-heart surgery, brain surgery, anything truly complicated—those are beyond our capabilities."

"And you perform all surgeries?"

"Oh, heavens, no. I'm an OBGYN. However, I did spend several years working in the Central Baptist emergency room, so there isn't much I haven't seen or had to deal with." Wiseman drew in a deep breath before continuing. "Here's how it works. We try to schedule each patient based on his or her needs. It doesn't always work out that way, but most times it does. If, say, we have three patients complaining of ear, nose or throat problems, we bring them in on the same day. And Dr. Alexis Brooks is here to see them. Those are her specialties. If it involves a pregnancy or female issues, naturally, they see me. For a dermatology problem, they see Donald Carlisle. You get the picture. We have physicians for virtually every problem area. As for walk-ins or accident victims or children with a fever and sore throat, well, that's when my emergency room experience comes in handy. I handle those cases, along with my three RNs. It may sound chaotic, but believe it or not, things usually go rather smoothly."

"I'll need the names and contact information for your full-time employees," Dantzler said.

"Call my wife later this morning. She'll give you names, addresses, phone numbers."

"Thanks." Dantzler watched as the sun cleared the horizon. "Did you have any kind of back-up procedure in place, or did you lose all records in the fire?"

"Oh, no, nothing was lost. It would be careless of us to not have a back-up system. Careless and stupid. Patients' files, records, insurance data, billing, payments, X-rays—everything is copied at the end of each day and then transferred to a computer in Greg Novotny's house."

"Who is Greg Novotny?"

"Greg is our Lab Tech. And like many young people today, he is extremely computer savvy. There seems to be nothing about computers he doesn't understand. Given his computer knowledge, Greg also serves as our IT guy. Any computer issues, he handles."

"And all information goes to him every day?"

"That's correct. The data is stored on a computer I purchased with clinic funds about four years ago. Actually, it was at Greg's insistence to put in such a safety procedure. Prior to doing so, some data was stored on a computer at my house. But much of it wasn't. We were living dangerously. If a catastrophe like this had happened back then, we would have lost virtually all of our records and files. It would have been a disaster."

Dantzler finished scribbling some notes, looked up at Wiseman and said, "Tell me about Carly Shelton."

"She was a terrific friend and confidant, a valued employee and a wonderful human being. Like I told you, Detective Dantzler, she was with the clinic from the very beginning. Without Carly we would never have been so successful."

"Can you think of anyone who would want to hurt her?"

"If you knew Carly, you would know how ridiculous such a question is. Carly simply did not have enemies."

"What reason would she have for being at the clinic at such a late hour on a Saturday night or Sunday morning?"

"I can't think of one."

"How many employees have a key to the clinic?" Dantzler said.

"All of them."

"Isn't that a little unusual?"

"Perhaps. But I trust my people. If I didn't, they wouldn't be working for me. Besides, this is the medical field. We sometimes work odd hours. I want my employees to have complete access in case they get called in late at night or on the weekend."

"Are there drugs in the clinic?"

"Sure. We have a limited amount of drugs on hand. Nothing remotely resembling a full pharmacy, though, if that's what you're asking."

"Are they locked away?"

"Of course."

"Did Carly have a key to that lock?"

"Yes. And in anticipation of your next question, Carly and I are the only ones who do."

"Is it possible she had a drug problem? Or maybe she was selling drugs?"

Wiseman's expression hardened. "I understand you have to ask these questions, Detective Dantzler, but you are not listening to my answers. Carly Shelton was one of the most decent, honorable human beings I have ever known. She did not have a drug problem, nor was she a drug dealer. I can't begin to tell you how absurd that notion is."

"Any chance she might've been meeting someone here?"

"Carly wasn't a nurse, so there would be no reason . . ." Wiseman shook his head, his eyes narrowing. "Wait a second. What you're really asking is whether or not Carly was meeting a man here tonight. A romantic encounter of some type. Is that right?"

Dantzler nodded.

"No. I can assure you she was not."

"How can you be so positive?"

"Because . . . she wouldn't do it."

"People, even the best of people, keep secrets hidden from others."

"I've no doubt about that. But Carly had no lover. Take my word on it."

"So her marriage was perfect?"

"I wouldn't go that far. Who knows what really goes on when the doors are shut and the blinds are closed." Wiseman rubbed his reddened eyes. "But I never heard Carly complain or indicate there were serious problems in the marriage. Like all couples, I imagine they experienced their share of ups and downs. All marriages ebb and flow. That's pretty normal."

"Are you and Paul Shelton close?"

"Surprisingly, no," Wiseman said, shaking his head. "Truth is, we're not even friends, which is odd considering how close Carly and I are . . . were. Paul travels in a different circle than I do. Has different friends, different interests. He's a golfer, and I play . . . well, as you know, I play quite a bit of tennis. Over the years Paul and I have attended various functions and been to the same dinner parties, but we rarely ever spoke."

Wiseman stood, turned and looked back at the place where only hours earlier his beloved clinic had been. Now, as the sun began its steady climb upward in the sky, the smoke from the fire rose to meet it.

"How many more questions, Detective?" Wiseman said. "I'm exhausted, yet I have a million things to do. Can we hurry this along?"

"I need to ask you about the trouble you had at the clinic last year."

"Oh, the troubles. What do you want to know?"

"It had to do with complaints about abortions, didn't it?"

"*Abortion*." Wiseman snapped. "A single abortion, not plural. Despite the picture our brain-addled critics tried to paint, we are most certainly *not* an abortion clinic."

"You only performed one abortion?"

"No, over the years, there have been four. All were deemed necessary, and all were agreed upon by the individuals involved. But the fourth one—the one performed last summer—caused the controversy. It's the only one performed during the latter stages of the third month."

"A late-term abortion?"

"If that's how you choose to label it, yes, a late-term abortion."

"What were the circumstances?"

"How is any of this going to help you find the person responsible for Carly's death and the destruction of my clinic?"

"Come on, Rafe, think about it. One of those 'brain-addled critics' very well might be the person who did this."

Wiseman let Dantzler's words sink in for several seconds before speaking. "The circumstances? Well, the expectant mother was sixteen and severely mentally challenged. She had no clue who the father was, or that she was even pregnant. It wasn't until midway through the third month before her parents realized the child, who was quite heavy, was pregnant. Naturally, when they did, they brought the child to me. I examined her thoroughly, and knew right off that there were major problems with the fetus. I explained everything to the parents. They didn't even have to think about it. They said the pregnancy needed to be terminated, and they asked me to do it. I did, and all went well. Trust me, it was the wisest and best decision they could have made given that awful set of circumstances. Everything went smoothly. The child recovered and went home to her parents."

"How did word get out that you had performed the procedure?"

"Good question. I have no idea. What I do know is that within two days a bunch of crazies were in the parking lot, yelling the vilest obscenities, throwing rocks, holding up signs with the most dreadful slogans on them. I got threatening phone calls, hate-filled letters and some rather frightening e-mails. It was not a particularly pleasant time for any of us at the clinic. Thankfully, it only lasted a week or so."

"Do you still have the letters and e-mails?"

"The letters are at my house, the e-mails on Greg's computer."

"Excellent. I'll need to go through them." Dantzler closed his notepad and stood. "Is there anything else you can think of that might be helpful?"

"No. Just find the bastard who did this to Carly?"

"We will."

CHAPTER FIVE

It was a little past eight on what was shaping up to be a beautiful Sunday morning. The sun was bright, the skies clear, the air clean and fresh. Almost the exact opposite from the scene Dantzler left less than an hour ago, where death and destruction ruled the night like a pair of evil spirits raging through the smoky darkness on wings of fire.

Thinking about what had happened to the Wiseman Clinic, Dantzler was reminded of a line written by Tennyson: *The fire of Heaven is not the flame of Hell*.

Dantzler promised to keep that thought in mind as he pursued this case.

Taking out his notepad, he flipped open his cell phone and dialed the home number Rafe Wiseman had given him. A woman answered after the second ring, identifying herself as Sally Wiseman.

"Yes, Detective Dantzler, my husband said you would be contacting me. If you will give me an hour or so, that should allow enough time for me to collect the information you need. Would, say, nine o'clock be acceptable?"

"That would be perfect," Dantzler answered.

"Do you know where we live?"

"Yes. Rafe gave me the address . . . 3668 Kenesaw Drive. Right across from Hartland Park."

"I will see you in an hour."

Dantzler closed his phone and dropped it onto the seat next to him. Looking at his watch, he realized he had an hour to kill and nothing to do. He thought about calling Laurie but decided against it. She was essentially going through a boot-camp type training exercise at Quantico, and with Sunday being her one day of rest she could use all the sleep she could get. Waking her simply to say hello would be cruel, to say the least.

A sudden stab of hunger reminded Dantzler that he had not eaten since early yesterday afternoon. Having neither the time nor inclination for a heavy breakfast, he drove to Panera's on Nicholasville Road, parked, grabbed his cell phone, went inside the restaurant, ordered a plain bagel with cream cheese and a glass of orange juice.

Judging by the lack of customers and the number of empty tables dotting the normally busy establishment, he had picked the perfect time to show up. The early Mass Catholics had already come and gone, and the Sunday-service Protestants had yet to arrive. His timing couldn't have been better. He secured a table near the front window, sat and went to work on the bagel.

After taking a couple of bites his cell phone buzzed. He washed down the bagel with a gulp of orange juice, opened the phone and answered. The call was from Eric Gamble.

"What's up, Eric?" Dantzler said, taking another sip of juice.

"I know you told me to get some shuteye, but I felt the need to be active. Sleep doesn't come easily for me when we begin a new investigation. I know you're the same way."

Yeah, you got that right. "So, what did you do?"

"I did a quick canvass of the apartment complex nearest the Wiseman Clinic, focusing primarily on those units facing the clinic. I spoke with individuals from twelve apartments. None of them saw or heard anything prior to the explosion and fire. However, one lady—Amanda Woolcott—remembers seeing a pick-up truck drive past the clinic at approximately ten-thirty. According to Tank's timeline, that would be thirty minutes to an hour before the blast went off. Could be the doer checking to make sure Carly Shelton was inside."

"Can Amanda recall anything more specific about the truck? Make, model, color?"

"No. Only that it drove very slowly past the clinic, and then speeded up as it drove off."

"Well, that's pretty thin, but it's better than nothing." Dantzler was silent for a few seconds, then said, "Did you speak with everyone who lives in apartments facing the clinic?"

"Just the thirteen who were at home. The building is four stories high, so I would estimate there are twenty to thirty units with windows facing the clinic. There are still plenty of people I need to interview."

"Later this afternoon, you and Milt revisit the place. Find out if anyone else remembers seeing or hearing anything suspicious. Again, it's a long shot, but, who knows, maybe we'll get lucky and catch a break."

"Have you met with Wiseman's wife yet?" Eric said.

"I'm heading in her direction right now."

* * *

The Wisemans lived in a two-story brick house with a small front yard hidden behind a wall of shrubbery that separated the residence from the sidewalk and street. There was a front entrance off the main street, and a side entrance where the two-car garage was located. It was one of the smallest houses in the expensive neighborhood, cozy, neat, unpretentious. Much like Dr. Wiseman himself, Dantzler concluded.

Dantzler parked on Kenesaw, walked up the short walkway and rang the doorbell. As he waited for a response from inside, he looked across the street at Hartland Park, where several laughing children were in swings being pushed by their mothers and fathers. A few older children were climbing on the monkey bars, or hurtling themselves down the many sliding boards.

Enjoy it while you can, kids, because the fun times don't last forever.

Seconds later, Sally Wiseman opened the door, forced a smile, then motioned for him to come in. He waited until she closed the door before following her into the den.

"Would you like a cup of coffee, Detective Dantzler?" Sally said, as Dantzler took a seat on the leather sofa. "I'm up to my eyeballs in Maxwell House, but I'll be more than happy to get you a cup."

"No, thanks. I've already had breakfast."

Sally Wiseman sat next to Dantzler on the sofa. A tall woman with dark brown hair and a still-youthful figure, she was wearing Levis, a white blouse and New Balance tennis shoes. She wore no makeup or other accoutrements, and it was obvious from the puffiness around her eyes that she had been crying. Despite the train wreck that had shattered her life, she appeared to be holding herself together fairly well. Judging by her demeanor, Dantzler immediately concluded that she was a strong woman. She was also very attractive.

"You are something of a hero to my husband," Sally said. "He is in awe of your ability as a tennis player. More than once I have heard him say he would gladly sell his soul to Satan if he could play tennis at your level."

"Rafe isn't bad," Dantzler said. "In fact, he's an excellent doubles player. Much better than your average hacker."

"I'm sure you are being very generous in your assessment, Detective." She noticed Dantzler looking at the small cross on the wall. "Unlike my husband, I am not Jewish. Born and raised a Methodist. However, it has been years since I last attended church on a regular basis. Perhaps it's an area of my life I need to re-evaluate."

"How long have you and Rafe been married?"

"Almost seven years. We were both about a year out from nasty divorces when we met. A mutual friend introduced us. I immediately fell head over heels in love with the man, despite my best efforts not to. The last thing I wanted at the time was another relationship. Six months later we were married. So much for my strength and resolve, right? What I quickly learned was that although Rafe loved me, I would always be his second love. The clinic came first. That's where his true affections are and always will be. And he will say as much if you ask him. It cost him his first marriage, and . . . well, it has not always been easy for me, either. You see, no wife wants to be second to anyone or anything. But . . . the state of my marriage is not what you came to talk about, is it?"

Sally picked up a manila folder from the coffee table and handed it to Dantzler. Then she leaned forward, lifted a large box from the floor and set it on the coffee table. The box was filled to the top with letters, envelopes and cards of various sizes.

"This should be everything you need," she said.

Dantzler opened the folder. Inside, were two pieces of paper, upon which Sally had listed the name, home address, e-mail address and phone number for each of the ten full-time clinic employees, along with the same information for the visiting physicians.

"You are very thorough," Dantzler said, closing the folder. "I appreciate this. Having this information at my fingertips will make my job a lot easier."

"It's the least I could do," Sally said. "I may be terribly jealous of the clinic, but I would never want something this awful to happen. This incident has devastated Rafe, and I ache for him."

"Do you think he will rebuild?"

"Oh, definitely. He has already said he would. It's the first thing he told me after he got home this morning. The clinic was well insured, so we're covered in that area."

"What will he do while the clinic is being rebuilt?"

"He has already contacted a friend of his who rents office space. Rafe is meeting with him tomorrow to see if anything is available that might serve as a temporary clinic. I know this sounds preposterous, but Rafe will be seeing patients somewhere within the next week to ten days. He will not let this incident break him or keep him from helping those who need medical attention. For many people, especially those who feel somewhat disenfranchised or forgotten, my husband is a real hero."

"How well do you know the employees?" Dantzler said, pointing at the manila folder.

"I am the director of a rape crisis center, which takes up most of my day, so I don't tend to spend much time at the clinic. Nor do I mingle with Rafe's employees. There are the occasional functions, but those are rare. Therefore, I don't know any of them all that well."

"What about Carly Shelton?"

"There isn't much I can tell you about her, other than she was the first person Rafe hired when he opened the clinic. I do know he relied heavily on her. If the clinic was the United States, Rafe would be the president, Carly the vice president, and Greg Novotny the secretary of state." Sally thought for a second, and then said, "Jenny Saunders is the one I know best. The only reason is because her sister, Kim, and I were good friends in high school. Jenny is several years younger than us, but she was always hanging around when Kim and I were together."

"Jenny is an RN?"

"Yes, but she is also a PA. Physician's assistant. She sees many of the patients who come in with minor illnesses or injuries, the ones Rafe or the other doctors don't need to see. I know Rafe relies heavily on her as well."

"That's good to know. I will meet with her first."

"You might want to speak with Barbara Pearlman, too. She handles billing and insurance, been with the clinic almost as long as Carly has. Barbara and Rafe attend the same synagogue. She has known Rafe since they were kids."

Dantzler pointed at the box filled with letters and cards. "Correspondence from Rafe's fan club, I take it."

"Oh, please, don't get me started on those," Sally said. "Hateful, vile, scary ranting from a bunch of loonies. What you'll read in there will make you sick to your stomach. It is hard for me to believe people can be so ugly. I begged Rafe to turn this nonsense over to the police or the FBI, but he wouldn't. He'd just shrug, say something like 'what good would that do?' Well, look what happened. I wouldn't be at all shocked to learn that a letter or card in this box is from the person or persons who bombed the clinic tonight. Truth is, I would almost bet on it."

"I can guarantee you we'll check out each and every one."

"Those right-wing, pro-life fanatics simply have no clue," Sally continued. "And they have no compassion. Hell, I'm as pro-life as anyone. Any sane person is pro-life, for God's sake. And in a perfect world, there would never be a need to terminate a pregnancy. But we don't live in a perfect world, do we? No, far from it. Therefore, any sane person should also be pro-choice. Remember, I work at a rape crisis clinic, so I've seen plenty of instances where terminating a pregnancy was the only sane and rational choice. The situation at Rafe's clinic, the one that sparked last summer's outcry, well, when you take a close look at it, when you consider the individual involved, there was but one logical choice: terminate the pregnancy. Tragic, yes, but absolutely necessary."

"Rafe gave me the details," Dantzler said. "Sounds like he did what was best for everyone."

"Everyone except those idiots whose priorities are so misguided and hypocritical. The ones who wrap themselves with the flag and wave the Bible like it is a sword." Sally snickered. "Know what really angers me the most? The hypocrisy. Those right-wing, pro-lifers only seem to care about life during the period between conception and birth. Once a baby is born, all bets are off. Think about it. Right-wingers believe in the death penalty. They believe in the death penalty for teenagers. They are the first ones who want us to go to war. They think a person should be allowed to own as many guns as they can afford. They murder innocent people who work at clinics where abortions are performed. And, of course, they do all of this in the name of God. Well, I only pray God isn't so forgiving when they come face to face with him."

"I'll leave God's work to God," Dantzler said, standing. "My task is to catch the person or persons who did this. Once that happens, I'm confident the jury won't be in a forgiving mood. They'll do what's right."

"Amen to that."

* * *

As Dantzler was concluding his talk with Sally Wiseman, another meeting was taking place in Shillito Park. In the bright Sunday morning daylight, with an African-American family gathering for lunch beneath an open shed less than fifty yards away, three men sat at a picnic table, each man silently observing the surrounding activity with detached indifference.

Two of the men were father and son, and although there was a considerable age difference between them, they had on more than one occasion been asked if they were twins. The father considered the suggestion a compliment, the son less so.

The third man, the one sitting across from father and son, couldn't have been more different in looks, dress or demeanor. Whereas father and son were short, stocky and fair skinned, not good looking by any set of standards, the third man was tall, dark and classically handsome. It was as if George Clooney was sharing a table with Don Rickles and Dom DeLuise.

Clooney reached into his suit coat and came out with a thick envelope. He held onto it for several seconds before offering it across the table.

"The first half, as promised," he said. "You get the rest when the job is completed. And I want it done within the next week."

The son eagerly took the envelope and started to open it. Before he could get it open, Clooney reached across the table and grabbed his hand.

"How stupid are you?" he said to the young man.

"Stupid? Who said I'm stupid? I ain't stupid. Anybody says I'm stupid, I'll kick his ass."

"*I* just said it."

"Well, you shouldn't say things like that," the boy muttered, his tone of aggression long gone.

"Then don't count money in public," Clooney ordered. "It's dangerous, and it shows a lack of trust. Twenty-five grand—it's all there."

"Give it to me," the boy's father snapped. He took the envelope and tucked it into his pants pocket. "He's right—you don't flash this kind of cash in a public place."

Clooney stood, closed his eyes, breathed in deeply and then slowly exhaled. "Damn, what a glorious day. Almost makes me believe there's a God. Almost."

"You'd better believe in God," the boy said. "You don't, you're doomed to hell."

Clooney grinned. "Well, I won't be alone, will I?"

"What's that supposed to mean?"

Clooney put his sunglasses on and started walking toward his car. "You want the rest of the money, then take care of business here on Earth. Worrying about my salvation isn't gonna get you the other twenty-five grand."

CHAPTER SIX

Dantzler went home, took a quick shower and grabbed three hours of much-needed sleep. Waking at one-thirty, he shook the disorientation cobwebs from his head, dressed, went into the kitchen, ate some warmed-up spaghetti and drank a Diet Pepsi. When he'd finished eating he dumped the plate and glass into the sink, sat at the table and was about to dial Eric's number when the phone began to buzz. The call was from Laurie.

"Hear you're working again," she said.

Dantzler smiled. Typical Laurie—always thinking work first.

"And how have *you* been?" he answered, a hint of playful sarcasm in his tone.

"Cut the BS. I'm fine, you're fine, everybody is fine. Okay? Now, tell me what's going on with the Wiseman Clinic situation?"

"How did you hear about it?"

"Scott's father called about an hour ago. He told Scott, Scott told me, and now I'm in search of details. Who better to supply those details than the great Jack Dantzler?"

"Two weeks with the Feds and you've become a smart ass. No, let me amend that. You've become an even bigger smart ass."

"Didn't think it was possible, did you?"

"Anything is possible when you hang out with the FBI too long."

"It's your punishment for exiling me to this Hades in the first place."

"You're conveniently forgetting that it was Rich who suggested you and Scott go through the training program."

"*Suggested?*" Laurie laughed out loud. "It was no suggestion. It was an order."

"Then blame Rich, not me."

"Actually, the training is pretty cool. Tough and challenging, but definitely worthwhile. Okay, so what's going on with the Wiseman case?"

"The clinic was bombed and it burned to the ground. Happened around midnight. One of the clinic employees, Carly Shelton, was inside. Death likely resulted from the blast, but the coroner won't know for sure until he performs the autopsy. Rafe Wiseman has no idea why Carly would have been in there so late at night. Eric did a quick canvass of the apartment building near the clinic earlier this morning but didn't come up with much. One lady said she saw a truck drive slowly past the clinic, then speed off just minutes before the blast. No make, model or plate numbers, so it's pretty much a nothing lead. That's about all I know at this stage."

"Wasn't the Wiseman Clinic the one where there was some trouble a year or so ago?"

"It was. Some rather rowdy marchers protesting a late-term abortion Dr. Wiseman performed. A few actually spent a night or two in jail for tussling with the police."

"Shouldn't be a problem accessing their names. That will give you a starting point, at least."

"I met with Sally Wiseman this morning. She gave me a box filled with letters and cards Dr. Wiseman received in the days and weeks following the incident. I haven't gone through them yet, but Sally says they are vile, ugly and threatening. Exactly what you'd expect from a bunch of religion-soaked loonies. He also received threatening e-mails. I'll get them later today."

"Sounds like a lot of work for three people to handle. Should Scott and I cut it short here and get back to the real world?"

"No. You guys stick it out and finish what you started. I've already asked Rich to get me Jake Thomas. Rich has agreed to make it happen. If I need more personnel later on, I'll ask for it."

"I know Jake. He's a sharp guy, tough, professional. And I know he really wants to join the Homicide unit."

"I've also heard good things about Jake. Looks like he's going to get his chance to show us if all the praise is justified."

"Is Milt still set on retiring in two weeks?" Laurie said.

"He hasn't indicated otherwise. But you know Milt. If this case is still hot and we need him, he won't walk away. The guy's a pro's pro. He'll see it through to the bitter end."

"Well, if you do need Scott or me, we're only a phone call away."

"Laurie, you'll be back in three weeks, for Christ's sake. You're making it sound like you've been sent to Siberia."

"When they blow the whistle at five a.m. and roust my weary ass out of bed, I wish I was in Siberia."

Dantzler laughed. "It's good for you. It builds character."

"Sleep builds character. Getting up before the rooster opens his eyes is not what God had in mind for humans when he created us."

"Hang tight. And call me when you get a chance."

"I will. And, by the way . . . I really miss you."

"Same on this end."

* * *

Dantzler punched off, stood and was on his way toward the front door when his phone buzzed again. This time the ID box on the phone read "Caller Unknown."

"Hello," Dantzler said.

"Detective Dantzler, my name is Jay Matthewson. I'm Paul Shelton's attorney. He has asked me to set a meeting with you, hopefully sometime later this afternoon. He is scheduled to arrive from Los Angeles in about two hours. The purpose of the meeting is two-fold. He knows you'll have questions for him, and he would appreciate it if you would fill him in regarding any information you have relating to his wife's death. Would a four-thirty meeting at my office be agreeable?"

"Four-thirty is fine," Dantzler said. "But my office, not yours."

"Shouldn't be a problem," Matthewson said. "We'll see you there."

* * *

Dantzler checked his watch. It was a few minutes past three. He punched in Eric's number, informed him about the meeting and asked him to let Milt know. Eric said he and Milt would meet Dantzler in the War Room at three forty-five.

Next, Dantzler phoned David Bloom, his old college roommate and tennis teammate. Bloom, a well-respected psychiatrist, had often worked with the Homicide Department in the past, and Dantzler never hesitated to go to him for advice or information. Bloom answered after three rings.

"What can the Hebrew Hammer do for you, my goyish friend?" Bloom said.

"Hebrew Hammer? That's your new moniker? Where'd it come from?"

"Me and Richard Goldman just slaughtered a pair of Philistines in straight sets. Beat 'em love and love. A thing of beauty, Jack, true art. Even you would've been impressed. Anyway, as we're walking off the court, this one guy, obviously awed by my lethal serve, called me the Hebrew Hammer. It's a bit over the top, I admit, but I kind of like it."

"Funny, but I've never been overly impressed by your serve."

"Well, no, you wouldn't, since you are supremely gifted whereas I'm only moderately talented. While I bow to your superiority, I do not spurn praise when it comes my way."

"Nor should you." Dantzler turned serious. "I guess you've heard about the Wiseman Clinic."

"Yes. And believe me when I tell you it is a genuine tragedy. Rafe Wiseman is as close to a saint as this city has to offer. The man has helped more poor, indigent people than you can imagine. He turns no one away, whether they have insurance or are uninsured. How many doctors or hospitals can make a similar claim? None, that's how many."

"Have you spoken with him today?"

"I called him a couple of hours ago to let him know that if he

needed to talk, I am available. He's a badly shaken man, but he'll perse-
vere. I am confident of it."

"Did you know Carly Shelton?"

"No."

"What about Paul Shelton?"

"Him I do know," Bloom said. "Matter of fact, I saw him earlier
this morning. He and I have served together on a couple of commit-
tees over the years. We've never been social pals, but I've spent some
time with him."

"Are you sure about seeing him today? His attorney told me Shelton
wouldn't be getting back into town until later this afternoon."

"Must be a mix-up, because I passed Paul on Nicholasville Road a
little before noon."

"I'm meeting with him at four-thirty. Anything relevant I need to
know before I talk to him?" Dantzler asked.

Bloom chuckled. "Only this . . . you'll despise him."

"Why do you say that?"

"You'll see."

* * *

"Did you come up with anything new during the follow-up canvass of
the apartment complex?" Dantzler asked Milt.

"Big waste of time," Milt answered, shaking his head. "Nobody saw
or heard anything prior to the explosion. They were either asleep, or
had their eyes glued to the idiot box when the blast went off. And
when they did look out the window, no truck in sight. Only fire and
smoke."

Dantzler, Milt and Eric were seated at the long rectangle table in
the War Room. The box of hate mail from Dr. Wiseman's house was
sitting in the middle of the table. Eric plucked a letter from the box
and began reading. Milt sipped from a cup of coffee, while Dantzler
thumbed through his notepad. They had fifteen minutes before the
meeting with Paul Shelton and Jay Matthewson.

Milt looked up, said, "Wonder why Shelton felt the need to bring
his attorney with him? Pre-emptive strike, you think?"

"That would be my guess," Dantzler answered. "How did he sound when you informed him his wife was dead?"

"Shocked, outraged, saddened."

"Sincere?"

"Yeah, I guess so. But who knows if it was genuine or an acting job? Hell, I'm sure O.J. sounded genuine when he was told Nicole had been murdered, and we all know how that turned out. It had to be the best acting performance the bastard ever gave."

"Great football player," Dantzler said.

"Who gives a shit? He skated on a double murder charge, which kinda sucks. The man was guilty and he should've been made to pay." Milt sipped more coffee. "How well do you know Paul Shelton?"

"Don't know him at all," Dantzler said.

"His attorney, Matthewson. He's the guy Dan talked to during the Victor Sammael case. Best I remember, Dan liked him. And Dan didn't like many barristers."

Eric waved the letter he was reading. "Man, listen to this. 'You will burn in hell for what you did to that unborn baby. You ripped a living being from the holy womb. God will show you no mercy for such a heinous act. There will be no forgiveness for the crime you committed. Justice on this Earth must be dispensed immediately. You must be held accountable for the sin of murder. An eye for an eye, a life for a life. The poor unborn child must be avenged. You are not safe, you murderous kike doctor. I am taking aim on your life, as God is taking aim on your eternal soul. Be ready for Judgment Day. It's not far off.' Eric tossed the letter onto the table. "Scary stuff, and unsigned, of course."

"I'll make you a bet, Eric," Dantzler said. "The person who bombed the clinic and killed Carly Shelton didn't send a letter or an e-mail. Going through all this nonsense, which we'll have to do, will end up being nothing more than a wild goose chase."

"What makes you think so?" Eric asked, putting the letter back in the box.

Dantzler shrugged. "A couple of reasons. First, killers rarely advertise. Second, I'm not convinced this had to do with the abortion. I think something else is at play here, something that's going to come at us from left field. I may be wrong, but my gut tells me we're looking at something other than a hate crime."

Milt stood and pointed toward the door. "Looks like our guests have arrived."

"Show them in," Dantzler said, standing.

CHAPTER SEVEN

David Bloom nailed it—Dantzler vibed negative the moment Paul Shelton walked into the War Room. If arrogance was a perfume, he immediately concluded, Shelton would smell like an overpriced French hooker. The man reeked of self-importance and egotism.

Shelton's haughty demeanor wasn't what turned Dantzler's stomach, though. Nor was it the expensive tailor-made suit, the cold reptile eyes, the two-hundred dollar haircut or the permanent salon-baked George Hamilton tan. It was the smirk, a dismissive sneer that said, *Why must I waste my valuable time with these peasants?*

Dantzler, Milt and Eric stood as Shelton and Jay Matthewson entered the room. Matthewson acknowledged the detectives with a nod, pulled back a chair and sat. Dantzler motioned for Shelton to take the chair across from him. Shelton remained standing for several seconds, as though he was trying to decide whether to stay or go. Only after glancing at his Rolex did he finally take the chair next to Matthewson.

Dantzler read the Rolex check for what it was: *My time is more valuable than your time, so let's make this brief.*

"We appreciate you coming in at a time like this," Dantzler said to

Shelton. "And I—*we*—want to express our condolences for the loss of your wife. I can promise you we will do everything within our power to find the person or persons responsible, and to see that they are brought to justice."

Shelton didn't respond and his expression remained unchanged. The smirk lingered.

Matthewson said, "I want it noted for the record that my client came in of his own volition and that he willingly submitted to this interrogation."

"This isn't an interrogation," Dantzler pointed out. "It's a fact-finding interview."

Matthewson started to respond but Shelton raised his left hand in a silencing gesture. Dantzler read the move as this: *Quiet, peon, I'll speak for myself.*

"I'm no idiot, Detective," Shelton said. "I'm well aware that in cases such as this, the surviving spouse is always at the top of the suspect list. Or at the very least, a 'person of interest.' Isn't that the term you folks use?"

Folks, as in civil service peasants. Dantzler fought the urge to reach across the table and slap Shelton. While his instincts said go, his sense of restraint won the internal debate.

"Like I said, Mr. Shelton, our goal is to gather facts and information that might be useful in helping us solve the case. We have no reason to suspect you had anything to do with the murder of your wife."

A lie.

"And your willingness to come in and cooperate is another reason why we aren't considering you a person of interest at this time."

A second lie.

Paul Shelton wasn't buying it. "Detective Dantzler, I have no doubt you'll turn over every rock in an effort to prove my guilt."

"Did you murder your wife?" Dantzler asked.

"I did not."

"Did you pay someone else to murder your wife?"

"I did not."

"Then you have no reason to worry about what we might find when we turn over those rocks, do you?"

Another Rolex check. "Then ask your questions, Detective. I have funeral arrangements to make."

Dantzler looked at Matthewson. "Do you have a problem with us taping this conversation?"

"I don't. Do you, Paul?"

"No."

"Excellent," Dantzler said, turning the tape recorder on. To Shelton, he said, "When did you leave for Los Angeles?"

"Last Wednesday."

"What was the purpose of the trip?"

"Business mixed with pleasure. I had to attend several business-related meetings with certain clients of mine. I also have a very good friend in the Los Angeles area I wanted to spend some time with, which I did. We drove up into Napa Valley and bought some excellent wine. We also spent a night in Carmel."

"When was the last time you spoke with Carly?"

"The day I departed for L.A. We had breakfast together and then she left for work. Must have been around seven-thirty. A couple hours later I drove to Louisville, where I caught my flight to Los Angeles."

"You didn't speak to her while you were out of town?"

"No."

"Not one phone call? No text message? No e-mail?"

"We did not communicate while I was away." Shelton leaned forward. "Why? Are you bothered by the fact we didn't converse while we were apart?"

"Not at all."

A third lie.

"We are not young lovers who pine for each other when we are apart," Shelton said. "We would have spoken if, indeed, there had been a reason to. But there wasn't."

"Do you have any idea why Carly would have been at the clinic so late at night?" Dantzler asked.

"No."

"Can you recall other instances when she did go in after hours?"

"No. She wasn't a nurse, so she wasn't needed in emergency situations. There have been times when she stayed late, but on those occasions she was always home by eight or eight-thirty."

"Is it possible she went there to open the clinic for one of the other employees?"

"It's my understanding that all employees have a key. So my answer to your question would be no."

"Do all of the visiting physicians have a key?"

"I don't know. You would have to ask Wiseman."

"Can you think of anyone who might have wanted to kill Carly?"

"My wife was collateral damage, Detective Dantzler. The fucking clinic was the target. She just happened to be at the wrong place at the wrong time. I don't know who bombed the clinic, but I will tell you this: Rafe Wiseman is every bit as guilty as the person who lit the fuse."

"Why such a harsh opinion of Dr. Wiseman?"

"He's a baby killer, that's why."

"Baby killer seems a little extreme."

"Performing late-term abortions *is* extreme."

"How did you feel about your wife working for a doctor who performs abortions?"

"How do you think I felt, Detective? I didn't like it. And I made my feelings known countless times. I tried to impress upon her that working for a man like him was no different than working for a murderer like Hitler. She wouldn't listen. To her, Rafe Wiseman was a saint. Talk about deluded."

"What is your relationship with Dr. Wiseman?"

"Relationship? I have no relationship with the man. I detest him and everything he stands for." Shelton gave another quick Rolex glance. "How much longer, Detective? I really have other matters I need to take care of."

"You're free to leave anytime you like."

"Do you have other questions?"

"A couple."

"Ask them."

"When the clinic was being picketed last year, did Carly receive any hate mail or threatening e-mails?"

"Not that I'm aware of."

"Did she ever mention a specific individual or individuals who might have posed a serious threat to Dr. Wiseman or the clinic?"

"No."

"How did you feel about what was going on?"

"I was one-hundred percent in support of the protesters. They were on the side of the angels."

"Weren't you worried about your wife's safety?"

"When you dance with the devil, Detective Dantzler, you are always going to find yourself in someone's crosshairs. I told her that, but she wouldn't listen."

"Is it possible your wife was having an affair, and perhaps that is why she was at the clinic so late at night?"

"No." Shelton stood and pushed his chair back. "And with that asinine question, this little chat has clearly run its course. If you have additional questions you know how to contact me. I'm not difficult to find. Come, Jay, let's go."

"One final question: What time did you get back from California?"

"About an hour ago."

"What would you say if I told you that someone said he saw you on Nicholasville Road before noon?"

"I would say he needs to have his eyes checked."

"Thank you for coming in, Mr. Shelton," Dantzler said. "And again, we are very sorry for your loss."

Shelton left without responding.

* * *

"Is the word asshole in the dictionary?" Milt asked.

"I don't know," Eric replied.

"Well, if it's not, it should be. And Paul Shelton's picture should be right next to the word. Man, what an arrogant prick."

"He's also a liar," Dantzler said. "David Bloom saw him this morning, and I believe David."

"That means Shelton probably was in town when I spoke with him," Milt said.

Dantzler rewound the tape in the recorder. "Know what's strange? Not once did Shelton mention Carly by name. It was either she or my wife. Never Carly."

"I noticed that, too," Eric said, adding, "I know people grieve in different ways, and it's always dangerous to make snap judgments, but I didn't detect much genuine grief in his demeanor. To me, he came across as cold and remote and not in much pain."

Milt said, "Jack, I think you asked the wrong person about an affair. I would love to know who was with him when he bought the wine and spent the night in Carmel. My money says his 'friend' is a female. We need to take a long look at his phone records, find out who he's been talking to, here and in L.A."

"It certainly doesn't sound like they had a marriage made in heaven," Dantzler said. "Definitely a lot of friction there."

"And his hatred of Dr. Wiseman," Eric said. "Calling him a baby killer and comparing him to Hitler? Jesus, what's that all about?"

"It's the only time during the entire interview that he displayed any emotion," Milt pointed out. "His anger was genuine."

"A zealot's anger is always genuine," Eric said. "Often misplaced, but never lacking sincerity."

Dantzler opened the manila folder on the table and took out the two pages with Wiseman Clinic names and contact information. "These are the clinic employees. We'll eventually meet with all of them, but I want to get with three of them this evening. Milt, you take Greg Novotny. He's a lab tech and their IT guy. He'll have the e-mails Rafe received. Have him print them out for you. Eric, you take Barbara Pearlman. She's a receptionist. She has known Rafe since they were kids. See if she can give us a better insight into the state of the Shelton marriage. I'll take Jenny Saunders. She's a physician's assistant. According to Sally Wiseman, Rafe relied heavily on Jenny. I'll see what light she can shed on all this."

Dantzler stood. "Let's meet tomorrow at ten. We can bring Rich up to speed, see what suggestions he might have. Hopefully, Jake Thomas will be there as well, so we can fill him in on what's going on."

Eric said, "Tell me, Milt. How many meetings do you figure you've been to in all your years on the force?"

"About eight million."

"Just think—two more weeks, no more meetings."

"You know, I'm gonna miss all this," Milt said, after jotting down Greg Novotny's phone number and home address. "It's tough walking away from something you've loved doing for almost forty years. Hard to believe the end has finally arrived."

"Let's solve this case, Milt," Dantzler said, "so you go out on a high note."

"Yes, let's do," Milt answered.

CHAPTER EIGHT

The Long Branch Saloon was formerly The Library Club before Neil Raymond bought the place in 1972 and changed its name. Neil, a one-time bit actor in Hollywood, named his new establishment after the old TV Western *Gunsmoke*, on which he spent three years playing one of the Dodge City locals. It was his only steady gig in what was a thoroughly undistinguished acting career.

In 1967 Neil managed to land a small role in *The Flim-Flam Man*, a con artist caper movie starring George C. Scott. A big part of the movie was filmed in and around Central Kentucky. While on location for the movie, Neil met a local girl named Betsy Gilbert, whom he wooed and married. She reluctantly followed him to Hollywood, but when the acting roles for Neil failed to materialize and the financial struggle became too great, Betsy laid down an ultimatum: Move back to Kentucky with me and find a real job, or we're kaput. Neil agreed. The couple packed up and relocated to Lexington. Neil worked a variety of jobs over the next three years, but with no discernible skills and only a high school education, no job lasted more than a few months. As a last resort, out of money and in desperate financial trouble, Neil approached Betsy's father and asked for a loan. The old man agreed. With money in hand, Neil purchased The Library Club and christened it The Long Branch Saloon as a tribute to his old pals on the TV show.

In keeping with the *Gunsmoke* theme, Neil covered the walls with photographs of him with series regulars James Arness, Amanda Blake, Milburn Stone, Ken Curtis, Buck Taylor, Dennis Weaver and Burt Reynolds. Some were shots of him with the actors, others were scenes from various episodes. There were photos of him with *Gunsmoke* guest stars Lee J. Cobb, Leslie Nielsen, Steve Forrest, Warren Oates, a young Jon Voight and a much younger Jodie Foster. The largest picture, one dominating the wall behind the bar, featured Neil standing between James Arness and John Wayne.

The Duke, Matt Dillon and Neil Raymond. Three amigos hanging loose.

There was one other *Gunsmoke*-inspired tradition Neil brought to The Long Branch. Throughout the decades at least two dozen women had worked behind the bar, and although their names varied, each one was affectionately called "Miss Kitty."

Neil and Betsy had one child, Neil junior, nicknamed Buddy to distinguish father from son, although given their different personalities and attitudes the comparison rarely occurred. In fact, the same name was about the only thing the two had in common. They were as different as night and day. Neil may have lived in Hollywood at one time, but he was a straight arrow by-the-book citizen. He didn't drink alcohol, nor did he tolerate drugs or drug use in the bar.

Conversely, Buddy was a rebel and a troublemaker. Not surprisingly, the relationship between father and son was strained, due in large measure to Buddy's propensity for violence and his admittedly heavy drug use. As a teenager, Buddy had more than a dozen brush-ups with the law, and on several occasions only managed to escape incarceration thanks to his father's willingness to bail him out of trouble. The money was usually forked over at Betsy's insistence.

Despite their differences, when Neil's health began to fail he sold the saloon to Buddy for one-hundred dollars and two promises—keep the *Gunsmoke* motif, and refrain from selling or allowing the use of drugs on the premises. Buddy, twenty-seven and desperate for money at the time, agreed to his father's demands, although he had no intention of keeping the promises made to the old man.

Gunsmoke didn't mean shit to him—he'd heard his father's me-and-Jim Arness stories so many times they made him want to puke—and there was simply too much money to be made from selling drugs to give any serious thought to ending that enterprise.

Besides, nostalgia was for suckers and old farts. Buddy had no desire to surround himself with reminders of his father's failed dreams and sorry life. His plans for the future were simple: Once the old man checks out, down comes the *Gunsmoke* nonsense and up goes the NASCAR stuff. So long, Matt Dillon, hello, Dale Earnhardt and Jeff Gordon.

Fuck you very much, John Wayne.

Buddy was sitting at the bar gabbing with the latest Miss Kitty when Rufus Young came charging in like a rampaging pit bull. His nostrils flared and fire burned in his eyes. Rufus, who always appeared pissed off about something, was hotter than usual today.

"You seen that damn boy of mine?" Rufus growled.

"Which one?" Miss Kitty asked. "You have three."

"You know which one. Oscar. The one who's stickin' his pecker into places it ought not go."

"And where might that be?" Miss Kitty teased.

"A non-American gash."

"Rufus, if crude was gold, you'd be richer than Bill Gates."

"I'm just bein' honest. That boy needs to stop banging foreigners."

"The one thing I know about a man's pecker is it definitely does not suffer from the sins of prejudice or discrimination," Miss Kitty said. "It will happily go anywhere, anytime. I'm convinced that the world would be a better place if a man's brain behaved with the same lack of bias as his pecker."

"Look, if you want to shack up with some taco eater, that's your business," Rufus said. "But that won't cut it for my boys. They'll stick with their own kind or I'll turn them into geldings. It's a sin to mix races. Whites will soon be the minority in this country, and when it happens, there goes the United States of America."

Miss Kitty laughed. "Rufus, you are so full of shit you could float down the Mississippi like a barge."

"You serve the beer and keep your lips zipped. I don't need advice from a cunt like you." Rufus quickly cut his eyes toward Buddy. Realizing he had stepped over the line with his last statement, he saw the need to make amends. "Well, you ain't a cunt, Miss Kitty. Sorry for sayin' so."

The reason for Rufus's rare apology was simple—Buddy Raymond. By his own admission, Rufus Young feared only one person on Earth, and it was Buddy. He always had . . . and with good reason. Buddy was simply not someone to tangle with . . . ever. Rufus was tough—plenty tough—but Buddy was kill-you-in-a-split-second bad. He didn't look the part—tall, thin, wiry and quiet—but he was strong, and he was absolutely fearless. People tended to misread Buddy because of his easy going, laconic manner. But make him angry—like Rufus had just done —and the change was startling. His eyes turned black like a shark's, and he had a certain look that said your next course of action had better be the right one or it could mean instant death.

Rufus knew all too well what Buddy was capable of doing. He found out two decades ago during one of their early criminal endeavors —boosting high-end automobiles and selling them to a chop shop in Tampa, Florida. On what turned out to be their final trip to the Sunshine State, Buddy had a slight financial disagreement with Ernesto Avila, the shop's owner. Buddy judged Ernesto's accounting practices to be a bit on the shady side, with the numbers decidedly in Ernesto's favor. Buddy said Ernesto owed the boys another ten grand. Ernesto held his ground, then ordered Buddy and Rufus to leave. He also told them he expected another shipment of cars within the month. Buddy smiled, picked up a tire iron and savagely beat Ernesto's head until his skull cracked like an egg and his brains spilled out onto the garage floor.

"Bet he didn't expect that," Buddy said, using a canvas rag to wipe blood from the tire iron. "Bastard would still be alive if he was a little better at math."

They looted almost twenty-five thousand from Ernesto's safe, grabbed a bite to eat, then drove back to Lexington. Two nights later

Buddy tossed the tire iron into the lake at Jacobson Park. After getting rid of the murder weapon, he got back in the car, lit a joint, took a hit and passed it to Rufus.

"I won't tolerate being cheated or lied to," Buddy said. "Someone cheats me or lies to me, I'll kill him."

Rufus did not want to cross swords with a man that volatile.

"Let's chat," Buddy said, pointing to a table near the front window. "We need to get some things straight."

Rufus followed Buddy to the table, pulled back a chair and sat. "Sorry for what I said to Miss Kitty. I shouldn't have called her a cunt. But that damn Oscar. He's got me all worked up. Slippin' the meat to some greasy Mexican whore. What's he thinkin', anyway, going for the dark stuff when he knows how I feel about such things? Hell, there are plenty of white girls out there he could screw."

"You need to back off, Rufus, and cut the kid some slack. At his age, all he wants is some trim. He couldn't care less about race, religion or creed."

"I'm tellin' you, Buddy, you made the right decision by not gettin' married. By stayin' away from women."

"I didn't stay away from women. I stayed away from a wife."

"Well, it was the prudent thing to do. You can take my word on it. I sired a brood, and look what it's done to me. Made me a madman."

"You've always been a madman, Rufus. Only no one other than me has the nerve to tell you you're a madman."

Rufus grinned. "You got nerves and you've got smarts. There's no denying it."

"Smarts . . . an excellent subject to talk about."

"What do you mean?"

Buddy leaned forward, both elbows on the table, fingers steeple-shaped at his lips. "This clinic thing was dumb, Rufus. Not a smart play at all. You should've steered clear of that one."

"Fifty G's. Hard to say no to so much cash."

"Fifty? I heard twenty-five."

"Well . . . the job ain't done yet."

Buddy shook his head. "If this bleeds over and interferes with the other thing, I'm not going to be happy. And you'll be the one I hold responsible."

"Won't happen. There couldn't possibly be any way to connect the two. If I thought there was any danger of it happening, I would not have taken the job. I'm not that stupid."

"Yeah, Rufus, sometimes you are."

"Well, this ain't one of those times."

"For your sake, you'd better hope not."

CHAPTER NINE

Dantzler phoned Jenny Saunders's home number and got the answering machine. Next, he punched in the cell number given to him by Sally Wiseman. Jenny answered immediately. Because of the background noise, he could barely hear her. Dantzler identified himself, then asked if she would be willing to meet him sometime tonight.

"I can meet with you right now, if you'd like," Jenny said. "I'm at Harry's Bar with my partner, Renee Connelly. We're drowning my sorrows."

"I can be there in twenty minutes," Dantzler said.

"Terrific. That will give us even more time to drown."

"How will I recognize you?"

"We're sitting at a table in the back. Renee is the gorgeous red-head drinking wine, and I'm the almost-pretty brunette mixing Heineken and tequila shots." Jenny giggled. "By the time you get here my eyes will match Renee's hair."

"I'll see you in ten minutes, then."

Dantzler made it to the bar on Tates Creek Road in eight minutes. He parked, went inside and immediately spotted the two women. In tandem, they waved and motioned for him to join them. Dantzler wondered if he looked *that* much like a cop.

As he worked his way toward their table, he realized Jenny's assessment had only been half right. Renee was, indeed, a stunningly beautiful woman. She had a proud, almost regal air about her. Could have been a Kennedy, Dantzler concluded. But Jenny's assessment of herself wasn't even close to being accurate. It was way off the mark. In every way, Jenny's beauty rivaled Renee's. She was slightly shorter than Renee, with dark hair and dark eyes, and she appeared to be a few years younger, but definitely a beautiful lady. Together, they looked like a Hollywood A-list couple.

Jenny tapped her watch. "Under ten minutes. Faster than a speeding bullet."

"That's me—Superman."

"Sorry, but being the Man of Steel won't help you at this table," Jenny said. "You have landed at table Kryptonite"

"What do you mean?"

"It means you are about to chat with a couple of lesbians."

"Well, then, I guess I should tuck my cape away."

Both women laughed. "I think this guy's okay," Jenny said to Renee. She turned toward Dantzler. "Would you care for a drink, Detective? Or are you going to hit me with the boring I'm-on-duty cliché and take a pass?"

"I am on duty, but this late on a Sunday night, why not? But only if you allow me to buy the next round."

"Chivalry won't get you into bed with either of us, Detective, but it is certainly appreciated." Jenny motioned to the waiter. "Another glass of wine for Renee, another beer and shot for me, and . . ."

"Smithwick's," Dantzler said. After the waitress took the order and left, he said, "Are you up to answering a few questions?"

Jenny nodded and finished off the Heineken. "Can I ask you a question first?"

"Sure."

"Is it true about Carly? That she is dead?"

"I'm afraid so."

"That's beyond tragic. Carly was a genuinely nice person. I can't imagine the Wiseman Clinic functioning without her."

Dantzler waited until their drinks were served before taking out his notepad and pen. After taking a pull from the bottle of Smithwick's, he said, "The big mystery seems to be why Carly was at the clinic so late on a Saturday night. Any thoughts?"

Jenny downed the tequila and followed it with a long drink of Heineken. "The only reason would be if she was meeting someone. It's the only thing that calculates for me. But I can't imagine who it would be."

"One of the visiting physicians, maybe?"

"Possibly. But they all have keys to the clinic. They wouldn't need Carly to let them inside. And even if one of the doctors was there, for whatever reason, they wouldn't need Carly's assistance. She wasn't a nurse. Her being there simply doesn't make any sense."

"Any chance she was there to get drugs?"

"Carly didn't smoke, and she rarely drank alcohol. There is no way she had a drug issue. And the thought of her selling drugs is even more ludicrous."

"Could she have been meeting a man?"

"I don't think so. Although . . ."

"What?"

"Considering who she's married to, I wouldn't blame her if she was having an affair."

"We'll discuss him in a minute," Dantzler said. "But I want to cover a few other bases first."

Renee said, "Should I excuse myself, Detective? You won't hurt my feelings if you say yes."

"No, you're fine." He turned to Jenny. "Last year, when the clinic was under assault, did you receive any threatening phone calls, hate mail or e-mails?"

"No. But I did get threats and curses when I tried to enter the building. On the last day, when the police were called, I was shoved to the ground and kicked by one of the protesters. It happened almost immediately after I got out of my car. Fortunately for me, a policeman witnessed the incident. He got to me in about two seconds, handcuffed the guy and put him into a patrol car. I'm pretty sure he was arrested."

"Did you know any of the protesters?"

Jenny finished off the Heineken. "Let me assure you, Detective, when you are making your way through an angry mob, you don't study faces. You keep your head down and move forward, praying no one has a gun or a knife."

"Can you recall if any of the clinic employees ever mentioned a specific protester?"

"No. Sorry."

"Okay, let's talk about Paul Shelton?" Dantzler said.

"If you insist upon discussing him, we definitely need more booze." Jenny motioned to the waitress and indicated another round of drinks. "Paul Shelton—not one of my favorite people."

"What can you tell me about him?"

"Not nearly as much as Renee can. Right, honey?"

"Unfortunately." Renee took the glass of wine from the waitress and sipped. "Are you familiar with the law firm of Sandberg, Wilson and Connelly?"

"I am," Dantzler said.

"Well, I'm the Connelly. Our firm has represented Paul's financial services company for almost fifteen years. We do a lot of work for him. I also teach a Corporate Law class at the University of Kentucky, and once each semester I have Paul come in as a guest lecturer. He's a jerk, but he's exceptionally good at what he does, as painful as it is to admit. Over the years I have attended several parties Paul also attended. In other words, I have interacted with him on far more occasions than I care to."

"You don't like him?" Dantzler asked.

"Not in the least. Aside from being the single most arrogant man I've ever met, he is also a professional flirt. I don't know a woman he hasn't come on to at least once, and that includes me."

"He hit on you?"

"Not fifteen minutes after I first laid eyes on him. This was several years ago, at a party hosted by our firm. He strolled over to where I was standing and said—and these are his exact words—'Hey, Doll, you look lost, lonely and in search of the perfect man. Well, this is your lucky day, because I'm that man.' Even if I weren't gay, even if I was the horniest straight woman on the globe, I wouldn't respond positively to such a pathetic line as that one. I didn't know whether to laugh out loud or throw up."

"Tell Detective Dantzler what you did say," Jenny urged.

"I said, 'Can't the perfect man come up with something better than a horseshit line like that? You couldn't get laid in a whorehouse with that stinker.' Then I gave him my nicest smile, turned and walked away. He hasn't bothered me since."

"You go, girlfriend," Jenny said, hoisting the Heineken. "Paul Shelton is a rat bastard. I don't know how Carly tolerated the man."

Dantzler could tell Jenny was starting to feel the effects of her drinking. Along with beginning to slur her words, her voice had gone up several decibel levels. He hoped Renee was behind the wheel when they drove home.

"Did Paul hit on any of the other women at the clinic?" he said.

Jenny shook her head. "He hates Dr. Wiseman and everything the clinic stands for. I doubt he's ever said one word to any of the clinic employees. He would consider himself too good for lowly mortals like us."

"Did Carly ever indicate if she suspected him of having an affair?"

"Not to me, she didn't," Jenny said. "But a guy like him—I wouldn't be surprised if he was having multiple affairs."

Dantzler closed his notepad and put it in his coat pocket. He hadn't learned anything new from the two women, but he had confirmed what he did know—there was no obvious reason for Carly to have been at the clinic at midnight, and his assessment of Paul Shelton as being arrogance personified wasn't off the mark. Still, he considered the chat worthwhile. During any homicide investigation, it was always better to turn over too many rocks than leave a single rock untouched. You never knew which rock might be hiding the answer to the puzzle.

"Do either of you think Paul Shelton is capable of murder?" Dantzler said. "Could he have killed his wife?"

"Anyone is capable of just about anything, including murder,"

Renee said. "Being a homicide detective, you know this better than I do. But Paul Shelton as a cold-blooded murderer? I don't see it. In the end, I think he would lack the guts to commit an act like that."

"He could always pay someone else to do it," Dantzler pointed out.

"True. But . . . What do you think, Jenny?"

"I think I'm too drunk to offer an opinion. Ask me tomorrow, after I sober up."

"Come on, honey, let's get out of here before you order another round."

"Why leave now? It's still early. And as of right now, I'm unemployed. One more round. Come on."

"You've had enough, Sweetie." Renee waved to the waitress. "What's the damage?"

The waitress went to a computer terminal, punched in some numbers and waited for the tally. She came back and handed the bill to Renee.

"Ouch! Eighty-two bucks," Renee said. "I had no idea we were such alcoholics."

Dantzler pulled out a roll of bills, peeled off two tens and a five, and laid them on the table. "For my drink and your time."

"If I weren't gay I'd go after this man," Renee said to Jenny. "He would be a keeper."

"Right now, I'm too drunk to go after anybody," Jenny mumbled. "But if you feel the need to go over to the dark side, he's yours. Just make sure he's out of the house when I do sober up."

"My dear, I would never leave you for any man."

"Of course you wouldn't. Why would you even consider it?"

Dantzler helped Jenny out of her chair. To Renee, he said, "Are you okay to drive?"

"I'm fine."

"Thanks for talking to me tonight. And if either of you think of anything else, give me a call." He handed two cards to Renee. "You can reach me at this number, night or day."

"I've heard that line before," Jenny said.

CHAPTER TEN

At eight the next morning Dantzler walked into the morgue, hoping his early arrival would allow him to suit up and observe Carly Shelton's autopsy. Viewing the desecration of a human body wasn't part of the job he particularly cared for, but he did see it as necessary in most cases, if not so much for what he learned during the gruesome procedure as for his own desire to be a frontline participant during all aspects of an investigation. He had always believed the more he knew, the better his chances of solving the case. Information yields results.

Dantzler moved through the morgue area, which was dark and smelled of chemicals and death, and headed toward the two offices in the back. In the office to his right, he saw Arnie Edwards sitting at his desk furiously typing on his computer. Edwards, a small man with a disproportionately large head, swiveled in his chair and smiled when he heard Dantzler knock on the door.

"Detective Dantzler," he said, rising and extending his hand. "The very chap I'm looking for. However, I didn't expect to see you this early."

Dantzler shook the man's hand, then said, "Thought I would come by and observe the Shelton autopsy."

"Already done." Edwards sat back down. "I'm almost finished with my final report. If you can hang around for another thirty minutes or so, you can take a copy with you."

"Sure, no problem."

"Care for a cup of coffee or some juice? Maybe a crème horn? There are a few left in the break room."

Dantzler couldn't imagine how anyone could possibly eat or drink in this place. "I'll pass. Thanks, anyway."

Dantzler was surprised—and pleased—to learn the autopsy was completed. It meant Edwards performed it sometime Sunday, or very early this morning. Either he was a workaholic, or as the new man on the job he was trying to make a positive impression on his superiors. Neither scenario mattered to Dantzler. With the autopsy completed, he would not have to wait for the information gleaned by the coroner.

"Anything important you can tell me off hand?" Dantzler asked.

"Dental records confirmed the deceased was Carly Shelton," Edwards said, as he continued typing. "Other than that, not a lot. As I suspected from the beginning, death resulted from the explosion and not the fire. There was virtually no smoke in her lungs, which means she wasn't breathing when the fire and smoke began to spread. I would consider it a blessing. Being burned alive is a horrible way to die."

"What was the cause of death?"

"Two large pieces of metal, probably from a cabinet or desk, penetrated her back. One did extensive damage to a kidney and the spleen, the other, the one which likely caused instant death, went straight into her heart. I can't say for certain which injury occurred first. My guess would be they happened almost simultaneously. She died within seconds of the impact."

"Did you take X-rays?"

"Of course."

"Any sign of old fractures that had healed?"

"No."

"Nothing indicating she had been physically abused?"

"I saw no signs of previous breaks."

Dantzler was silent for a few seconds, then said, "Could you tell if there had been recent sexual activity?"

"When a body has been so extensively damaged, some things are impossible to know. Sexual activity falls into that category. I can't even tell you what the woman had eaten, or when her last meal might have taken place. Keep in mind, Detective, Carly Shelton's body burned for nearly two hours before the fire was extinguished. It sustained about as much damage as a human body can sustain. There was virtually no tissue or muscle remaining."

Edwards turned in his chair and resumed typing. It took him less than twenty minutes to finish his report. When it was completed, he printed out a copy and handed it to Dantzler.

"Wish I could give you more, but under the circumstances this is the best I can do."

"Thanks. And I really appreciate you getting it done so promptly." Dantzler folded the report and put it in his coat pocket. He shook Edwards's hand. "If I have any questions, I'll be in touch."

"I'll be here," Edwards said.

* * *

After leaving Edwards, Dantzler drove downtown, parked and went into the Police Station. He exchanged small talk with veteran desk sergeant Bruce Rawlinson, climbed the steps to the second floor and tapped on Captain Richard Bird's door. He went into the office before Bird had time to respond.

"I got you Jake Thomas," Bird announced. "He's in the War Room with Milt and Eric. You have him as long as necessary."

"Thanks." Dantzler sat in the chair across from Bird's desk. "I just came from meeting with the coroner. Carly Shelton's autopsy didn't give us much to go on."

"Body that badly burned . . . no surprise there." Bird took off his glasses and leaned back. "Any preliminary thoughts on the case or how you're going to approach it?"

"Given what happened at the clinic last year, the hate crime angle is the most obvious route to take," Dantzler said. "And we will have to pursue it. But something in my gut tells me that's not what this is all about."

"Why not? It's no stretch to believe one of those lunatics went over the edge and decided that marching outside the building wasn't enough, that more drastic action needed to be taken. So, he blows the place up, probably thinking no one would be inside at the time. His intent was to destroy, not kill. Carly was collateral damage."

Collateral damage. People toss the phrase around as if it were meaningless.

"But the trouble occurred more than a year ago," Dantzler said. "Why wait all this time before taking action?"

"It took time for his anger to stew and his courage to grow."

Dantzler shook his head. "You're overlooking another possibility, Rich. What if Carly Shelton was the intended victim all along?"

"Then Paul Shelton moves up the suspects' list—with a bullet by his name." Bird rubbed his eyes with the palms of his hands. "Eric and Milt think the guy could have done it. They said he's a jerk who doesn't rate very high on the likeability scale."

"Being an arrogant prick doesn't make him guilty of murder."

"True. But if you are right about Carly being the intended victim, hubby then becomes the prime suspect. He wouldn't be the first husband to off his wife."

"If Paul Shelton is guilty, we'll get him."

Dantzler stood, remembered something else, and sat back down. For the next few minutes he recounted his Saturday-night conversation with Nikki Bradford about the death of Danny Tucker, and how Nikki had pleaded with Dantzler to look into the case. Bird listened intently but remained silent until Dantzler concluded his presentation.

"And you think it would be worthwhile to investigate?" Bird asked. "You don't see it as a waste of your time and our resources?"

"I think there might be something to it."

"The cyanide is what troubles you, right?"

"How many suicides have you heard of where the person died by ingesting cyanide? Exactly as many as I have—none. Plus, Danny lived in Lexington. That gives us a reason to look into it."

"If you feel so strongly about it, I'll contact the right people in Woodford County," Bird said, jotting some notes on a notepad. "I'll also get in touch with Woody Porter at KSP. He's a friend, but he might not be thrilled about us investigating a case that has been signed, sealed, delivered and closed. He could tell me to back off."

"If he does, we drop it." Dantzler stood and walked to the door. "If he says okay, we look into it."

"A word to the wise. The Danny Tucker investigation, if it does get the green light, takes a backseat to the Wiseman Clinic bombing and Carly Shelton's death. That's order number one. And if we do look into it, I don't want you stepping on anyone's toes. That's order number two. I already have enough enemies. I don't need more names added to the list."

"Charmer like you couldn't possibly have enemies, Rich."

"Oh, how I wish that was true."

CHAPTER ELEVEN

In the War Room Milt sat at the table, stirring cream into a cup of steaming black coffee. Eric sat opposite Milt and was sorting through his notes. The new guy, Jake Thomas, stood next to the large chalkboard at the far end of the room. A half-empty box of assorted Krispy Kreme doughnuts rested on the middle of the table.

Upon Dantzler's arrival, Jake pulled back a chair and sat next to Eric. Dantzler took his usual place at the head of the table.

"First off, welcome aboard, Jake," Dantzler said. "We need you, and it's good to have you with us."

"Thanks. It's an honor to work with you guys."

"Did Milt and Eric bring you up to speed on what we know so far?"

"Yes, sir. They copied their notes for me. They also gave me an overview of the situation as it now stands."

"I'm Jack around here. You don't have to be so formal. You're not in the military anymore."

"Yes, sir. I mean, yes, Jack."

Jake, a local kid, was a senior in high school when the Twin Towers were hit. Like many people his age, he was angered by what happened and eager to give some payback. With enough credits to graduate in December, he left school early and joined the Marines, with an eye on

Afghanistan and the hunt for bin Laden. However, when President Bush sent the military on a questionable detour into Iraq, Jake was dispatched to that country, where he served eighteen months fighting Saddam's forces instead of al-Qaida. During his time in country, Jake was involved in some of the war's fiercest and bloodiest battles. After being wounded a second time, he was shipped back stateside, spending nearly six months in the hospital recuperating from his injuries. For his heroic efforts, he was awarded a host of medals, including the Silver Star, Bronze Star, Legion of Merit, and Purple Heart (twice). Following his discharge from the Marines, Jake joined the Lexington Police Force, quickly working his way up to the Robbery Unit, where, to no one's surprise, he established a reputation for being an exemplary cop.

Dantzler had no idea what kind of homicide detective Jake would make, but he did know one thing for certain: He would never have to worry about Jake's courage under fire. The kid had proved his bravery many times over.

Dantzler said, "Okay, Milt, did you get a chance to meet with Greg Novotny?"

"I was with him for about an hour last night," Milt replied. "He's the chatty type, and he has a rather high opinion of himself. According to him, he's the one who keeps the clinic going. In his words, 'without me, the place would crumble.' He is a sharp guy, there's no question about it. But . . . there's something a little off about him. He's squirrelly, nervous, never looks you in the eye. Shifty is the word I would use to describe him."

"Did you detect any signs of animus toward Rafe?"

"That's where it gets a little odd. He praises Dr. Wiseman, but always in a roundabout way. It's difficult to tell what his true feelings are for Wiseman. There's something else that caught my attention. Novotny tends to make himself out to be some kind of big hero. Take the abortion situation last year. Novotny said he's the one who detected problems with the fetus. Said he discovered it through blood work. He also says he's the one who urged Dr. Wiseman to perform the procedure. And, of course, Novotny also says he's the one who stood up against the protesters. Like I said, Jack, the guy has delusions of grandeur."

"Where was he Saturday night?"

"At the Kentucky Theatre with a chick named Allison Vincent. They went to see a midnight showing of *Pink Floyd The Wall*. I haven't been able to contact Allison yet. I'll give her another call later this morning."

"Midnight is midnight. The blast occurred between eleven and eleven-thirty. Novotny's alibi isn't rock solid."

"All the more reason to speak with Allison Vincent. Maybe she can firm it up for us."

"Does Novotny drive a pickup truck?" Dantzler asked.

"Blue Toyota RAV4."

"Maybe . . ." Dantzler shuffled through Eric's notes, "Amanda Woolcott confused the Toyota for a pickup. Was she a credible witness, Eric?"

"She would have no reason to lie," Eric answered. "If you want me to, I'll meet with her again, show her a picture of a RAV4 and see if that's her notion of a pickup truck."

"Good idea, but let Jake do it. He has the puppy-dog charm all elderly ladies love."

"What? I don't have charm?" Eric said, feigning mock indignation. "I'm a walking billboard advertising charm."

"You're a walking black dude who probably scared the shit out of poor old Amanda," Milt said. "You can bet she breathed a sigh of relief when you walked out the door and all her valuables were still inside."

"Come to think of it, Milt, since you and Amanda are both in the senior citizen age bracket, you should have interviewed her. No doubt she would have felt more comfortable chatting with an old codger like you."

"She would have come on to me, no question about it."

"Yeah, Milt, I see you as a real chick magnet."

"Chick magnet?" Milt said, nodding his head. "That works for me."

Dantzler nudged Jake's shoulder. "In the Marines, did your commanding officer hear silly nonsense like this?"

"No, sir," Jake said. "But my CO never had to put up with guys like these two."

"Oh, the rookie shoots, the rookie scores," Eric announced in his best play-by-play broadcaster's voice. "A three-pointer nailed from downtown. This kid has all-star potential, Milt. Don't you agree?"

"Tell me, Jake. Did you ever meet Dan Matthews?" Milt asked.

"No, sir. But I've heard plenty of good things about him. Why do you ask?"

"He would have loved you," Milt said. "The smart-ass answer you gave is exactly the kind of thing he would have said. And if it had been said about him, he would have cracked up. Yeah, kid, you'll fit right in with us."

"It took weeks before Scott shed his fear of us," Eric said. "Jake did it in ten minutes."

"After what Jake's been through, I don't think we're going to scare him," Milt said. "Welcome aboard, Jake."

"It's only a temporary assignment," Jake pointed out.

"You never know when temporary might become permanent. I'm out of here in less than two weeks. Who knows? Maybe you'll get the call and Captain Bird will replace an old Vietnam vet with a young Iraqi vet."

Dantzler said, "Let's get back to business. Milt, can you see Greg Novotny as the doer?"

Milt pondered the question for several seconds. "Yes and no. If the intent was to kill Carly Shelton, then I vote no. I don't see him as a killer. However, if the intent was to destroy the clinic and Carly just happened to be there, then I think yes is a possibility."

"What reason would Greg Novotny have to bomb the clinic, his place of employment?" Jake asked. "It doesn't make much sense."

The three veteran detectives stared at Jake, surprised the rookie had asked the question, and pleased that he had.

"It's a long shot, I agree," Milt answered. "And at this moment I don't see him as a serious suspect. If his alibi holds up he's not a suspect at all. But like I indicated earlier, there is something *off* about the guy. I can envision a scenario where he bombs the clinic so he can help Dr. Wiseman rebuild it from the ground up, with Novotny offering expert advice on all facets of the new structure and on how the clinic should be run."

"He has *that* much ego?" Dantzler asked.

"Greg Novotny loves Greg Novotny. That much I can tell you."

"Novotny stays on the radar until Allison Vincent makes or breaks his alibi." Dantzler turned to Eric. "What did Barbara Pearlman have to say?"

"Nothing that is going to help us find out who bombed the clinic," Eric said. "Like everyone else, she could not imagine why Carly would be at the clinic so late at night. She wouldn't even venture a guess. She did say Dr. Wiseman had been somewhat preoccupied in the past couple of weeks. 'More into his own thoughts' was how she phrased it."

"Did she give a reason why he was preoccupied?"

"No. Only that he seemed more distracted than usual."

"Maybe his wife could answer that for us," Jake offered.

An impressive debut for the kid. "That's a good call, Jake," Dantzler said. "At some point, we'll need to ask her about it."

Dantzler opened the manila folder and took out the two pages listing the Wiseman Clinic employees. He read off the names of those who had not been questioned, then assigned each one to a detective. Next, he removed the paper clip binding together the e-mails Greg Novotny printed out for Milt.

"Jake, I want you take a look at these," Dantzler said, handing the stack to the new detective. "There aren't as many as I was led to believe—thirty-one in all—so it shouldn't take too long. Some will be from cranks who love to shout from the mountaintop, some from individuals who genuinely believe abortion is wrong. Those you can dismiss. What you're looking for are the ones that make your skin crawl. Look for certain buzzwords, specific insights indicating the sender knows what he's talking about. Whoever did this is filled with hate and rage combined with a high level of self-righteousness. Use your best judgment. Pull out the ones you consider worth looking into."

"Got it."

"We'll divide up the letters and postcards sent to Rafe and go through them," Dantzler said to Milt and Eric. "There are almost two-hundred, so it's going to take us some time. We need to get on it ASAP."

"What's the priority?" Eric asked. "Interviews, or going through the correspondence?"

"Call the employees and set a time to meet. If they can see you immediately, do that first. If they can't meet until later today or sometime tomorrow, work on the letters and postcards. Same with you, Jake. If you can get with Amanda Woolcott this morning, great. If not, look through the e-mails."

Milt said, "And, Jake, when you do phone Amanda, let her know you aren't the big, threatening black dude who interviewed her the first time."

"Fuck off, Milt," Eric said.

"Now *that* I did hear in the Marines," Jake said.

CHAPTER TWELVE

For the next two days the homicide squad alternated between interviewing Wiseman Clinic employees and sifting through correspondence received by Dr. Wiseman. Neither avenue provided much in the way of relevant information. Dantzler hadn't expected it to. He continued to believe the crime was about something other than hate for Rafe Wiseman or his clinic.

All but two employees were interviewed. Amy Galloway, one of the scrub techs, was out of town attending a funeral and wouldn't be back until Thursday afternoon. Anna Davis, a receptionist, could not be reached.

Those employees who spoke with the detectives echoed what had been said by Dr. Wiseman, Jenny Saunders, Barbara Pearlman and Greg Novotny—there was no reason for Carly to have been at the clinic so late at night. Nor could they imagine why she was. They were unified in their respect and admiration for Carly, and they were in agreement that her loss would leave a big hole at the clinic that might be impossible to fill. They all seemed profoundly upset and disturbed by her death.

As for Barbara Pearlman's observation regarding Dr. Wiseman

"being more into his own thoughts" than usual, none of the employees had picked up on it.

"Dr. Wiseman was by nature a deep thinker," Eva Landon, one of the RN's, said. "He was a true intellectual, easily the smartest, wisest man I've ever been around. But I haven't noticed him being distracted. Not in the least. He's always focused. I can't imagine what Barbara was alluding to."

"No, Dr. Wiseman hasn't seemed distracted," Kevin Brothers, the anesthesiologist, told Eric. "I mean, he's always dealing with distractions—sometimes five or six at a time—but as for him *being* distracted, no way. The guy is sharper than a razor blade."

Jake Thomas's search through the e-mails sent to Dr. Wiseman proved to be another dead-end pursuit. Of the thirty-one received by Wiseman, only two were judged to be worth following up. They were traced to a pair of elderly males who lived next door to each other and attended the same church. Jake spoke with the two men, both of whom had solid alibis for the time of the bombing. They were part of a large Christian group that spent Saturday evening at a Joel Osteen Crusade in Cincinnati. The group traveled in three busses, and did not return to Lexington until well after midnight Sunday morning.

Although the two men—William Tartar and Wayne Coffman— were not responsible for the bombing, they were pleased to learn "one of God's soldiers" had the fortitude to "do God's work."

"The wicked shall reap fire and brimstone, in this life or in the next life," Wayne Coffman told Jake. "The sinners who lived in Sodom and Gomorrah incurred the wrath of God, and they paid the ultimate price. Doctors who kill the unborn are not deserving of mercy, here or when they stand before the Almighty on Judgment Day. The Wiseman Clinic went up in fire just like those Cities of the Plain, and the abominable Dr. Wiseman's soul will burn for eternity in a lake of fire."

Of the nearly two-hundred letters, postcards and notes sent to Dr. Wiseman, only six were deemed worthy of further investigation. Four of the six individuals were interviewed by Milt and Eric. Three had alibis excluding them as viable suspects. The fourth sender, who signed the letter R. J. White, turned out to be Rhonda Jo White. Although she could not provide an alibi—"I was home alone . . . unfortunately"—the detectives were convinced the bomber was not female.

The remaining two possible suspects had yet to be located.

Not much payoff for two days of hard work by the detectives.

"Jack, you predicted we would shoot blanks on the hate crime angle," Milt said, when the squad gathered in the War Room late Wednesday afternoon. "Unless, of course, one of these remaining two turns out to be the doer. And based on what we've run into thus far, I'm not counting on it."

"I'm not ready to totally write off the hate crime angle," Dantzler said. "It's very likely that whoever bombed the clinic is not much different from those who sent letters or e-mails. Philosophically, anyway. He's filled with the same hate, rage and self-righteousness. But the difference is the doer is a man of action. He's not going to waste time making threats when he can spend time making bombs."

Dantzler opened a bottle of water and took a long drink. "Having said that, I still can't shake the feeling that this is not about the abortion or what transpired at the clinic last year. There's something else at play here and we need to find out what it is."

Jake pushed away from the wall and took the chair next to Dantzler. "Are we all in agreement that the doer did not send an e-mail or letter to Dr. Wiseman?"

"Yeah, I think we can agree on it," Milt said.

"Okay," Jake continued, "based on our interviews with the clinic employees, are we all in agreement that none of them set off the bomb?"

"I'll go along with that, too," Milt said.

"All right, then . . ."

"Slow down, Jake," Eric interrupted. "There are two clinic employees we still haven't talked to. And unless Allison Vincent backs up Greg Novotny's alibi, he's worth a second look. In addition, two people who sent letters are still unaccounted for. That adds up to five people we can't eliminate. So we need to do some follow-up work before we start waving the magic wand and dismissing potential suspects."

"Eric's right," Dantzler said, looking up at Jake. "Those doors can't be closed just yet. But go on. What were you about to say?"

"If the employees are innocent, and if it turns out the doer is not among those who sent letters or e-mails to the clinic, then we need to go back and re-interview Dr. Wiseman. It could be he knows more than he's telling."

"You talked to the guy, Jack," Milt said. "And you know him better than any of us do. Any chance the rookie could be on to something?"

"There is always a chance an individual is hiding secrets or withholding information. I don't know Rafe all that well, so I'm in no position to offer much insight on the man, other than he has a weak forehand. However, when I spoke with him he didn't give off a negative vibe. I didn't sense or detect anything hinky in his demeanor or his answers. He was in shock, and obviously distraught but very forthcoming in his response to my questions."

Dantzler took another drink of water, and then said, "But Jake is correct. We need to speak with him again, see if we can dig more information out of him. Or at the very least, get a sense of whether or not he is holding back on us."

"What about insurance money?" Eric said. "There's an area we haven't even touched on yet."

"Good point," Milt said, looking at Dantzler. "Was the clinic well insured? And if it was, how will the money be paid out, and who does it go to?"

"Sally Wiseman showed me the policy while I was with her," Dantzler answered. "There was more than enough coverage. As for where the money will go, it goes to Rafe. But this isn't an avenue we want to pursue. Money is not what motivates the man. He's all about helping people. He'll use the money to rebuild. In fact, he has already begun looking into rebuilding in the same location."

"Sounds like Dr. Wiseman is a good guy," Eric said, adding, "Damn, I hope he's not involved in this."

"Where do we go from here, Jack?" Milt said, nodding at Jake. "I thought I had better ask before the rookie beat me to the punch."

"The two individuals we haven't spoken to—we need to contact them. And there are two clinic employees we still need to talk to. Amy Galloway should be back in town sometime tomorrow. Who had her?"

"I did," Milt said.

"Try to reach her and see if she can tell us anything useful. Who had Anna Davis?"

Eric raised his hand.

"Jake, get the contact information from Eric and see if you can track her down. If not, check with the neighbors and see if one of them can help you locate her. Also, try to contact Allison Vincent. We need to know if she really was with Greg Novotny."

"Got it," Jake said.

Anticipating Eric's question, Dantzler said, "Eric, unless we hear from Allison, you and I are going to meet with Greg Novotny. We need to look this guy in the eye and knock some cockiness out of him."

"Sounds like fun," Eric said, smiling.

CHAPTER THIRTEEN

Buddy Raymond leaned against the bar, his eyes focused on the six men squeezed into a booth near the front window. They were Long Branch regulars who came in almost every night of the week, a group Buddy had known since they were kids. And there wasn't much to like about them. Not then, not now. They were all in their mid-twenties, cocky and full of themselves, with a look and attitude Buddy detested. Long hair, scruffy beards, worn out jeans, flannel shirts, boots, earrings and plenty of tattoos, some prison cheap, some expensive and well done.

A table occupied by clichés, Buddy thought. Cut-rate cowboy types who dream of being true rebels like Willie Nelson or Waylon Jennings or Johnny Cash or Kristofferson. But no matter how much they might want it, they weren't even close to measuring up to their heroes. Those Highwaymen guys bucked the system, spit in the face of conventional wisdom and carved out the careers they wanted. They were the real deal, men who lived life on their own terms. But these toads were dreamers, frauds who strive for the outlaw image, too stupid to understand that if you have to work at being a rebel, a non-conformist, you are nothing more than a conformist. This bunch was, Buddy knew, more fake than Monopoly money.

Three of the men stared forward with a dull, vacant look in their eyes. Two were gawking at a table where four well-dressed woman were seated. All five men were sending the same message to the sixth man, who was talking nonstop. Their message: We are bored stiff and can't wait for you to shut up. Judging by the indifference etched on their faces, it was clear they were being held captive and would rather be anywhere but here. Speak your piece and shut the hell up was what their faces and body language seemed to be saying.

The sixth man was Oscar Young, and given his reputation as a long-winded talker, the discourse could last for hours. The trouble with Oscar was he rarely had anything worthwhile to say. He could hold court for hours and say nothing of interest or substance. He was a classic bullshit artist. But he could get away with boring his friends because Rufus Young was his father, and Rufus was tight with Buddy Raymond. In short, Oscar was backed by power-packed patronage. Given Oscar's status, his friends had little choice but to sit there and listen. And they certainly knew better than to criticize.

The Long Branch was uncharacteristically busy for a Wednesday night. The crowd was different, too. Fewer regulars than usual, and more new faces, which, Buddy reckoned, would be good for business in the long term. New faces tended to become regulars. The Long Branch was, after all, a great watering hole.

"Wonder why we're having such an influx of new inhabitants?" Miss Kitty asked Buddy. This Miss Kitty, a college senior named Donna Potter, only worked Wednesdays and Sundays, both typically slow nights. "I've never been this busy on a Wednesday."

Wonder why we're having such an influx of new inhabitants? Only Donna would come up with a line like that. "What are you studying, Miss Kitty?" Buddy said. "Law or literature?"

"Psychology. Why do you ask?"

"Because lawyers and literature teachers are full of shit."

"Not to worry. I'm going to be a child psychologist."

"Yeah, well, they're full of shit, too."

"Who's *not* full of shit?"

"Me."

One of the new customers, a man Buddy had never seen, slowly approached the bar. He was in his late twenties or early thirties, a stocky, balding man dressed in a suit and tie. Holding a nearly empty bottle of Corona in his hand, he was looking at the wall above the bar.

Buddy knew exactly what the man was going to say. He'd heard it a million times.

"Hey, who's the dude in the picture with John Wayne and Matt Dillon?" the man said, pointing at the photo. "I don't recognize him. Was he famous, too?"

"Neil Raymond. And, no, he's not famous. He's an asshole, that's what he is."

"Well, he's a lucky asshole, being in a picture with those two guys." The man finished off the Corona, politely asked Miss Kitty for another, returned to his table and began informing his drinking buddies that the third man in the photo was some lucky asshole named Neil.

Miss Kitty started to slice a lime, paused and looked up at Buddy. "Why do you say such ugly things about your father?"

"Because I can't stand the man, that's why." Buddy edged away from the bar and headed toward the table occupied by Oscar and his pals. Tapping Oscar on the shoulder, he said, "Follow me. We need to talk."

Oscar went silent, his bravado vanishing faster than shaved ice in a microwave. He'd been around long enough, heard enough stories, to know a summons from Buddy Raymond could have grave consequences. Standing, Oscar looked at his friends, who were no longer bored. Now they were extremely interested. He made a valiant attempt to show them a brave face, but it didn't work. Oscar was scared and his friends knew it.

Buddy led Oscar out of The Long Branch to a bench in front of a Rite-Aid drug store. Oscar wanted to ask Buddy what this chat was all about but had the good sense to remain silent. In Buddy's presence, it was best not to speak until spoken to. When Buddy sat, Oscar slid down next to him.

"Rufus still on your case for screwing the Mexican girl?" Buddy said.

This is what he wants to talk about, the old man bitching about who I bang? Oscar breathed a sigh of relief. "He's on my case about everything. The man's a jerk-off."

"You ever tell him he's a jerk-off?"

"Nah."

"I didn't think so." Buddy put his hand on Oscar's knee. "What were you talking to your friends about?"

"Nothing, really. Just telling them about a couple of chicks I banged last week."

"You must be quite the swordsman, Oscar."

"Awe, I get my share of 'tang, there's no denying it."

"You talk too much, Oscar. And I don't care for big talkers."

Oscar rubbed his hands together. "I never talk about anything important. Not to those guys. Basically, they're idiots."

"Who do you talk to when you talk about important things?"

"No one."

"No, Oscar, what you said was you don't talk about important things to your idiot pals. However, you implied that you do talk about important things to others. I want to know who those 'others' are."

"I don't. Swear. I've been around you and Dad enough to know when to keep quiet."

"For your sake that had better be true. Too much talk can put you in a precarious situation."

"I don't know what precarious means," Oscar said.

"It means you can get your ass killed."

"Look, Buddy, I'm not even sure I know what you're talking about. But even if I did, I wouldn't say anything to anybody. You can trust me."

"I'm not sure you are worthy of my trust, Oscar."

"Come on, Buddy, you know I am. Hell, you've known me all my life. If you can't trust me, who can you trust?"

"Now there's a great question, Oscar. And I'm going to give it some thought."

"Well . . . you can trust me." Oscar stood. "I really need to get going, so if it's okay with you I'm heading home."

Buddy looked at his watch. "Nine-thirty? A legendary swordsman like you calling it a night before ten? What's up with the early bedtime?"

Oscar grinned. "Got a four a.m. wake-up call. Need to hit the sack."

"Have a good night, Oscar."

"You, too, Buddy. Be seeing you."

"Be smart, Oscar. It's the safe way to travel."

"You got it, man."

Buddy watched Oscar climb into his pick-up truck and drive away. He would have to keep a close watch on Oscar. A *very* close watch. The kid's mouth could be more dangerous than a rifle. Buddy didn't worry about Rufus—he could be controlled. But Oscar was a loose cannon who could cause problems. And Buddy wasn't about to tolerate problems from an idiot like Oscar.

As Buddy strolled back toward The Long Branch, he considered the very real possibility that the loose cannon might have to be permanently silenced.

CHAPTER FOURTEEN

I t had now been five days since Carly Shelton's murder and the investigation was going nowhere fast. There were no new leads, no witnesses, no serious suspects. Nothing but dead ends and closed doors. Most homicide investigations yielded scraps of information along the way, and if you could put enough scraps together, put the pieces of the puzzle in the proper places, even the most challenging case could be solved. Thus far, the scraps had yielded no information worth noting.

The puzzle continued to baffle.

Dantzler had never failed to solve a homicide case. His record was perfect. "Flawless, like God's soul," as Dan Matthews used to say. But now, almost a week into this investigation, a feeling stirred in his gut that he might be staring at his first failure.

He wasn't about to let it happen, but to achieve success he needed to find some piece of evidence important enough to open those closed doors. He needed a break.

As expected, the clinic employees came up clean, and although there were two who had yet to be interviewed, both were females. Dantzler had already ruled out a woman as the killer. This indicated to him that the crime was not the result of an inside job.

He had the same negative expectations regarding the two as-yet-to-be-interviewed men who sent letters to Dr. Wiseman. They would be tracked down and questioned, but nothing beneficial or helpful would come from those interviews. It would turn out to be another dead end. He was convinced the person or persons responsible for the Wiseman Clinic bombing and Carly Shelton's murder did not communicate in any way with Wiseman or the clinic prior to setting off the deadly blast.

What was to be made of Greg Novotny, the lone clinic employee who couldn't be dismissed outright? He was an odd duck, to be sure, cocky and self-absorbed, but was he capable of committing an act such as blowing up his own place of employment? Was he a criminal? Milt didn't think so, and neither did Dantzler.

But without question the biggest disappointment in the investigation thus far revolved around the phone records. Dantzler had hoped phone calls might provide a solid lead, a direction for the detectives to follow. They hadn't. He had been particularly keen to find out about phone calls made to and from Paul Shelton prior to his California trip, and those calls he made, if any, while he was on the West Coast. Dantzler wasn't sold on Shelton as the doer, but by virtue of him being the surviving spouse, the man could not be excluded as a suspect.

According to phone records Shelton made a total of thirteen calls while in California, all on his cell phone. Nine were made to his office in Lexington, four to a Danielle Melendez in L.A. Eric spoke with her, and she reluctantly admitted to being the "friend" who accompanied Shelton to Carmel. Danielle said she and Shelton had been seeing each other "several times a year" for the past three years. She went on to say they parted ways early in the morning, and she wasn't sure when he left for Kentucky. She did say that he traveled on a private jet.

"He's an arrogant prick *and* a scumbag," Milt said, upon hearing the news. "But even more important, he has motive. Get rid of the wife and replace her with the hot young California babe. Sure works for me."

Dantzler also had Eric check on Carly Shelton's phone records during the period when her husband was in California. She received two calls on the land phone, and three on her cell phone. There were no out-going calls on the land phone and only one on her cell. All calls except one could be traced either to the clinic or to Carly's sister. The lone exception was a call on the land phone from Carly's beautician.

Dead ends on all fronts.

A knock on the War Room door startled Dantzler out of his near-trance. It was Jake Thomas. *Barely seven a.m. and the kid is on the job. He's working hard at making a good impression, and he's succeeding.*

"Morning, Jake."

"You can ditch the Greg Novotny interview," Jake said, taking a seat at the table. "His alibi is solid. He was with Allison Vincent."

"The whole time?"

"Yep. She said he picked her up around nine-thirty. They drove into town and hooked up with another couple at the Rosebud Bar. After a few drinks they walked to the Kentucky Theatre and watched the Pink Floyd movie. When the flick ended Greg took her home and left. This was around three a.m."

"You believe her?"

Jake nodded. "Oh, yeah. She's on the up and up."

"Is she romantically involved with Novotny?"

"Allison says they are just friends. They both belong to an archery club, which is where they got to know each other. She said they've competed as a team at several co-ed tournaments, but this was the first time they had been out together for drinks and a movie. I didn't get a sense she has special feelings for Greg."

"Archery, huh? There's a world I know nothing about."

"I served with a guy in Iraq who was a world-class archer," Jake said. "Always said his one goal was to make the Olympic team. It was his big dream. His name was Aaron Franklin. He was KIA in Fallujah."

Dantzler was about to respond but hesitated when he saw Captain Bird standing in the doorway. Bird wore the look of a man about to bear bad news. It was a look Dantzler had seen many times in the past.

"We've got another homicide," Bird said. He paused and grimaced, as though he would rather take a bullet than continue speaking. "Raphael Wiseman has been murdered."

CHAPTER FIFTEEN

Captain Bird informed Dantzler that the murder occurred in Hartland Park almost directly across the street from the Wiseman house. His body had apparently been discovered by a young couple out for a morning walk. They phoned 911. A patrol car was on the scene in less than ten minutes.

By the time Dantzler and Jake arrived, there were four patrol cars blocking Kenesaw in all directions, an ambulance and a white Honda Civic belonging to Arnie Edwards. A large crowd drawn like vultures to a rotting carcass had already gathered on both sides of Kenesaw, some watching from their front yards, others edging as close to the body as possible before being stopped by the yellow crime scene tape.

As Dantzler climbed out of his vehicle he looked across the street at the Wiseman house. With this much commotion in a normally quiet neighborhood, he couldn't help but believe Sally Wiseman was already aware of her husband's grim fate. A wave of sadness swept through him.

"Who was first on the scene?" Dantzler asked the first patrolman he encountered.

"The first responder was Stafford, sir," the man said, pointing toward one of the uniformed officers fifteen feet away. "Stafford and his partner, Belinsky."

Dantzler nodded. "Make sure the crowd stays behind the tape. Inevitably, someone will try to get as close to the body as possible. There is always one morbid weirdo who wants an up-close look at the blood and gore. I don't want the victim's body splashed all across the Internet. And if anyone from the media shows up, direct them to me."

"Yes, sir."

Jake said, "Want me to get Stafford down here?"

"Not yet. I want to take a look at the body first." Dantzler opened his briefcase and removed a camera. "Ever take any crime scene photos?"

"Yes, sir. But never a homicide."

Dantzler handed the camera and a pair of latex gloves to Jake. "Well, it's not very difficult . . . your subject isn't going to move on you. Take as many as you feel necessary. Arnie Edwards is the guy kneeling next to the body. He's the M.E. Ask him for advice if you need it. Or ask me. Make sure to watch where you're stepping. There could be a lot of blood, and you'll want to avoid stepping in it."

"I'm no stranger to blood, sir," Jake said.

Rafe Wiseman's body lay in a small ditch running parallel between a brick pathway and the park. He was on his back, eyes open, with his left leg bent at an odd angle, his left foot hidden beneath his right leg. He wore a white sweat suit and white sneakers. There was a large circle of blood on his chest, blood on both hands, and blood around his mouth. Blood could also be seen on both of Wiseman's sneakers. Dantzler's immediate conclusion was the fatal bullet struck Wiseman in the chest, nicking or shattering his heart, a devastating wound certain to cause considerable blood loss and instant death. The man never had a chance.

Dantzler was still fifteen feet away from the body when he noticed a large pool of blood on the pathway. He also saw bloody footprints extending out of the main puddle. Some were obviously human and had likely been made by Dr. Wiseman—hence the blood on his shoes —while the others, judging by the shape and size, appeared to have been made by a small animal, most likely a dog or a cat.

His discovery of a large pool of blood forced Dantzler to revise his initial scenario. The new one went like this: Wiseman takes a bullet to the chest, knocking him down. He lays there for an unknown amount of time, bleeding heavily. Somehow he finds the strength to stand, places both hands on the wound in an effort to stem the flow of blood, and begins walking. He makes it only a few yards before collapsing into the ditch, where he bleeds out and expires.

A painful, ugly, lonely death. No way for anyone to die.

While Jake introduced himself to Arnie Edwards and began taking crime scene photos, Dantzler made his way to Officer Stafford. Taking out his notepad and a pen, he said, "Bring me up to speed, beginning with when you and Belinsky took the call."

"The dispatch came at oh-six-forty-eight, sir. We were on Trent Boulevard, so we were on the scene by oh-six-fifty-seven. A couple, Bonnie and Michael Hannigan, led us to the deceased. Upon viewing the body, we radioed for backup and the M.E., and began securing the scene."

"Were other civilians at the scene when you and your partner arrived?"

"Yes, sir. But they were either across the street or up in the park area. And we had the tape up within minutes after arriving."

"So to the best of your knowledge none of them disturbed the crime scene?"

"That would be my assessment, sir."

"Excellent." Dantzler collected his thoughts, then said, "Did you speak with the couple who found the body?"

"Yes, sir."

"What did they tell you?"

Stafford took a deep breath. "It's kind of an O.J.-type thing, sir. They were taking their dog for a morning walk, which they do every day, usually around five-thirty. They were up near the monkey bars when they heard a dog begin to bark. Bonnie Hannigan said it sounded more like wailing than a dog's normal bark. Anyway, the dog kept barking . . . or wailing, or whatever you want to call it. The Hannigans became concerned the dog had been hurt, so they walked toward the sound. The dog was running back and forth on the pathway. Michael

Hannigan summoned the dog—his name is Hillel—and he went straight to Michael. Bonnie and Michael noticed blood on the dog's paws. At first, they assumed the dog was bleeding from an injury. Michael Hannigan checked the dog for cuts or scrapes but didn't find any. The dog bolted away, ran to a certain spot next to the ditch and began wailing again. The Hannigans followed the dog and saw blood on the pathway. Michael walked around the blood and went to restrain the dog. That's when he saw the victim. He told his wife to call nine-one-one, which she did."

"Was it still dark when they found the body?" Dantzler said.

"No, sir. It was maybe fifteen or twenty minutes after daybreak."

"Did you ask if they heard a gunshot?"

"We asked the Hannigans; they said no. We also asked most of the others who showed up. No one heard a gunshot. The shooter must have used a silencer."

"Good work, officer."

"Just doing my job, sir."

Dantzler looked around at the crowd, which had more than doubled since he arrived. Close to a hundred, he estimated, and the numbers would continue to grow once word of what happened began to circulate. Humans are naturally curious, and nothing triggers their curiosity faster than a good old-fashioned murder involving a famous neighbor.

Like all homicide detectives, Dantzler understood that a crime scene had to be preserved and protected as though it were a perfect diamond. Once flawed, crime scenes, like diamonds, can never be made perfect again. You only get one shot at keeping a crime scene perfect; any damage to its integrity can prove disastrous to a homicide investigation. A single screw-up by anyone working a crime scene is all a diligent defense attorney needs to get a murderer acquitted.

Presently, the on-lookers were far enough away from the yellow tape circling the crime scene to not pose much of a problem. This wasn't what bothered him. The problem was, he really had no clue how far the crime scene extended into the park. Or if it even did extend into the park. Right now, that was anything but a certainty. The shooter may have been in the park, or he may have been elsewhere. He could just as easily have been across the street, or in the middle of the street when he pulled the trigger. Dantzler had no way of knowing the direction from which the shot was fired. Hopefully, Arnie Edwards could provide an answer based on the direction of blood spatter.

"Detective Dantzler," Edwards said, looking up and shielding his eyes from the rising sun. "We meet again under dreadful circumstances. I suppose, given our chosen professions, this is destined to be the norm."

"What was TOD?" Dantzler asked.

"Sixty to ninety minutes ago."

"Between six and six-thirty? Correct?"

Edwards looked at his watch. "Yes, that would be my preliminary time frame. I'll know with more certainty once I do the autopsy."

"Can you tell from the wound what caliber weapon was used?"

"A bullet did not kill this man."

"What did kill him?"

Edwards pointed to a large oak tree across the street, maybe twenty to thirty yards away. Protruding from the tree was an arrow.

"A bow and arrow was the murder weapon?" Dantzler said.

"Went straight through the victim and imbedded in the tree. Happened so fast I doubt the poor man felt any pain. I'm sure he was more shocked, confused and stunned than anything. He didn't suffer long, though. Not with this much blood loss."

"A bow and arrow?" Dantzler repeated, as if he were trying to convince himself of the improbable. He looked at Jake. "Know what this means, don't you?"

"Yes, sir, I do. Means the interview with Greg Novotny has been given a second life."

"It also makes me wonder if Greg Novotny has *taken* a second life."

CHAPTER SIXTEEN

Even under the best conditions, preserving the integrity of a crime scene presents any investigator with a host of difficult challenges. For starters, and most important of all, it demands nothing less than perfection. No mistakes or oversights can be tolerated or excused. All potential evidence must be photographed, numbered, bagged, tagged, logged in and carefully transported back to headquarters and the lab.. Nothing, absolutely nothing, can be missed. A single screw-up by anyone working a crime scene could potentially lead to disastrous results, the worst of which would be allowing a guilty person to go free.

Totally unacceptable.

A crime scene in a very small room or enclosed space was difficult enough for investigators to work. This meant the one Dantzler was facing now, with it vastness and unknown parameters stretching in all directions, was especially daunting. Yet, despite the challenges facing him and his team, there was only one way to proceed—slowly, cautiously and step by tedious step. As if they were panning for gold, which, in a way, they were.

Dantzler spent the next hour making sure everything went as

smoothly as possible. He dispatched a dozen uniformed officers to speak with the onlookers, hoping maybe one of them might remember seeing or hearing something that would prove beneficial. Eric was tasked with searching the area, looking for a spot where the killer might have been hiding. Jake continued to photograph the crime scene and surrounding areas. He also photographed many of the onlookers, on the chance that one of them might act suspicious, overly curious or perhaps guilty. Killers have been known to return to the crime scene to admire their work and to revel in the chaos they caused. Dantzler knew it likely wouldn't yield positive results, but even a thousand-to-one shot was worth playing when working a murder investigation.

Dantzler gave the two most difficult—and thankless—tasks to Milt. First, he sent Milt across the street to the Wiseman house, to officially notify Sally that her husband had been killed. Then Dantzler gave Milt the job of retrieving the arrow that was presumed to be the instrument of death.

"I want that arrow in pristine condition," Dantzler said. "If you can get it out with little or no damage to the tree, fine. If not, then I don't care if you chop the tree into kindling. Get the damn arrow bagged and tagged. Maybe we'll catch a break and lift a fingerprint."

After leaving Milt to do his thing, Dantzler crossed the street and was in the Wiseman's front yard when his phone rang. The caller was Captain Bird.

"How are things going, Jack?" Bird asked.

"Everybody's working, but as you might expect, it's slow going."

"Any preliminary thesis?"

"All I know for sure at this stage is that Robin Hood didn't do it."

"Bow and arrow? Jesus, that's a first for me."

"Yeah, me too."

"This is gonna be big, Jack. I'm thinking maybe I should call Laurie and Scott, get them back here."

"Hold off on that for the time being. We can always bring them home later in the investigation if we need them."

"How is Jake Thomas doing?" Bird said.

"He's smart, sharp and highly professional. When Milt finally calls it quits, I'm going to fight to have Jake assigned to Homicide."

"You won't have to fight, Jack. I'll make sure it happens."

"Good. The kid's a keeper." Dantzler paused, then said, "I need to go inside and see how Sally Wiseman is holding up. I'm not looking forward to this visit."

"Oh, before I let you go," Bird said, "I wanted to tell you that you've been given the green light to speak with Amos Garland concerning the Danny Tucker case. My counterpart in Woodford County said okay, but was quick to add that you will be wasting your time."

"He's probably right, but it's my time to waste, so I'll talk to Amos."

"I also spoke with Woody Porter at the Kentucky State Police," Bird continued. "A little less enthused with us poking around, but he eventually said okay. Keith Davis, the guy who found the body, is off for a few days. Lucian White is working days, so you can reach him just about any time. I'll text you his and Keith's cell phone numbers."

"I had no idea you could text, Rich."

"You kidding. Text, Tweet, Facebook . . . I can do it all. You have to know this stuff when you have teenage daughters. That's the only way they communicate with their mom and me."

"Well, text me what you've got. I'll get on it first chance I have."

"Just keep in mind what I said—Danny Tucker takes a backseat to the Wiseman case."

"Not a problem, Rich."

Dantzler closed his phone and dropped it into his coat pocket when it began to ring. He dug it out, flipped it open and said, "Hello."

"Detective Dantzler, this is Amos Garland. I was told that you would be contacting me, so I figured I would beat you to the punch. Hope this is not an inconvenient time."

"I appreciate you making the call. And, no, this is not an inconvenient time."

"It's my understanding that you want to discuss the Danny Tucker case. Is that correct?"

"Yes. Is that a problem for you?"

"Not at all. However, I think you'll be wasting your time."

Dantzler said, "You may be right. Still . . . I do have a couple of things I would like to ask about."

"I'm off work tomorrow and will be taking care of some personal business in Lexington. Would it be possible for us to meet, say, around noon?"

"Sure. Where do you want to meet?"

"O'Neill's Irish Pub on Richmond Road. You familiar with it?"

"Yes, I know where it is."

"Then I will see you at noon."

Dantzler punched off, put the phone back in his coat pocket and walked around to the side of the Wiseman house. He climbed the half-dozen steps leading to the landing that overlooked the garage, hesitated, then knocked on the door. Seconds later, it was opened by a tall woman who bore a striking resemblance to Sally Wiseman. Dantzler immediately concluded that the two women had to be related.

The woman seemed to read the look on Dantzler's face. "I'm Lynn Stokes. Sally is my sister, younger by sixteen months." She extended her right hand. "And you are Jack Dantzler. Famous homicide detective and equally famous tennis whiz. Pleased to finally meet you, although the circumstances certainly suck."

"How is Sally holding up?" Dantzler asked, taking Lynn's hand.

"Not too well, I'm afraid. She's upstairs, asleep. We had to have her sedated." Lynn fought back tears. "I can try to rouse her if you want me to."

"No, let her sleep. She needs rest more than anything else. She'll have some difficult days ahead."

Dantzler looked through the doorway into the living room. From what was a relatively limited view of the downstairs area, he could see more than a dozen people standing around. Most were women, but a few men drifted into sight. If there were this many people in the living room, he figured there were probably another dozen or so in other parts of the house. Friends, co-workers and family members seeking to give comfort to a stricken woman who was going through a dark time. Good, decent people at their best. But Dantzler knew from personal experience, having lost both parents before his fifteenth birthday, that their best efforts would not begin to ease the pain Sally Wiseman was suffering, and would suffer for the remainder of her life.

"Would you care for something to eat, Detective?" Lynn said. "As you might expect, there is plenty of food."

"No, thanks. But if you don't mind, I would like to ask you a few questions."

"By all means. I don't know if I have anything positive to contribute, but go ahead and ask away."

"The obvious first question is, can you think of anyone who might want to kill Rafe?"

"No, I can't. Rafe Wiseman was as close to a perfect human being as I've ever met. He was put on this earth to help people, and that's what he did. And he often did it for little or no remuneration."

"But he did have enemies," Dantzler said, adding, "especially after what happened last year."

"That was most unfortunate," Lynn said, shaking her head. "But we're talking about something that happened such a long time ago. Things have calmed down and gone back to normal since that bunch of crazies behaved so pathetically. Why? Do you suspect one of them?"

"That's an avenue we'll pursue."

"It's strange, but Rafe never appeared to be worried about those nutcases. Sally was, and so was I. But not Rafe. He'd just shrug it off and say something like, those who scream the loudest are the ones you worry about the least. Maybe he was wrong."

"How well did you know Carly Shelton?" Dantzler said.

"Well enough to say hello and maybe chit-chat for a few minutes. But we were more acquaintances than friends. I do know that Rafe thought very highly of her."

"You're going to judge this a terrible question, but I have to ask anyway. Is it possible that Rafe and Carly were more than friends and co-workers?"

"You mean lovers? Having an affair?"

Dantzler nodded.

"No, Detective Dantzler, that's one avenue you don't have to pursue. That never happened, and would never happen under any circumstances." Lynn tried her best to smile, but it didn't quite work. There was a hint of anger in her eyes. "Have you spoken with all the clinic employees? If you have, and if you asked them that question, I'm positive you received the same answer."

"We've spoken to all but two of Rafe's full-time employees," Dantzler said. "Anna Davis and Amy Galloway. I'm hoping to get with them within the next couple of days."

"Can't help you with Anna Davis, but Amy Galloway is here. I'll get her if you want me to."

"That would be great."

"Just a sec and I'll be right back."

Dantzler pulled back a chair and sat at the kitchen table. He could hear the quiet murmur coming from other parts of the house. It sounded like a soft, steady buzz. A woman he didn't recognize came into the kitchen carrying a bucket of KFC chicken. She smiled, set the food on the counter, nodded and left without uttering a word.

Lynn returned a few moments later, followed by a short woman in her late twenties, somewhat on the plump side, with brown hair, blue eyes full of tears and a face covered with freckles.

"Amy, this is Detective Jack Dantzler. Detective, Amy Galloway."

Dantzler stood and shook Amy's hand. Then he pulled back a chair and motioned for her to sit. After she sat and scooted her chair forward several inches, Dantzler sat back down.

"I was supposed to meet with one of your detectives," Amy whispered. "I can't recall his name."

"Milt Brewer."

"Yes, Detective Brewer. That's the one."

Amy spoke so softly Dantzler had to lean forward to hear her. He said, "If you feel up to answering a few questions now, you won't have to meet with him later on."

Tears began to stream down Amy's face. Lynn took a small package of Kleenex from her pocket, extracted one and handed it to Amy.

Dantzler waited until Amy blew her nose, then said, "It's obvious that you held Rafe in high regards."

"After my father, Dr. Wiseman was the best man I've ever known," Amy said. "He was just . . . the best."

"How long have you worked at the clinic?"

"Almost five years."

"Did any of the clinic employees ever have problems or serious disagreements with Rafe?"

"Never. We adored the man."

"What about Carly Shelton?" Dantzler nodded at Lynn, letting her know that he was staying away from a certain avenue. "What can you tell me about her?"

"In many ways, she ran the clinic," Amy said. "Without her, things wouldn't have gone as smoothly as they did. She was the glue that held things together."

"Do you know her husband? Paul Shelton?"

"Seen him a few times, but I don't know him."

"Did Carly ever discuss her marriage?"

Amy shook her head. "Not with me, she didn't."

"Barbara Pearlman said she thought Rafe had been acting different lately. That he had been more into his own thoughts than he normally was. Did you pick up on that?"

"No, not at all. I can't imagine what Barbara was referring to."

Dantzler said, "What can you tell me about Greg Novotny?"

"Greg? What do you want to know?"

"Your opinion. Your assessment."

"Greg's okay, I guess. He's very intelligent, very, ah, how do I put this without sounding judgmental? Very confident. He has an extremely strong belief in himself."

"How would you describe Greg's relationship with Rafe? Did they get along okay?"

Amy let the question float for a few seconds before answering. "I think Greg respected Dr. Wiseman, but he didn't worship him like the rest of us did. I always felt that Greg thought of himself as being on the same intellectual level as Dr. Wiseman, which, of course, he wasn't. Dr. Wiseman was far more intelligent than Greg Novotny, a fact that Greg would argue with until his dying breath."

"That's pretty much the scouting report we've gotten on Greg," Dantzler said, standing. "Everyone is in agreement that he's doesn't lack for self-confidence."

"I don't mean to be finking on Greg or putting him down in any way," Amy said. "He is good at his job, and he is particularly good with computers."

And how good is he with a bow and arrow, Dantzler wanted to ask but didn't.

CHAPTER SEVENTEEN

Dantzler arrived at the office a few minutes past seven the next morning carrying his briefcase, a bag of bagels and a container of cream cheese. After setting the bagels and cream cheese on the War Room table, and dropping the briefcase in his chair, he went into the break room in search of something to drink. Unlike the other detectives (and practically everyone else he knew), Dantzler was not a coffee drinker. His beverage of choice was Diet Pepsi, which he secured from the machine for a buck and a quarter.

Within the next twenty minutes, Eric, Jake and Milt showed up, arriving in that particular order, each man going first to the coffee pot before attacking the still-warm bagels. Food and drink in hand, they settled in at the table.

"Who bought the bagels?" Milt asked.

"I did," Dantzler answered.

"No way, Ace. I can't remember the last time you bought anything."

"Milt, your memory is shorter than your pecker," Dantzler replied. "I brought bagels one day last week. Monday, if I'm not mistaken."

"He's right, Milt," Eric said.

"You would take his side," Milt said. "I thought black guys were supposed to stand up to their white slave masters. Malcolm X would reject you."

"Malcolm X might, but Halle Berry wouldn't. She would be all over me like that cream cheese on your bagel."

"In your dreams, Eric. In your dreams."

"That's one gorgeous woman," Jake said. "Did you guys see *Monster's Ball*? Halle Berry rocked in that movie, with or without her clothes."

"I didn't buy it for a second," Eric said, shaking his head. "In what universe would Halle Berry ever do the big nasty with a guy as ugly as Billy Bob Thornton? Something that perverse could *only* happen in the movies."

Dantzler cleared his throat, signaling an end to the Halle Berry discussion. "Milt, you can scrap your interview with Amy Galloway. I spoke with her yesterday at the Wiseman's house."

"What did she have to say?" Milt asked.

"She echoed what everyone else has told us. Rafe Wiseman was a saint, Carly Shelton was an angel and Greg Novotny has an ego bigger than Donald Trump's."

"Where do we go from here?" Eric said.

"Keep turning over rocks until we find something."

"Jack, is there even a remote possibility that Sally Wiseman is behind this?" Milt asked.

"No." Dantzler leaned back in his chair and rubbed his eyes with the back of his hands. "Right now, we have two prospects—Greg Novotny and Paul Shelton. Paul, being Carly's husband and a guy who detested Rafe Wiseman, is the most likely, but the one I like least for this. I don't see him as having the guts to do it. Greg Novotny doesn't really fit the profile of a cold-blooded killer either, but the fact that he belongs to an archery club makes him a candidate we can't write off."

Milt said, "We need to get his squirrelly ass in here and crunch his nuts big-time. He might think he's smarter than we are, but he's not. Under real pressure, he'll melt like butter."

"We'll bring him in, but not until after I've done some research," Dantzler said. "I need a quick tutorial on archery, learn as much as I can about bows and arrows. Once I do that, Eric and I will question Greg."

"Allison Vincent told me she and Greg belonged to Wolfe's Archery Club," Jake said, after thumbing through his notes. "It's on Moore Drive. Want me to speak with the owner?"

"No. Eric and I will do that later today. I want you to meet with Amanda Woolcott and show her photos of a RAV4. You might take along photos of several other SUVs and trucks as well. Maybe she'll recognize one of them."

Dantzler turned toward Milt, said, "What's the status of the arrow?"

"Mint condition. We're just waiting to see what forensics comes up with."

"Let me know when they have something, positive or negative." Dantzler paused a few seconds, then said, "There's another matter I need to let you guys know about. Do any of you recall reading about the state trooper who committed suicide in Versailles a few weeks ago? His name was . . ."

"Danny Tucker," Jake interrupted.

"Did you know him?"

"Sure, I knew Danny. He and I played baseball against each other from Little League through high school. Pretty good player, too. Lot of power with the bat."

"What does Danny Tucker's death have to do with the price of sausage in Poland?" Milt said.

"I'm taking a look into his case," Dantzler answered.

"Why? And on whose authority?" Milt asked. "He died in Woodford County, not here. And if the coroner ruled it suicide, then it's a done deal. Why would you stick your beak into a closed case?"

"A friend of his asked me to. Said she didn't buy the suicide ruling. And I'm not sure I do, either."

"Why not?" Eric said.

"He killed himself by drinking cyanide. I'll bet any of you a hundred bucks that Danny Tucker didn't know a damn thing about cyanide. And I'll bet you another hundred bucks that he didn't voluntarily drink the stuff. If I win those two bets, then it had to be homicide."

"Who investigated?" Milt said.

"A detective named Amos Garland. I'm meeting with him at noon."

"Ah, shit."

"What's wrong, Milt?"

"I've known Amos for decades, since the early eighties."

"And?"

"He has a reputation for being lazy and sloppy. He's also a big-time boozer. Or he used to be. Maybe he's been able to get off the sauce in the last few years, I don't know. I haven't seen him in a long time. But once upon a time he hit the stuff hard."

"I'm meeting him at O'Neill's. Either he's still a drinker, or he's testing his resolve. Guess I'll find out when I get there."

"First, a bow and arrow," Eric said, standing. "Now, cyanide. What-ever happened to simple guns and knives?"

* * *

O'Neill's was busy, with more than two-thirds of the large establish-ment filled with the noon lunch crowd. Most of the tables and booths were occupied, and another half-dozen or so were sitting at the bar. Dantzler had eaten supper here on a few occasions in the past, but never lunch. He was surprised the place did this well so early in the day.

Dantzler entered through the side door, so he made a left turn and began looking for Amos Garland. It didn't take but a second to locate him; he was sitting alone in one of the booths. And he wasn't one of those enjoying lunch. The only item on his table was an empty shot glass.

Amos Garland didn't look well, Dantzler thought. His hair and mustache had gone gray, and his skin was an almost off-yellow color. His eyes were sunken, lifeless, showing no sign of hope or enthusiasm. He looked like a man worn down by his job, by the years and by who knows what else? A man who looked twenty years older than he really was.

Dantzler introduced himself, then slid into the booth across from Amos. He offered his hand, which Amos reluctantly accepted.

"Let me be frank here, Detective Dantzler," Amos said. "I'm not thrilled that you're looking into one of my cases. I consider it unprofessional and a breach of ethics. It's also a personal affront, a challenge to my integrity and my ability."

"Let me be equally frank, Detective Garland," Dantzler said, leaning forward. "I don't give two shits what you think. I was asked to look into the case and . . ."

"Yeah, by that crazy Bradford broad." Amos motioned to the bartender that it was time for a refill. "I don't give two shits what she thinks. That damn boy killed himself."

"How long have you worked homicide, Amos?"

"Twenty-three years."

"And how many cases have you worked that involved cyanide? How many times have you even heard the word cyanide in one of your cases, whether it was homicide, suicide or an accident? I'll tell you how many. Same as me. Zero."

"Just because we haven't seen it in the past doesn't mean it didn't happen in this instance. There's a first time for everything."

"What are the odds?"

"I'm a homicide detective, not a bookmaker. I deal with facts. Odds don't matter in my world."

Amos waited until the waitress placed his drink on the table, then said, "Look, I get it. You're the hot-shot homicide detective from the big city and I'm just some lowly country-bumpkin shnook detective from Hooterville. But what you think of me doesn't mean squat. That boy died because he drank the poison. That conclusion was corroborated by the coroner. And no matter what Miss Bradford thinks, that's just how it is. She needs to accept it and move on."

Appearing exhausted from his speech, Amos quickly emptied his glass. After setting it on the table, he motioned to the bartender to hit him again.

"You think I drink too much, don't you, Detective Dantzler?" Amos said. "You've already concluded that too much booze kept me from seeing the truth in the Danny Tucker case. Well, regardless of what you think, I called it right."

Dantzler wasn't sure how much more he wanted to put up with Amos's belligerence, whether fueled by alcohol, professional envy or personal failures. It was becoming clear that Amos was not a friendly drunk. So, Dantzler knew, the more Amos drank, the worse his behavior and snarly attitude would get. The smart play would be to get up, walk away and forget about trying to learn anything relevant from this asshole. Under a different set of circumstances, that's what he would do.

Still . . . there were a couple of questions he needed to ask.

"Were you the first person to enter the house?" Dantzler said.

"The coroner and I went in at the same time. Of course, Keith Davis had already been in the house. But he was outside waiting when we showed up."

"Was the door locked or unlocked?"

"Locked. In fact, we had to break the glass in order to open it."

"Everyone is in agreement that cyanide was the cause of death," Dantzler said. "That the poison was in the coffee. And I'll grant that Danny drank the coffee without being forced to do so."

"You have just made my case for me," Amos said, sounding almost boastful.

Dantzler was stunned that a veteran detective would make such a statement. By uttering those eight simple words, Amos Garland had revealed two things about himself and the case—he had only looked at one side of the evidence coin, and he was a shitty detective.

"But who put the cyanide in the coffee?" Dantzler asked. "That's the question yet to be answered."

"Danny, of course."

"How can you be so sure?"

"Because there was no evidence that anyone else was in the house when he drank the poison."

"Did he empty the coffee cup, or was there some remaining?"

"There was enough left in the cup to detect the presence of cyanide."

"Was there coffee still left in the pot?"

Amos took a drink and nodded. "It was more than half full."

"Did it contain cyanide?"

"We didn't test it."

"You've gotta be kidding. Why wouldn't you?"

"What was the point?" Amos said, after taking another drink. "The coffee was in the cup, the poison was in the coffee, Danny Tucker drank it and died. End of story."

Dantzler didn't know how to respond. What he did know was that if one his detectives had performed in such an irresponsible manner, that detective would be looking for a new way to make a living.

"The point, Amos, is if all the coffee contained cyanide, it ups the odds that someone other than Danny Tucker put it there. That would mean Danny was unaware of the cyanide when he poured and drank the coffee. And that means it was a homicide, not suicide."

"There you go again, talking odds while ignoring the facts."

Dantzler stood and started to walk away. But not before he got in a final word. "Well, Amos, here is one fact that can't be ignored—you let someone get away with murder."

* * *

At noon, The Long Branch Saloon, an alcohol-only joint, was home to exactly three customers, none of whom were regulars. One was an elderly gentleman seated at the bar who was about to finish off his fourth Bloody Mary. The other two were beefy leather-clad biker types who had commandeered a table by the front window and were drinking Bud Lite. The trio had been there for more than an hour.

Miss Kitty came out from behind the bar and asked the two bikers if they were ready for a refill. They declined, so she went back to slicing lemons and limes. This Miss Kitty's name was Ruth Anderson. She was the oldest Miss Kitty, and the lone holdover from the days when Neil Raymond ran the place. No one knew her actual age, and no one had the courage to inquire. Better to ask your local priest how many young boys he's molested than to probe Ruth Anderson about her age. Rumor had it that she was in her eighties, but how was one to know for certain? Rumor also had it that she was always in possession of a .38 Smith & Wesson pistol, holstered to her side during the day, under her pillow at night. That particular rumor was generally accepted by everyone as being true.

Rufus Young charged into The Long Branch in his typical bull-like fashion, stopped when he saw who was behind the bar, snarled and muttered something under his breath. He looked as though he had come face to face with his worst nightmare, which wasn't far from the truth. Rufus and Miss Kitty had a long history and none of it was good. Bad blood between them went back decades. As a result, he detested her, she despised him.

"Is Buddy here?" Rufus growled.

"In the back, in his office," Miss Kitty answered.

"Alone?"

"No. He's getting a hand job from Nicole Kidman."

"You're about as funny as a root canal, you know that?"

"I have two words for you, Rufus. Fuck off."

Rufus started to answer but didn't. He was well aware of the rumor involving the .38. Better to walk away than find out that Mr. Smith and Mr. Wesson were on the premises.

Rufus walked past the bar, turned left and proceeded down the narrow hallway. On his right were doors leading to the men's and women's restrooms, straight ahead was a door with an "Office" sign on it. He entered without knocking, reached into his back pocket, took out a thick envelope, tossed it onto the desk and stood back, grinning.

"What's this?" Buddy said, picking up the envelope.

"A little something for you."

"How much 'something'?"

"Twenty large."

"Why are you giving this to me?"

"Call it a goodwill gesture," Rufus said. "I know you weren't pleased with my last venture, so I'm giving this to you as a kind of peace offering."

Buddy opened the envelope and used his thumb to fan through the bills. When he finished, he closed the envelope and tossed it back onto the desk.

"Keep your money, Rufus," Buddy said. "That was your deal, not mine. And I still say it was a dumb thing to do. It was a risk that wasn't worth taking."

"It was worth fifty grand. That's not exactly small potatoes."

"What do I keep telling you, Rufus? Think big picture. We're about to make a lot more than fifty grand. What you did could have jeopardized my plan. Who knows? It still might."

"It won't," Rufus said, pouting. "We're in the clear."

"You'd better hope so."

"When are you putting your plan in play?"

"In a couple of days," Buddy said. "I'm still working on a few items, making sure everything is airtight."

"Still gonna ask for half-a-mil?"

Buddy shook his head and held up two fingers.

"Two million?" Rufus said. "No way he'll pay that much."

"Then he'll go to prison."

"Yeah, and he won't be the only one," Rufus said.

"He'll pay up. That's not an issue. A guy like him wouldn't last a day in prison. He'd be some big Bubba's bitch before the sun went down."

"Two million? Boy, we could crap into a diamond toilet if we land that kind of scratch."

"You do realize there is one loose end that will have to be taken care of?"

Rufus nodded, said, "Yeah, I do. Give me the word and I'll see that it gets done."

"You don't do anything until I tell you to. Is that clear?"

"Yes."

"I hope you do. We've been friends a long time, Rufus, and I would hate to see that friendship come to an end. But if you do anything to screw up my plans, *anything* that keeps me from getting the money, you'll be a dead man. Is that understood?"

"Damn, Buddy, you talk to me like I'm an idiot child."

"Sometimes you are an idiot, Rufus. And I'm not about to let an idiot cost me two million dollars."

CHAPTER EIGHTEEN

When Dantzler saw the large building with the Wolfe's Archery Range sign on the front, he recognized the place immediately. A big grin spread across his face.

"I know this place," he said. "Used to come here a lot when I was a kid.""Thought you didn't know anything about archery," Eric said, puzzled."I don't. But this was once a bowling alley. I bowled here countless times. I know you won't believe it, but back then, this area was mostly woods. There was nothing but trees. Certainly none of these businesses were here. The bowling alley was the only building on this street. If I'm not mistaken, this was the first bowling alley in Lexington that had automatic pinsetters. Prior to that, guys had to set them up."

"Were you in first grade with Fred Flintstone?" Eric said. "Second grade with Moses?"

Dantzler ignored the digs. "The guy who ran the place was a big-time World War Two hero. Fought the Japanese all across the Pacific. Everyone called him Sarge. He was awarded all kinds of medals for bravery. He's the first person I ever knew who had a tattoo."

"You hate tattoos, so you must not have cared much for Sarge."

"Nah, Sarge was cool. Nobody messed with him, though. He was a legitimate tough guy."

Dantzler made a right into the parking area and pulled up alongside a battered red pick-up. He cut the engine, unsnapped his seat belt and climbed out. A minute later, he and Eric were inside the bowling alley turned archery range.

The place was brightly lit and more spacious than a warehouse. To their right was the area Dantzler remembered as having been the concession stand. The enclosed glass case that once upon a time was home to M&M's, Snickers, Milk Duds and a multitude of other types of teeth destroying sugar-filled candy now held a host of archery equipment that included arrowheads, targets, bow sights, hunting knives, stabilizers and various other items unfamiliar to either Dantzler or Eric.

Bows, arrows and quivers hung from the wall behind the glass cage. Since there were no prices listed, Dantzler figured they must be for renting. There was a small trophy case to the right, and above it the wall was covered with photos, plaques and a large Honor Roll board.

The guts of the place had been completely torn up and reworked, making the length from front to back much deeper than it ever had been when it was still a bowling alley. The lanes, gutters and pinsetter machinery were long gone; now the floor was hard wood and had been divided into twelve vertical sections. Each section was approximately six feet in width. There were twelve targets located at the end of each section. Each target was attached to what appeared to be a three-legged easel. Closer to the front, where the archers stood, were a series of lines, each one marking a different distance from the target. Dantzler wondered how the archer recovered the target once he finished shooting. Did the archer walk to the target, which would be dangerous if others were still shooting, or did the target have a mechanism that brought it to the archer, much the same as it was done in a gun range? Dantzler simply didn't know enough about archery to make much more than an uneducated guess.

Lenny Wolfe, the owner, was a tall, wiry guy with black hair pulled into a ponytail, a thick beard and eyes that resembled coal chips. He was wearing Levis, a flannel shirt and combat boots. He was not wearing a smile, and seemed disinclined to do so under any circumstances. Dantzler could picture him playing a key role in a biblical epic. Not Jesus, but one of the Apostles. Peter was the one who immediately came to mind, but then Dantzler remembered that when things got dicey, Peter turned out to be a chickenshit. Lenny Wolfe did not look like a chickenshit. Probably not as tough as old Sarge, but definitely not a pushover.

"Thanks for taking time to speak with us," Dantzler said, offering his hand, which Lenny accepted. "As I told you when we spoke on the phone, neither Eric nor I know much about archery."

"Tennis is your sport, right? I've seen your picture in the paper." Lenny looked at Eric. "What's your sport?"

"I was a decent basketball player," Eric answered. "So if I have a sport, I suppose that's it."

Dantzler said, "You know why we're here. We have a man killed by a bow and arrow. That's not a murder weapon we're familiar with. Like I said, we need help."

"Sure. What do you want to know?"

"What can you tell us about the kind of bow the killer might have used?"

"Compound bow, no question about it. Probably one with seventy-pound draw weight. Maybe even eighty-pound."

"Like that one?" Eric said, pointing toward the wall.

"No. That's a crossbow," Lenny answered. "Could be the weapon; it would certainly get the job done. But I'd bet on a compound bow."

"Why?" Dantzler said.

"Convenience. It's easier to transport. Plus, it's a little less conspicuous."

"What type of arrow?" Eric said, looking up from his notepad.

"Believe it or not, the arrow is almost incidental. The critical factor is what type of tip was used. My money is on a fixed-blade broadhead. Maybe a razor blade arrowhead."

"Would it surprise you to learn that the arrow went through the victim and embedded in a tree twenty-two yards away?" Dantzler asked.

"It would surprise me if it hadn't." Lenny stroked his thick beard, said, "It's not unusual for an arrow to go clean through large prey like a male deer, an elk or even a moose. A human's body mass is nothing compared to a full-grown buck. So, no, I'm not at all surprised."

Dantzler looked at Eric and nodded. Eric said, "Do you know Greg Novotny?"

"Sure. Greg's a member here. He comes in three or four times a week. His usual days are Wednesday and Friday in the evening, Saturday and Sunday sometime in the afternoon. Why are you inquiring about Greg?"

"How would you rate his skill as an archer?" Eric said, ignoring Lenny's question. "We heard he competed in tournaments, so we're assuming he must be fairly competent."

Lenny snickered but didn't smile. "Make that *barely* competent and you're gaining ground on the truth. His enthusiasm far out distances his talent. As for his competing, he takes part in club events here, which is very low level competition. He's no big-time shooter."

Lenny reached into a small cooler, took out a bottle of water, opened it and took a big swig. "Listen, guys. If you're even remotely considering Greg Novotny as your killer, then you are going to be traveling down the wrong path. He's not who you're looking for."

"Who are we looking for?" Dantzler said.

"A hunter, pure and simple." Lenny took another drink. "This might be his first human kill, I don't know. But I can guarantee you he has taken down more than his share of big game. He's no virgin when it comes to killing.

"From what I read in the newspaper, the killing took place at dawn," Lenny continued. "That means there was not yet full light. Plus, the victim was walking, maybe slow, maybe fast, who knows? But he was a moving target. This guy scored a clean hit. He knows what he's doing."

"Can you think of anyone who fits that description?" Eric said.

"I can name a hundred guys and a dozen women who do," Lenny said. "But I can't name one who is a murderer. Sorry."

"Who's your best archer?" Dantzler said, standing.

"Three or four come to mind," Lenny said. "One of them was just here. You must have missed him on the way in. His name's Oscar. He's definitely among the very best."

"He a hunter?" Dantzler asked.

"Oh, yeah. A good one, too. He lives for the kill."

"Thanks for your time," Dantzler said. "If we have more questions, you might be seeing us again."

"I'm not hard to find. I spend most of my life in this place."

The battered red pick-up was gone, leaving Dantzler's Forrester as the lone vehicle in the parking area. As he was opening the door, his cell phone buzzed. He looked at the number, but didn't recognize it.

"Jack Dantzler," he said.

"Detective Dantzler, this is Nikki Bradford. Remember me?"

"Sure, Nikki. What's on your mind?"

"I was just wondering if you've had a chance to look into Danny's case. I don't mean to be pushy, but it's just that I'm curious."

"This is where things stand, Nikki. I have been given the okay to look into the case, which I will do. I've also spoken to Detective Amos Garland. But you need to know that Danny Tucker is not my number one priority at the moment. I'm investigating two homicides at the present time. They have to come first."

"I understand," Nikki said, sounding a little deflated. "Can I ask you one more question?"

"Fire away."

"Do you agree with what Amos Garland told you?"

Dantzler paused for a moment, then said, "Let's just say I have a few problems with his investigation."

"See, I told you," Nikki said, excitement in her voice. "Danny was murdered. He did not commit suicide."

"Don't jump to conclusions, Nikki. It could turn out that Amos Garland's investigation, problems and all, got it right. That Danny did kill himself."

"Please, Detective Dantzler. Promise me that you will keep investigating."

"I promise. But it might be a while before I know anything."

On the ride back into town, Eric said, "Based on what Lenny Wolfe told us, think we should cancel the Greg Novotny interview?"

Dantzler thought about Eric's question for a few seconds before responding. "No. Let's bring him in, put him through the ringer, see what he's made of."

"I agree."

"What time is he supposed to be in the office?"

"Four o'clock."

Dantzler nodded, but didn't respond. He drove on, silently, his thoughts lingering on something Lenny Wolfe said.

CHAPTER NINETEEN

Dantzler sat at his desk, sipping a Diet Pepsi while reading Tank Tankersly's official report on the Wiseman Clinic fire. The report was brief, and it reiterated what Tank suspected from the start. The bomb was small, homemade, not sophisticated by any means. Like Tank said, it could have been assembled in someone's house or garage. The bomb's purpose was to ignite the fire. Tank had also suspected that the clinic had been doused by gasoline, which turned out to be an accurate guess. What Tank didn't know for certain was whether or not the gasoline was inside or outside the clinic at the time of the explosion, although judging by the direction of the fire, he would bet on inside.

But if that were true, Dantzler wondered, how did the arsonist gain access to the inside of the clinic? And when? It had to be someone with a key, since the clinic had a professional-level security system in place. In addition, that person would not only have to be in possession of a key, he would also have to know what security code to punch in to disengage the alarm.

Add it all up and it led to one conclusion—the arsonist had to be a Wiseman Clinic employee.

Dantzler placed the report in a folder, picked up his cell phone and dialed David Bloom's number. Bloom answered after the second ring, said, "What can the Hebrew Hammer do for you, my good friend?"

"For starters, you can stop referring to yourself as the Hebrew Hammer," Dantzler answered. "As we both know, you're speaking to the one Philistine you have never defeated, and will *never* defeat. You'd be more accurate calling yourself the Tennis Trombenik."

"Boychick, I am more than impressed with your use of that Yiddish term, although I seriously doubt that you have a clue what it means."

"Why would I throw it out there if I didn't know what it means?"

"Enlighten me."

"It means blowhard, braggart, someone who toots his own horn. You, essentially."

Bloom laughed. "What can I do for you, Jack?"

"I need to speak with Sally Wiseman. Nothing too detailed, will only take a few minutes. Is she up to it?"

"I think so. She's a strong lady, and she is hanging in fairly well. Do you want me to contact her, set something up?"

"Yes, if you could. Make it around one tomorrow afternoon at her house. And it would be good if you could be there."

"Consider it done."

"Thanks. I'll see you tomorrow."

Dantzler closed his phone, looked up and saw Milt standing in the hallway. He caught Milt's attention and motioned for him to come into the office. Milt held up one finger, indicating that he would be there in a second. That second turned into five minutes, but eventually Milt stuck his head in and said, "What's up, Ace?"

"Call Jay Matthewson and have him set up a meeting with Paul Shelton," Dantzler said. "Tomorrow morning, if possible. Either here or at his office, I don't care which."

"Why not simply call Shelton?" Milt asked, sitting in the chair across from Dantzler. "Take the attorney out of the equation?"

"That'd be a waste of time. Paul Shelton will never agree to meet us without his attorney present."

"You like him for the Wiseman murder and the bombing?"

Dantzler shrugged. "He can't be ruled out."

"He does have an airtight alibi for the bombing."

"I know he has an alibi for the bombing, but I want to know where he was when Rafe was killed. I also want to question him about his California friend. What was her name?"

"Danielle Melendez."

"Shelton doesn't know that we know about her. We'll ask, see how forthcoming he is."

"Don't kid yourself, Ace. They've communicated. She's told him that we spoke with her."

"Be that as it may, I still want to see how he responds."

Jake Thomas knocked on the door and came into the office. "Boss, what . . ."

"Did he just call you Boss?" Milt said, looking at Dantzler. Then he looked at Jake. "Did you just call him Boss?"

"I did. Why? Is that a hanging offense?" Jake said.

"No. But it is a first." Milt looked at Dantzler. "I apologize for not referring to you as Boss all these years we've worked together. How disrespectful of me."

"When are you going to retire, Milt?" Dantzler said.

"Not until you give me permission, *Boss*."

"How about right now?" Dantzler turned toward Jake. "What were you saying before this moron interrupted you?"

"What do you want me to do with the stuff we took from Carly Shelton's house last week?"

"Has everything been thoroughly checked out?"

"Yeah. Brendon retrieved all the data from the computer, which gave us nothing. I went through bank statements, credit card receipts, phone records, some letters Carly had received and a journal she kept. We did not find anything suspicious."

Milt said, "You know, Ace. Paul Shelton was really quick to give us access to Carly's things. Especially the computer. I would expect an asshole like him to fight us tooth and nail. But he didn't. Makes me wonder if perhaps he got on the computer and deleted anything we might find interesting."

"No way, Milt," Jake pointed out. "Nothing ever really disappears from a computer. Once something is in there, it's there for good. Now, it's true that not everyone knows how to recover the data. Brendon does. He's a technology whiz. He showed me virtually everything that was on the computer. There was nothing helpful."

"Box up Carly's things and take them to her house sometime tomorrow," Dantzler said. "Call ahead to make sure someone will be there. You don't want to make a wasted trip.'

"Will do."

"Have you been able to show the vehicle photos to Amanda Woolcott?"

"I'll do that tomorrow, right after I return Carly's stuff."

Eric tapped on Dantzler's door, then pantomimed an archer pulling back a bow string and then releasing it. Eric's way of saying Greg Novotny had arrived.

"Wish I could be in on that little chit-chat," Milt said, adding, "make the cocky little bastard squirm, Ace."

* * *

Eric was waiting by the War Room door, said, "How do you want to go after this guy?"

"We'll start off soft, see how he reacts," Dantzler said. "If he gets antagonistic, we'll switch to hardball."

Eric opened the door and they went inside. Greg Novotny was sitting at the table, looking glum and uncomfortable. Like a man who would rather be anywhere but where he was. Like a condemned man awaiting execution. He was dressed in tan Chinos, a blue Polo shirt and brown loafers. A small diamond stud gleamed from his right ear lobe.

Dantzler had formed a mental picture of Greg Novotny but the man sitting at the table didn't come close to resembling that image. In his mind, Dantzler saw Greg as short, plump, with thin hair and thick black-rimmed glasses. In truth, Greg was tall, thin, had a head full of blond hair and wore no glasses. He wasn't the stereotypical geek Dantzler had imagined.

Dantzler and Eric sat across the table from Greg. Dantzler opened a folder and waited, knowing what Greg's first words would be. It took less than two seconds before Greg uttered them.

"Do I need a lawyer?" he said, quietly.

"That's up to you, Greg," Dantzler said. "You're not under arrest—you're here to answer a few basic questions—but if you would feel more at ease having an attorney present, then by all means make the call. We're in no hurry."

Greg's fingers drummed the table. "What questions, specifically?"

"Specifically, where were you on the morning Dr. Wiseman was murdered?" Eric said.

"At home, in bed."

"Alone?"

"Yes, alone."

"When did you first learn that Dr. Wiseman had been killed?"

"About ten that morning. Barbara Pearlman phoned to tell me."

"Were you still at home when you got that call?" Dantzler said.

"Yes."

"What was your immediate reaction?"

"Shocked, of course. I couldn't believe it. I still can't believe it."

Dantzler waited a few seconds, then said, "What was your relationship with Dr. Wiseman?"

"I had tremendous respect for him," Greg answered.

"Why do I get the feeling there's a but hiding around the corner?"

"Well . . ."

"Spit it out, Greg," Eric said, forcefully.

"I don't think Dr. Wiseman truly appreciated what I did for the clinic. I mean, I'm an exceptionally good lab tech. As good as you'll find anywhere. If that had been all I did, my contribution would be huge. But I also handled all the computer stuff. I was the one who put the back-up security system in place. If I hadn't done that, all records and files would have been lost in the fire. That took a lot of time and effort. I worked my ass off for Dr. Wiseman and the clinic. But he never seemed to appreciate or acknowledge my efforts."

"Maybe this will help to heal those bruised feelings of yours, Greg," Dantzler said. "When I spoke with Dr. Wiseman, he was quick to sing your praises, listing all the ways you helped him and the clinic. Your contributions did not go unrecognized or unappreciated."

"Really?"

Dantzler nodded.

"Wow. That's nice to know."

"Can you think of anyone who would want to kill Rafe Wiseman?" Dantzler said. "Anyone who might have had a grudge against him?"

"No. But after all the trouble we had last year, you might want to look at some of those idiots who picketed the clinic."

"We have. And for the most part, they've all been cleared."

"Well, then, I don't know what to tell you."

"Did you have a key to the clinic?" Dantzler said.

"Of course. We all did."

"Do you have yours on you now?"

"Sure, although now that the clinic is history, I don't know why I should keep it." Greg dug into his pants pocket, pulled out a key ring, found the key he was looking for and showed it to Dantzler. "It's this one."

"Did you ever loan yours to anyone?"

"Never."

"Ever have a copy made?"

"No, absolutely not."

Eric said, "It's our understanding that you enjoy archery."

Greg's interest level shot up two notches. His eyes came alive, his posture straightened and a slight grin danced at the corners of his mouth. "Yeah, sure, I love archery," he said.

"You any good at it?" Dantzler asked.

"Very good. I have a bunch of trophies to prove it."

Dantzler nodded, recalling Lenny Wolfe's assessment of Greg's archery ability: *his enthusiasm far out distances his talent.* It had taken a while, but cocky Greg Novotny had finally showed up.

"How long have you been involved with archery?" Eric said.

"About ten years now."

"What type of big game do you hunt?"

"I don't. Truth is, I've never been hunting in my life. I shoot strictly for recreation. And to compete in tournaments, of course."

"Do you use a compound bow?" Dantzler said.

"Sure."

"Broadhead arrows?"

"No. Broadheads are not used in competition."

"They're used for killing, right?"

"I suppose so."

Dantzler said, "Greg, can you think of anyone who would want to kill Rafe Wiseman? Anyone he was having trouble with, or had a serious conflict with?"

"No, I cannot," Greg said, shaking his head.

"You can go, Greg," Dantzler said. "Thanks for coming in. And if you think of anything that might be helpful, give me a call."

"Does this mean I'm no longer a suspect?"

"It means you can leave now, Greg."

After Greg was gone, Eric looked at Dantzler, said, "What do you think?"

"He's no killer, that's for sure."

"You got that right." Eric stood. "Where do we go from here?"

"I'm meeting with Paul Shelton tomorrow," Dantzler said. "Then I'm going to see Sally Wiseman. Hopefully, one of them might provide us with some new information that will give us a direction to follow. If they don't, then we're back to square one."

"Don't know about you," Eric said, "but I really hate square one."

* * *

At a little past eight, Dantzler grabbed his briefcase, exchanged a few words with Bruce Rawlinson and left the office. He was tired, hungry, in need of sleep. Home was his intended destination but somewhere along the way he made an unexpected detour. By eight-thirty, he found himself sitting at a table in O'Neill's drinking a pint of Guinness, his thoughts on the two cases he was now investigating.

First, Danny Tucker. Dantzler remained convinced that this was a homicide. But proving it was not going to be easy, if it could be proved at all. All the cards seemed to be stacked against him. There was no evidence, no witnesses, no clear-cut suspects. He still needed to inter-view Danny's parents, sister and wife, but what was the likelihood that one of them committed the crime? Slim, at best. He doubted whether any of them even knew what cyanide was, or where to purchase it. If that quartet was eliminated—and he was certain they would be—it meant the pool of possible suspects expanded into the hundreds.

Dantzler thought about calling Woody Porter, Danny's boss with KSP, and the Woodford County coroner to get their take on the situation. But that would only prove to be a waste of time. He knew what each man would say. Woody would tell him *the lead detective and the coroner both called it a suicide, so we saw no reason to pursue it any further.* The coroner would say *cyanide poisoning was the cause of death, and I saw no signs of struggle or that the victim had been restrained and forced to drink the poison. Therefore, I ruled it suicide.*

Trouble was, Dantzler couldn't argue with anything either man might say. Despite that, he was convinced they had jumped to the wrong conclusion. Danny Tucker had been murdered. But . . . how to prove it?

Then his thoughts switched to the Wiseman murder and the clinic bombing. A possibility had begun to nag at him that the two incidents might be related. It made sense that someone would want to destroy the clinic *and* murder the clinic's owner. But the break in that thread was Carly Shelton. Where did she fit in? Was her death planned, or was it accidental, the tragic result of her being at the wrong place at the wrong time? That was a critical question, Dantzler knew, and one he couldn't begin to answer.

Although Greg Novotny was no longer a suspect, Paul Shelton couldn't be dismissed as the possible doer. But was he capable of cold-blooded murder, or was he nothing more than an arrogant, philandering asshole? If Shelton could be cleared, that left Dantzler facing another almost endless pool of potential suspects.

Well, maybe not.

The killer had to be someone with access to the clinic. That meant it had to be someone with a key. One of the employees, or one of the visiting physicians. He also remained convinced that the killer was male, a fact that narrowed the list considerably. Of the clinic's full-time employees, only three were men—Greg Novotny, Kevin Brothers and Duane Black. Kevin and Duane would have to be thoroughly checked out. Primarily, he was interested in whether or not they could account for their whereabouts at the time Rafe Wiseman was murdered? And did either man's skill set include archery? What about the physicians? How many of them are men? He made a mental note to contact Jenny Saunders. She should be able to answer his question concerning the physicians.

If the killer was someone outside the clinic, then the pool of suspects really did become endless. Dantzler didn't want to think about that now. He was too tired, too weary. All he wanted to do was climb in bed and get a few hours of much-needed sleep. He finished his Guinness, paid his tab and left.

Murder investigations would have to wait until tomorrow.

CHAPTER TWENTY

When Dantzler walked into the War Room, Milt was sitting in a chair laughing like a madman at some tall tale Jake was telling. Milt pulled a chair back and motioned for Dantzler to take a seat.

"Sit down, Ace," Milt said. "You gotta hear this."

Dantzler remained standing. "Okay, what's got you giggling like a school girl?"

"Tell him, Jake."

Jake said, "This morning I went to show vehicle photos to Amanda Woolcott. Got to her house around eight-fifteen. She immediately invites me in and asks if I want some coffee. I told her no. Then I begin showing her the photos. While she's studying them, she's got this really strange look on her face. It's like something's really troubling her but she can't quite figure out what it is. I have her look at each photo three times. She points to a pick-up truck and says this one is close to what she saw. Only the one she saw was much older. While she's telling me this, she still has this weird look on her face. I thank her for taking a look at the photos and start for the door. As I do, she lets out this blood-curdling scream. I jump, turn around, wondering just what in the hell is going on. Now old

Amanda is standing there with her arms across her chest, pulled tight, like she was trying to stay warm. But now the look on her face has changed from puzzled to one of embarrassment. I asked her what was wrong. She cast her eyes down, grinned and said, 'I just realized that I'm not wearing a bra. I forgot to put it on this morning. I hope this didn't distract you, young man.' Guys, I got out of that place real quick."

"So you weren't turned on by Amanda's free-swinging boobs?" Milt said, still chuckling.

"Come on, Milt. As droopy as those things were, she could play soccer with them."

Dantzler said, "Bottom line, she was no help with the vehicle ID, right?"

"She saw a pick-up truck of undetermined color."

Milt opened a bottle of water, took a drink, said, "Is Paul Shelton coming here, or are we going to his place?"

"Believe it or not," Dantzler said, "the arrogant prick is coming here."

Dantzler looked at his watch. It was nine-thirty. "He's scheduled to be here at ten." To Jake, he said, "Did you return Carly Shelton's stuff to the house?"

"Not yet. The housekeeper gets there at eleven. I'll take it then."

Eric came into the room waving a single sheet of paper. "I found something that might be of interest," he said, taking the chair next to Dantzler. "I went back and took another look at the Wiseman Clinic protesters who were arrested last year. One of those who got locked up was a guy named Tommy Snodgrass. When I checked him out, a couple of things caught my attention. First, he's been arrested on two previous occasions for assault and battery. Never served any time, but he did get probation. But what *really* got my blood flowing was what he listed as his occupation: construction worker and, drum roll please . . . archery instructor."

"Huh. So we have a tough-guy bad ass who can handle a bow and arrow." Dantzler nodded. "Good catch, Eric. Work up a full background on the guy, then contact him and get his ass in here for a little chat. Don't tell him the real reason for the interview. Instead, play on his ego. Tell him we need information relating to archery and we've heard he's the guy who can provide it."

"Do you want me to set up a meeting for later today?" Eric asked.

"Tomorrow would probably be better for me. Milt and I have Paul Shelton coming in within the next few minutes. Then I'm going to meet with Sally Wiseman again. I want to check in, see how she's holding up. I also have a couple of questions I need to ask her."

Eric said, "Damn, I can't begin to imagine the hell that woman is going through. You gotta feel for her."

Dantzler stood. "Okay, guys, let's clear the room. Eric, do the research on this Snodgrass guy. Jake, take Carly's things to her house. Milt, you and I will wait in my office until Paul Shelton shows up."

"Yeah, like two court jesters waiting for the king to arrive," Milt said.

"Maybe so, Milt. But let's see who's laughing when the final curtain comes down."

* * *

Oscar Young parked his truck in front of The Long Branch Saloon, cut the engine and listened to the motor rumble on for several seconds before eventually shutting down. He grabbed the keys, looked at his buddy Randy Trent sitting in the passenger's seat, shrugged and opened the door. At this moment, Oscar Young was not a happy young man.

But he was a scared young man.

Earlier this morning, word had reached Oscar that Buddy Raymond wanted to see him ASAP. Why? Oscar must have asked himself this question a thousand times in the past hour. There was no reason for this summons. Or at least there was none that Oscar could think of. But reason really didn't matter. Not when Buddy was barking the orders. When he called, you went. No questions asked. To ignore Buddy Raymond was akin to playing around with a loaded pistol. He could go off at anytime.

And yet, as Oscar walked into The Long Branch, he couldn't help but wonder: *why in the hell am I here?*

Miss Kitty was at one of the tables, putting empty beer bottles onto a tray. After wiping the table with a rag, she picked up the tray and went behind the bar. She tossed the empties into a big trash can, looked up and smiled at Oscar.

"Buddy is in his office," she said. "You're to go straight in. Alone."

Oscar did not like the sound of that at all. Alone was not good. No way. If Randy could go in with him, that might lessen the chances of Buddy doing something crazy. Like pulling out a gun or a knife and start killing people. Oscar had heard the stories of how Buddy could go from good guy to heartless killer in less time than it takes to flip a switch. Oscar did not want to be anywhere in the vicinity when that switch was flipped.

Walking down the narrow hallway, Oscar realized that his heart was beating faster than a hummingbird flapping its wings. There was a knot the size of a basketball in his stomach, his head was queasy and he felt as though he was about to lose his breakfast. Every inch of his body was bathed in sweat.

Taking a deep breath, Oscar knocked on the door, slowly opened it and went into Buddy's office. Buddy was sitting at his desk, those cold eyes giving nothing away. They were neither friendly nor angry. Oscar felt a chill run down his spine. Unreadable eyes are the most frightening of all.

"You've been a busy little beaver, haven't you, Oscar?" Buddy said, motioning for Oscar to sit. "Naughty but busy."

"I don't know what you're talking about," Oscar managed to say.

Buddy pointed a finger at him. "That's a good answer, Oscar. One of the few times I've heard you say something that even brushes up against intelligence."

"Maybe I'm smarter than you think I am."

"No, Oscar, you're not. That's why I have to keep a close watch on you." Buddy opened a desk drawer, took out a hundred dollar bill and laid it on the table. "Here, take this."

"What is it?"

"What does it look like?"

"A hundred dollar bill."

"If you knew the answer, why did you ask what it is? See, Oscar, that proves you're stupid."

"Damn, Buddy, why are you always on my case? I haven't done a damn thing to deserve this kind of shit. No way. You're acting like a big bully."

"Listen to you, Oscar, getting all bold and brave," Buddy said. "It's good that you have a spine; shows me you're not a candy ass. Just be careful who you show it to. Someone could interpret it as a sign of disrespect. And I might just be that someone."

"Sorry, Buddy. It's just that . . ."

"Shut up and listen. Take that hundred dollars, go next door to Rite-Aid and buy a pre-paid cell phone. Then go to Wal-Mart and buy another one. Did you do like I ask and bring Randy with you?"

"Yep."

"Good. Then go to Walgreens and send Randy in. Have him buy one. When you have all three, bring them to me. Think you can handle that?"

"Sure, no problem."

"You and Randy can keep whatever money is left. Buy yourselves some beer."

"Thanks, Buddy." Oscar took the bill and stuffed it into his shirt pocket. "We should be back in less than an hour."

"I want to make this absolutely clear to you, and it's on your shoulders to make this absolutely clear to Randy: You tell no one that you've bought these phones for me." Buddy stood, his eyes now hard and cold. "I mean no one. Not even your father. If this gets out to anyone, then the world's population shrinks by two. Understand?"

"Yeah, Buddy, I understand."

"Good. Now get out of here."

* * *

Paul Shelton showed up at precisely ten o'clock with his attorney Jay Matthewson trailing a respectful two steps behind. The king had arrived along with his personal serf in tow. Jay was friendly, smiling, cordial, shaking hands with Dantzler and Milt. Paul Shelton was typically distant and aloof, his arrogance and sense of superiority on full display.

Like he did on his previous visit, Shelton remained standing until all others were seated at the War Room table. It was, Dantzler knew, Shelton's way of demonstrating power, his way of letting the others know that the meeting won't begin until the king gives his blessing. Once again, Dantzler fought the urge to reach across the table and slap Paul Shelton.

"Are you any closer to finding the person or persons who murdered my wife?" Shelton said, after finally sitting. "Have you made any progress at all?"

"We're working the case very hard," Dantzler said.

"So I take that as a no. Right, Detective? "

"We have several leads we're following up on, but, no, at the present time we aren't any closer to finding Carly's killer."

"And now you've turned your full attention to finding the person who killed that baby butcher Rafe Wiseman," Shelton said. "Which once again means you see me as the primary suspect. Hence, the reason for this meeting."

"Let's face facts, Mr. Shelton," Milt said. "You haven't exactly been shy about making known your animosity toward Dr. Wiseman."

"Oh, it was more than animosity, Detective. I hated the man and everything he stood for. I shed no tears when I heard he had been killed. My only thought was good riddance."

"Hate is an excellent motive for murder," Dantzler pointed out. "Ranks right up there alongside money."

"Well, sorry to disappoint you again, Detective, but I didn't kill Rafe Wiseman."

"Can you account for your whereabouts on the morning Dr. Wiseman was killed?" Milt asked.

"I most certainly can. I was in Chicago that entire weekend."

"Seeing the town with another 'friend'?" Dantzler said.

"I was with my business partner, Jonathan Daniels. On Friday night, we went to see a play at the Steppenwolf Theatre. Jonathan is from the Chicago area and is close friends with the actor Gary Sinise, one of the founders of Steppenwolf Theatre. John Malkovich, another friend of Jonathan's, was in the play. On Saturday afternoon, we were at Wrigley Field watching the Cubs play the Dodgers. That evening, we had supper at an Italian restaurant, a few drinks at a nearby pub, and then we went back to the hotel and called it a night. We drove home Sunday."

"Which hotel?"

"The Palmer House Hilton." Shelton leaned back and let out a long sigh. "This can easily be verified, Detective. I don't keep ticket stubs or programs as souvenirs but Jonathan does. Give him a call. He will be more than happy to provide proof that I'm telling the truth."

Dantzler said, "So at no time were you with Danielle Melendez?"

"I was wondering when her name would work its way into the conversation. The lovely Danielle. She told me you had contacted her."

"You didn't answer my question. Were you with her in Chicago?"

"No. She is strictly a West Coast fling. And before you let your imagination run rampant and conjure up some big love affair between us, the fact is, I've only slept with her maybe four or five times. My relationship with her is not serious."

"I wonder if Carly would have agreed with you that spending a weekend in Carmel with another woman isn't serious," Dantzler said.

"Sex is a secondary reason for seeing Danielle. The main reason is to offer financial advisement."

"What? You're her financial adviser?" Milt said.

Shelton nodded. "I am. I met Danielle several years ago in Las Vegas. We started talking and she informed me that she owned several businesses in the Hollywood area. She has three hair salons and a couple of those places where you go get a tan. During our talk, she told me she was making big-time bucks but she was also getting hammered by the IRS. Basically, she had no clue how to run a business, especially one making serious money. So I let her know that there are ways to avoid getting bled dry by the IRS. She asked me to help. I've been advising her ever since."

"And is Ms. Melendez satisfied with your services?" Milt said.

Shelton glanced at his Rolex, prompting Jay Matthewson to say, "If there are no further serious questions, Paul and I really need to get on our way."

"No, I have nothing else to discuss at this time," Dantzler said, sliding his notepad toward Shelton. "If you don't mind, would you please write down a phone number where we can reach Jonathan Daniels?"

Shelton shoved the pad toward Jay, who quickly wrote down two phone numbers. "Those are for his cell and office phones," Jay said.

"Thanks, Jay," Dantzler said, picking up the notepad. To Paul Shelton, he said, "I appreciate you coming in. And once again, I am sorry for the loss of your wife. From everything I've heard about her, she was a wonderful person."

Paul Shelton left without responding, Jay Matthewson a respectful two steps behind.

"Damn," Milt said, once he and Dantzler were alone. "I was hoping that prick was guilty. But he's got an air-tight alibi, which puts him in the clear."

"You know, Milt, there are alibis and there are alibis. Los Angeles when the clinic is bombed, Chicago when Rafe Wiseman is murdered. That's pretty damn convenient, if you ask me."

"If you still suspect his involvement, Ace, then you know what that means, don't you?"

"Yeah. An accomplice."

CHAPTER TWENTY-ONE

I t was twelve-thirty before Dantzler cleared up some overdue paperwork and was able to leave the office. He was hungry, but with less than a half-hour until his meeting with Sally Wiseman, lunch, even a quick snack, was out of the question. It was not the first time work came before food, nor would it be the last. But that didn't matter. Personal sacrifices are easy to make when trying to catch a murderer.

While driving toward the Wiseman residence, Dantzler reminded himself why he had asked to meet with Sally. Thinking about it now, he realized the meeting was set up for two reasons, and upon reflection, one of those reasons was no longer valid. Initially, he wanted to get her take on Kevin Brothers and Duane Black, the clinic's two male employees. He doubted that Sally could offer much perspective on Brothers and Black. For information about that duo, he would call Jenny Saunders. She worked with the two men, so she should have a better insight into them and their relationship with Rafe Wiseman.

The second reason why he wanted to meet with Sally was still valid, still very important. He wanted to see how she was holding up. Simple as that. He also didn't want her to feel forgotten or left out of the loop while the investigation was on-going. That's what happened when

Dantzler's mother was murdered. He spoke with a detective one time, then never saw the man again. He vowed then that when he became a detective he would never treat crime victims in such a shabby, indifferent manner.

David Bloom was standing in the doorway when Dantzler pulled up in front of the Wiseman house. Bloom let Dantzler in, then the two men walked into the den, where Sally and her sister Lynn Stokes were sitting on the sofa. Lynn stood, but Sally remained seated.

"Pardon me for not getting up, but I'm too tired to move," Sally said to Dantzler. "Lynn tells me you two have already met, so I'll skip the introductions. Please, Detective Dantzler, have a seat and make yourself comfortable."

As Dantzler sat in a chair across from Sally, Lynn said, "Would you care for something to drink, Detective Dantzler? Tea, water, a soft drink? I will be more than happy to get it for you."

"No, thanks. I'm good."

"Well, then, if you don't mind, I'll leave you guys alone." To Sally, she said, "If you need anything, just yell."

Sally nodded but remained silent.

When Lynn was gone, Dantzler said, "How are you doing, Sally?"

"Adjusting. I would say that's the most accurate word I can come up with."

During his twenty-five years as a homicide detective Dantzler had spoken to hundreds of family members whose loved ones had been murdered. The responses he normally heard could be counted on one hand. *I'm angry*; *I don't know how I can go on*; *please find the person who did this and make him pay*; *why, why did God let this happen to me?*; *what kind of an evil person would do something this horrible?*

But in all those years, never before had anyone ever used the word *adjusting*. It was, Dantzler felt, an absolutely perfect response. A single word that said it all. As the child of a murder victim, he knew as well as anyone that events beyond your control force you to make major adjustments emotionally, mentally and physically. It was essential to your well-being and your recovery. You adjust or you go insane.

"Sure you don't want something to drink?" Sally said.

"No, I'm good. David and I will get some lunch when we leave."

"Only if you pay," Bloom said.

Ignoring Bloom, Dantzler said, "Is there anything you need from me? Any questions you want to ask?"

"I'm tougher than you might think, Detective. I'll get through this. I have a wonderful family and plenty of friends that I can lean on. They will make sure I'm okay. As for questions, I really have none. I know you are doing everything possible to find the person responsible for this tragedy. I have faith that you will succeed."

Dantzler smiled. "Thanks for the vote of confidence. And you're correct—we are turning over every rock in an effort to find out who did this." He paused for a moment, then said, "I know you told me you weren't very familiar with the clinic employees so I won't ask about them. But there are two names I want to throw out there, and I would like to know if you have any idea what Rafe thought of them."

"What names?" Sally asked.

"Kevin Brothers and Duane Black. Did Rafe ever mention either of those guys, or say anything about them?"

Sally shook her head. "If he did, it didn't register with me. He often mentioned Carly and Barbara and Greg Novotny. Jenny Saunders, occasionally. But I don't recall him mentioning any of the other employees. Sorry."

"Don't apologize."

"Check with Barbara or Jenny. They can probably answer your questions."

"I had planned to call Jenny later today. If she's available, I'll get with her."

"Why are you so curious about Kevin and Duane?" Sally said. "Are they considered suspects?"

"At this stage everybody is considered a suspect," Dantzler said. "But, no, those two aren't any higher on the list than anyone else. It's just that I can't shake the feeling that the bombing of the clinic was an inside job. If that's true, the bomber had to have a key and knowledge of the security system alarm code. In short, it had to be someone who worked at the clinic. I also believe the bomber was male; females rarely use explosives. Greg Novotny has been questioned, and we don't think he had anything to do with the bombing. Since Kevin and Duane are the only other men working at the clinic, we need to know as much about them as possible."

"Do you think Rafe's murder and the clinic bombing are linked?"

"Logic says they are, but . . . there's one piece of the puzzle that doesn't fit."

"What's that?"

"Carly Shelton."

"I don't understand."

"I can believe someone had enough hatred to blow up the clinic and then murder Rafe. But why did Carly die? If her death was accidental, if she happened to be at the wrong place at the wrong time, the odds are one person is responsible for both crimes. However, if Carly was an intended target, those odds flip the other way and we're probably looking for two killers."

"I never thought about that," Sally said, adding, "but if I had to put my two cents in, I would bet that both crimes were committed by one person."

"For that to be a certainty, we have to find out why Carly was at the clinic so late at night. If we can somehow do that, we'll at least know which path to follow."

"I don't envy you, Detective Dantzler. The challenges you face seem almost impossible to meet."

"We'll meet them, Sally, that much I can promise you." Dantzler stood. "Come on, David. Lunch is on me."

Sally followed Dantzler and Bloom to the front door. Extending her hand to Dantzler, she said, "Good luck, Detective. May God be on your side."

"Luck or God . . . I'll take either one at this point," Dantzler said.

* * *

The maid working for Paul Shelton was Hispanic, not much taller than five feet and weighing no more than a hundred pounds. Despite her small stature, she was strong as a bull. When Jake Thomas handed her the computer and the box filled with Carly's paperwork, the maid handled the exchange with the ease of a running back taking the handoff from the quarterback.

"Is this everything?" she asked, with an accent so thick Jake wasn't sure he understood her. "Do you have more in the car?"

"No, this is all there is," Jake answered.

"Then I will make sure Mr. Paul gets it." She closed the door, backed away and said, "Gracias."

Jake had almost reached his car when he saw a woman frantically waving at him. One arm was swinging back and forth in an effort to get his attention, while at the same time she was trying her best to control the little rat dog pulling at his leash. The old biddy, who looked to be in her seventies or eighties, was dressed in a pink sweat suit and matching pink sneakers. She was so thin and bony Jake wondered if the woman ever consumed food. Surely, money to buy food wasn't a problem, Jake concluded. Judging from the house she was coming from—the biggest in McMeekin Place—the woman was filthy rich.

"Young man, young man," the lady yelled. She was moving at senior citizen warp speed, the dog leading the charge. "I want to speak with you. So you just hold your horses for a minute."

Jake closed the car door and moved in her direction. "Yes, ma'am, what can I do for you?" he said.

"Are you a police officer?"

"Yes, ma'am, I'm a detective."

The lady fought to control the dog, which couldn't have weighed much more than ten pounds. She yanked at the leash in an attempt to bring him under control but that didn't work. The more she tugged, the more the dog's energy levels seemed to rise. Admitting defeat, she finally bent down and scooped the dog into her arms.

"I am not very impressed with your police department," she said, breathing hard. "I don't think you handle things in a proper fashion. You most certainly don't behave like they do on those TV cop shows."

"What do you mean, ma'am?"

"Oh, cut the ma'am crap, will you? My name is Martha Schmidt. But everyone calls me Marty."

"Okay, Marty. What's your complaint?"

Marty gave the dog a gentle kiss, then said, "On TV, when a

dreadful crime has been committed, the cops interview the victim's neighbors. They go around and ask if anyone has seen anything suspicious. Or seen anyone who might be suspicious. When poor Carly was murdered, not one police officer or detective came around and spoke to any of us. I view that as shoddy police work."

"I'm sure that was just an oversight," Jake said. "I'll relay this information to the lead detective as soon as I get back to the office. I'm sure he will send someone out here to speak with Mrs. Shelton's neighbors."

"You're here," Marty said. "You can start by interviewing me."

"Are you saying you saw something suspicious?"

"That's exactly what I'm saying." Another kiss for the dog, then, "I saw something *very* suspicious on the night Carly was killed. The truck, the man . . . everything."

Jake took out his notepad and pen. "Marty, start from the beginning and tell me what you saw."

"I had taken Prince outside to do his nightly business—"

"What time was this?"

"A few minutes past eleven."

"Okay, go on."

"I saw headlights and heard the loud noise. You know, the noise a car makes when the muffler has gone to hell. Only, this wasn't a car—it was a truck. A beat-up old thing covered with dents and rust. Certainly not one I had ever seen in this neighborhood."

"What color?"

"Well, it was dark, so I can't be sure. But I think it was red. Or possibly maroon."

"What happened next?"

"The truck stopped in front of Carly's house and the driver got out," Marty continued. "He ran up onto the porch and rang the doorbell. I knew Paul was out of town, so I was somewhat surprised when Carly opened the door. I had never seen that man before, and he didn't look like someone who would be friends with the Shelton's. Not the way he was dressed. Ratty jeans, cowboy boots and a hooded sweatshirt. He looked . . . dangerous."

"But Mrs. Shelton did open the door? Correct?"

"Yes. They have an intercom, so she must have ask the man to identify himself. Whatever he said met with Carly's approval, 'cause she opened the door a few inches. The man said something to her—couldn't have been more than a few words—then he left, went back to his truck and drove away. About ten minutes later Carly drove off in her car."

"This would have been around eleven-thirty?" Jake asked.

"I would say closer to eleven-twenty."

"Could you identify the man if you saw him?"

"No. I never got a good look at his face. What I can tell you is he was short and stocky, he was dressed like a bum and he drove a piece-of-shit truck."

"Why didn't you report this to the police?" Jake said, closing his notepad.

"Because I thought one of you guys would come out and talk to me. That's what the TV cops do."

"Well, Marty, this isn't TV. And it sure would have been beneficial if you had come forward with this information."

"Why?" Marty said, setting the dog down. "Is my information beneficial?"

"Yes, Marty, it is. In fact, you may have answered a very important question for us."

"See, you could have known this much earlier if you had only been more like those TV cops."

* * *

Back in his office, Paul Shelton fought the urge to call her. He was desperate to speak with her, to hear her voice, to tell her how much he loved her, to hear her say she loved him. He missed her so much he ached inside. It had been almost three weeks since they last spoke; those three weeks seemed like ten years. He wasn't sure how much longer he could go on without hearing her voice.

Twice, he picked up his cell phone, opened it and let his fingers dance above the numbers. All he had to do was go to his Contacts List, scroll down to her name and press the button. Seconds later he would hear her voice for the first time in weeks.

But he couldn't make the call, no matter how much he loved her and missed her. And God, he did love her. More than he could ever have imagined. He had been with countless women over the years, but none of them affected him the way she did. She was special. She was the light in his life.

And yet . . . despite his yearning to hear her voice, remaining incommunicado until certain events had transpired was essential. This was the rule he established, and neither of them could break it. There could be no trace of anything that might connect them. No phone calls, no e-mail, no texting, nothing. Painful as it was, now was the time for discipline and patience.

He would have to wait until later to tell her he loved her.

Shelton was alone in his office, having let the others take off early. There were a couple of business calls he needed to make, but they weren't urgent, so he decided to put them off until tomorrow. He didn't feel up to taxing his brain with more work today. The blues had him down, and he knew why—because he missed her so much.

It was only then that he noticed the large envelope in his In Box. A brown 9x12 with only his name printed on it. No return address, no date, no postage. He couldn't begin to imagine who sent it or when it arrived. It didn't come from one of his clients, that much was certain. Correspondence from clients always had his name and office address, a return address and the proper postage. With none of those standard requirements present on the envelope, that meant it had not been mailed. Someone had hand delivered it to the office.

Strange.

Shelton opened the envelope and removed a single sheet of paper. On it was this typed message:

I WILL BE IN TOUCH

Puzzled, he read the message again, trying to make sense of it. A third reading failed to lift the curtain and allow the light of understanding to break through. The mystery remained. Who could have sent it, and why? And although "I will be in touch" is rather cryptic, its meaning couldn't be clearer. Someone, at some point in time, was going to contact him.

But why? For what reason?

Who?

He sat at his desk for thirty minutes, his thoughts zig-zagging in a million different directions. He tried to match a name with the message, only to come up empty. One by one he ran through dozens of scenarios that might end with an "I will be in touch" message. But none of those scenarios fit.

After nearly an hour of thinking and pondering, he had no answers to his many questions. He was still puzzled, baffled. But this much he did know: whatever it was, it spelled bad news.

CHAPTER TWENTY-TWO

Dantzler snatched the cell phone from off his desk, looked up the number for Jenny Saunders and punched it in. Jenny answered on the third ring, sounding out of breath.

"Hello. This is Jenny Saunders."

"Jenny, this is Detective Jack Dantzler. Did I catch you at a bad time?"

"No, not at all. Renee and I are playing tennis at Woodland Park. That's why I'm a little winded. Not used to such strenuous exercise. Why? What's up?"

"If you have the time, I would like to ask you about a couple of Wiseman Clinic employees."

"It's Detective Superman," Jenny whispered to Renee. Then to Dantzler, she said, "What about now? Are you close to the park?"

"I can be there in ten minutes," Dantzler said.

"Planet Kryptonite's two leading residents eagerly await your arrival."

When Dantzler arrived at the park six minutes later, he got out of his car, walked closer to the tennis courts and looked for Jenny and Renee. Not seeing them, he turned and walked into the park, where he immediately spied them sitting on one of the benches, sharing an energy drink. Their tennis gear was on the ground next to the bench.

"Looks like I missed a fierce battle," Dantzler said, as he approached the two women. "Who won?"

"No winner," Jenny said. "Since Renee and I are such poor losers, we decided long ago that for the sake of our relationship, keeping score was not a good idea. Therefore, we play for fun, exercise and to sweat out the last drops of alcohol we consumed last night."

"And we were not about to let you of all people bear witness to our utter and miserable incompetence on the tennis court," Renee added.

Dantzler said, "I think it's safe to say my reputation as a tennis player far exceeds my actual ability."

"You're being modest," Jenny said. "I checked with a friend of mine who coaches tennis. He confirmed what everyone says—you are by far the best player this town has ever produced."

"Must be one of those guys I pay to spread that nonsense." Dantzler knelt next to the bench. "Putting aside my questionable tennis reputation, my reason for seeing you is to ask about a couple of clinic employees—Kevin Brothers and Duane Black. What can you tell me about them?"

"Kevin and Duane? " Jenny said. "Well, for starters, they are two very different individuals. Personality-wise, that is. Not so much when it comes to the job. Both are exceptionally skilled at work."

"Kevin is an anesthesiologist, Duane is an RN. Did I get that right?"

Jenny nodded. "Yes. And they always performed at a high level. Dr. Wiseman could always count on them. We all could. They were talented and dedicated employees."

"How are they different?" Dantzler said.

"Kevin is outgoing, friendly, a big talker. Duane is quiet, somewhat distant, more deeply wound up. I mean, he's always helpful. But you have to seek his help. With Kevin, he'll volunteer."

"What was their relationship with Dr. Wiseman?"

"The normal employer-employee relationship, I would say. Dr. Wiseman expected them to perform at a consistently high level, which they did. He expected that from all of us."

"From a personal standpoint, how did they get along with Dr. Wiseman?"

"They got along with him very well. We all did. Dr. Wiseman treated everyone fairly and professionally. If you did your job, he was an easy man to work for."

"Never any personal conflict between Dr. Wiseman and either Kevin or Duane?" Dantzler said. "No arguments or disagreements?"

"With Kevin, no. He's not a confrontational guy at all. With Duane, I do recall a couple of times when he and Dr. Wiseman butted heads over certain things. It was nothing serious or big-time. They just weren't on the same page, that's all. There was no screaming, yelling or arguing. More of a friendly debate is how I would categorize it."

"Who won the debate?"

"Dr. Wiseman, of course."

"How did Duane handle that?"

"Like a pro," Jenny said. "Look, Detective, don't make this out to be more than it was. Duane is a good guy, and he truly respected Dr. Wiseman. I'm sure you have disagreements with your colleagues at work. I'm also sure you settle them and then move on. That's the way it was with Duane and Dr. Wiseman."

"Do you know if either Kevin or Duane is involved with archery?"

"I can't imagine either of them would be. They don't strike me as the bow and arrow type."

"How many of the clinic's regular physicians are men?"

"Let me think about that for a second," Jenny said. "There's Donald Carlisle, Ted Buckley, Anil Singh and Harold Pressman. That's it. The rest are women."

"Any interesting notes you can give me concerning them?"

"Not really. They come in, do the job, then skedaddle. They are all nice, professional and easy to work with. And in anticipation of your next question, no, I'm not aware if any of them are involved with archery."

Dantzler stood and stretched his legs. "Thanks for your time, Jenny. Renee, it was nice seeing you again."

"Same here, Detective," Renee said.

Jenny picked up her equipment bag and tennis racket. "We are heading down to McCarthy's for a few drinks. You are more than welcome to join us."

"Maybe some other time. Right now, I need to concentrate on trying to catch a killer."

Or killers, he thought as he walked back to his car.

* * *

Eric phoned to say he had tracked down Tommy Snodgrass and that Snodgrass agreed to meet with him. Eric asked Dantzler if he wanted to be in on the interview. Dantzler said he did, although he doubted that Snodgrass would prove to be anything more than an insignificant sidebar. He still held to the conviction that none of the clinic protesters were responsible for the deaths of Carly Shelton and Rafe Wiseman.

"Where are you meeting Snodgrass?" Dantzler asked.

"The Lexington Green parking lot in front of Joseph-Beth Booksellers."

"I'll be there in fifteen minutes."

"Wait till you see this guy, Jack. He's a giant."

Eric's description of Tommy Snodgrass was no exaggeration. Snodgrass was six-foot-eight and all muscles; there was not an ounce of fat on the man. Broad shoulders, thick neck, huge thighs. His was a physique most NFL players would kill for. He was dressed in a nice black suit, white shirt with the collar open, and a pair of black loafers. His head was completely shaved, and a large silver earring dangled from his left ear, a la Michael Jordan. All in all, Snodgrass was an impressive specimen.

Dantzler and Eric, both of whom stood six-three, were dwarfed by the man.

"Let's make this quick, fellas," Snodgrass said, tapping his wrist watch. "You're cutting into prime hunting time, and there's plenty of competition for the prey. I can't afford to fall too far behind."

"So, you're a hunter?" Eric said.

"Damn straight. And one of the best, if I may say so."

"What do you hunt?"

"Pussy," Snodgrass said, sounding as though he had just been asked the most unenlightened question of all-time. "What else is there to hunt? Nothing, that's what."

"We're not interested in your pursuit of women," Dantzler said.

"Well, hell, we got nothing to talk about," Snodgrass said, adding, "because that's really the only thing I know much about."

"You have multiple arrests for assault and battery, so you apparently know something about fighting," Eric pointed out.

"Come on, fellas, don't make me out to be some Al Capone-type thug simply because I'm a big guy. Basically, I'm a six-foot-eight, two-hundred-seventy pound Woody Allen. I don't go looking for trouble."

"Trouble just has a way of finding you, right?" Dantzler said.

"Fellas, I chase chicks. That's what I do. In the course of my pursuits, I occasionally end up with a chick that is married or has a boyfriend. Naturally, those dudes don't like me poaching their territory. So, they confront me. I understand that completely; I would do the same thing if a guy hit on my chick. Unfortunately for those guys, when they do challenge me, Woody Allen turns into the Hulk. I beat the shit out of them, they press charges and I end up spending a night in the slammer. It's the price I pay for being good at hunting cooze."

"We understand that you are also good with a bow and arrow," Eric said. "Is that an accurate assessment?"

"Where did you hear that nonsense?" Snodgrass said, reacting as if he had just heard the second-most unenlightened question of all-time. "I wouldn't even rate myself as average with a bow and arrow."

"When you were arrested, you listed construction worker and archery instructor as means of employment," Dantzler said. "We're particularly interested in the archery part."

Snodgrass laughed. "Fellas, archery instructor, coaching basketball or coaching softball—those are simply means to an end. You see, I only coach chicks. It's a perfect way to meet them. Hell, I once took a cooking class. Do you really think I was interested in how to bake a cake or make a meat loaf? Of course not. But I was the only dude in the class. Me and about fifteen chicks. Those are my kind of odds."

"You're telling us you have no skills at archery?" Dantzler said.

"I can fool a beginner, which is what those chicks were. Believe me, fellas, I was lousy with a bow and arrow. But they thought I was Robin Hood. And that was all I needed to seal the deal. From then on, it was smooth sailing."

"Okay, Casanova, we get the picture," Dantzler said. "You're a ladies' man. We don't care about that. But tell us about the incident at the Wiseman Clinic last year. The one that led to your arrest."

"A cop shoved me so I got a little rough with him. Personally, I thought he overreacted. I was trying to help one of the women—she was on the ground—and I guess he assumed I was the one who knocked her down. He was wrong. I didn't do a damn thing. I don't hurt chicks."

"Did you agree with the protesters?"

"Man, I didn't have a clue what they were protesting."

"Why were you there?" Eric asked.

"Do you really have to ask? I went to meet chicks."

"One last question, Romeo," Dantzler said. "Are you familiar with anyone who is good with a bow and arrow?"

"There is this one dude—I've only seen him two or three times—but he's exceptionally good. I'm talking world-class good."

"Got a name for us?"

Snodgrass thought about the question, then finally said, "I can't be sure, but I think his last name was Yewell. Yeah, I think that's it. Yewell."

"No first name?"

"Nah, don't believe I ever heard it mentioned. But like I told you, I only saw him a few times. Never did meet him or speak with him."

"Thanks for speaking with us," Dantzler said. "Hope we didn't derail your pursuit too much."

Snodgrass looked at his watch, said, "I'm running a little behind schedule but I won't have any trouble making up the time. Just means I'll have to hustle a little faster."

* * *

Dantzler sat on his deck, glass of Pernod and orange juice in hand, staring out into the darkness, watching the moon slowly make its way across the cloudy night sky. Sitting there, his thoughts on the trio of murders he was trying to solve—Danny Tucker, Carly Shelton and Rafe Wiseman—he felt as though those cases were moving more slowly than the moon. Three weeks of hard work and nothing of real consequence to show for it.

Frustrated as he was by the lack of progress, he was also angry with himself. Not because he had yet to solve the crimes, but for having agreed to look into Danny Tucker's death in the first place. That had been a mistake on his part. The case was a done deal, signed off by everyone involved. He should have left it that way, just said no to Nikki Bradford, and not given it a second thought. Instead, he said yes to what was turning out to be a time-consuming distraction. Despite his anger, he knew there was no way he could've said no. That wasn't possible, not when his detective's instincts kicked into high gear. Danny Tucker's death was suspicious, that much he was sure of. It had homicide written all over it. Justice would not be served unless a more thorough investigation was conducted.

More important, a murderer would continue to walk the streets.

Unacceptable.

But . . . that being the case, where to go from here? Dantzler asked himself. Interviewing Keith Davis and Lucian White topped his list of priorities. Hopefully, one of them might shed some light on the case. His list also included Danny's parents, sister and wife, although he didn't consider them serious suspects. At the time of Danny's death, his parents were in Florida, his sister, Kelly, was at work, and his wife was out of town. For one of them to be the killer meant concocting the poison, leaving it in the coffee pot, and then *hoping* Danny would drink it. That defied logic.

He could always have another chat with Amos Garland, maybe catch the detective on a day when he wasn't hitting the booze so hard. But what were the odds that would happen? Garland gave every indication of being a hard-core alcoholic; lifting a glass of bourbon came as easily to him as breathing. To his credit, though, Garland had graciously provided a copy of his case notes, which Dantzler had yet to find the time to really study. He would give them a detailed read, then decide whether or not another meeting with Garland was necessary.

That left Malcolm Kinnison, the Woodford County coroner, as the final interview possibility. But his notes and sketches were included in the folder provided by Amos Garland. Dantzler would study them before deciding if a face-to-face meeting with the coroner was necessary or a waste of time.

His thoughts began to drift away from Danny Tucker and toward Carly Shelton and Rafe Wiseman, but he quickly shut down the circuits. He was too tired, too beat, to think about those cases right now. He had but one thing on his mind—sleep.

He finished his drink, closed his eyes, and was snoring thirty seconds later.

CHAPTER TWENTY-THREE

"You are the man," Eric said, pointing at Jake. "Our big hero."

"Hear, hear," Milt said, hoisting his coffee cup into the air.

"Just a stroke of luck," Jake said. "Right place at the right time. I didn't do anything special."

"Never downplay luck," Milt said. "Sometimes it can be your best friend."

For the first time in nearly three weeks spirits were high in the War Room. So was the energy level. The detectives had an extra bounce in their step that hadn't previously been present. Positive news has a way of making that happen. Although no code had been broken and no secret uncovered, they were convinced that *something* critical to the investigation had come their way. It was, they felt, one piece of the puzzle. The challenge now—find the missing pieces.

Dantzler took a seat at the table, said, "Thanks to . . . what was her name, Jake?"

"Martha Schmidt. Marty."

"Thanks to Marty, we now know that Carly Shelton was not collateral damage. She was an intended target."

Milt said, "Alibis or not, it comes back to Paul Shelton. With his wife out of the picture, he's free to hook up with the mistress. Plus, we all know how much he detested Rafe Wiseman. Shelton eliminates his wife *and* the Wiseman Clinic at the same time. It's the perfect outcome for him."

"Does that mean you also like Shelton for the Wiseman murder?" Eric asked.

"I wouldn't put anything past this guy," Milt answered. "He's a first-class scumbag."

"We can't arrest a guy for being a scumbag," Eric said. "If we could, half the guys I know would be behind bars."

"Sounds like you need to pick better friends," Milt said, laughing.

"I didn't say they were friends, Milt. I said they were guys I know."

Dantzler popped open a can of Diet Pepsi, said, "Milt, I'm not discounting Paul Shelton as our killer. Not by a long shot. But there are several hurdles we have to clear before we can tag him as the guy. Those alibis are solid, which means if he is behind the murders, he had help. Right now, we don't have a clue who that person might be. Except whoever he is, he's damn good with a bow and arrow. We've dumped Shelton's phone records, we've checked his bank statements and credit card purchases, and there is nothing on any of them that is even remotely suspicious. If we're gonna hang this on him—if he's guilty—we've got some heavy lifting to do."

"Then let's get to the lifting," Milt said. "How do you want us to proceed?"

Dantzler looked at Jake, said, "Do you think it's worthwhile to speak with Martha Schmidt again?"

"Not really. She doesn't know anything more than what she told me. If you want me to, I can talk to her neighbors. Maybe one of them saw the truck or the driver that night."

"Okay, do that. Milt, Eric, you guys take a closer, more detailed look at Paul Shelton's paperwork. Go back at least six months. If he did hire someone to commit these crimes, he had to contact him and pay him. There has to be a connection somewhere, and we need to find it. Otherwise, we've got nothing on him."

"What about you?" Eric said. "What's on your plate?"

"I'm meeting with Keith Davis at noon."

"Isn't he the one who found Danny Tucker's body?" Jake asked.

"Yes, he was. Do you know him?"

"No."

"He wasn't particularly thrilled when I called and ask if we could get together. I felt like I was begging the guy. But he finally relented and agreed to see me. Later this afternoon, I'm going to pay another visit to the archery range. I have a question for Lenny Wolfe."

Milt said, "When will Laurie and Scott be back?"

"Sunday," Dantzler said.

"Hey, Milt, isn't Friday your last day?" Eric said.

"That's what the paperwork says. But I'm sticking around until we have people in custody for killing Carly Shelton and Rafe Wiseman. I will not walk away until that happens."

* * *

Body language can speak volumes and Keith Davis's body language screamed his displeasure with being interviewed by Dantzler. He slouched in his chair, shoulders slumped, a scowl on his face. When he spoke, it was in a gruff, hurried tone. He was not happy and he made no attempt to hide it.

"This is my day off," he said to Dantzler. "I have errands to run for a neighbor, my car is scheduled to be in the shop in less than an hour, and I have a date tonight. So, please, make this quick."

"This shouldn't take long," Dantzler said. "I only have a few questions for you."

"I don't know why you have *any* questions for me. I've already told the investigators what happened. If you want to know what I said, talk to Amos Garland."

"I did speak with him. But I would like to hear what you have to say. What you remember."

"The case is closed; I can't see any reason why you're asking me about it now."

"I'm doing it because I have a problem with the official ruling."

"What? You don't think Danny committed suicide?"

Dantzler shook his head. "No, I don't."

"I was the one who found him, remember? I was there. I saw the body. Danny Tucker killed himself."

"Did you see Danny drink the coffee?"

"No, I didn't. But I did see the coffee cup on the table. The cyanide was in the cup."

"How do you know it was cyanide?"

"I think Amos Garland mentioned it to me. Or maybe I heard it from Captain Porter. Yeah, I'm pretty sure it was the captain who told me."

"Let's start from the beginning, Keith. What time did you get the call from Captain Porter, where were you and what did he say?"

"All that information is in Amos Garland's notes. Get it from him."

"I'd rather get it from you."

Keith let out a long sigh, said, "Captain Porter called me at about ten-thirty. I was on New Circle near the Versailles Road exit. He told me Danny did not show up for his shift, nor had he called in sick. Captain Porter said he phoned Danny's apartment but got no answer. He asked me to go see if anything was wrong. That's what I did."

"Danny lived at the Racquet Club apartments on Crosby Drive, yet you went immediately to his parent's house in Versailles. How did you know to go there?"

"I think maybe Danny told me he would be staying there for a few days."

"Were you and Danny close friends?"

"I wouldn't say we were close. We got along, never had any problems."

"Okay, so you get to the Tucker's house. What happened next?"

"I parked, exited my vehicle, went up onto the porch and rang the doorbell. When no one answered, I knocked a few times. Still no response, so I went around to the back of the house. I thought maybe Danny was in one of the barns, or that he was feeding the horses. I called out his name but he didn't answer. Then I went onto the back porch and looked through the window. That's when I saw Danny sitting at the kitchen table. He was slumped to one side. I knew some seriously bad shit had happened. I went inside, took one look at

Danny and could tell right away that he was dead. I didn't even bother to check for a pulse. I went back outside and phoned Captain Porter."

"You didn't call nine-one-one?"

"I called the captain. He must've called the police and the coroner."

"The back door was unlocked, right?"

"Yep, it was."

"What about the front door?" Dantzler said. "Was it locked or unlocked?"

"Couldn't say. I never tried opening it."

"Where were you when the police and the coroner showed up?"

"Out front, sitting in my vehicle." Keith looked at his watch. "How much longer is this going to take? I am in kind of a hurry."

"We're almost done. Just a couple more questions and we'll call it quits."

"What else do you want to know?"

"Did Danny have any beefs with anyone? Either on or off the job?"

"How would I know that? Like I told you, he and I weren't bosom buddies."

"Do you know his wife?"

"Yes."

"Any problems in Danny's marriage that you're aware of?"

"I'm a state trooper, not a marriage counselor. So no, I can't speak to the state of their marriage."

Dantzler closed his notepad and stood. He took a card from his shirt pocket and handed it to Keith. "Thanks for your time," he said. "If you think of anything else, call me at either of those numbers."

"Keep this." Keith handed the card back to Dantzler. "There's nothing else to say."

* * *

When Dantzler entered the Wolfe Archery Club, Lenny Wolfe was standing behind the counter conversing with a father and his son. Lenny handed the man an application, then told him the cost of a membership for adults was twenty-five dollars a month or one-seventy-five for a year. For kids sixteen and under, the cost was fifteen dollars monthly or one-hundred for a year. The man thanked Lenny, said he would fill out the app, then bring it back within the next few days.

When the man and his son were gone, Lenny looked up at Dantzler and nodded. He made an attempt at a smile but couldn't quite pull it off. "You here to sign up for archery lessons?" he said.

"I think I'll take a pass on that. I've seen enough bow and arrow nonsense to last me for a while."

"Archery is much easier on the knees than tennis. You need to consider that as you get older."

"Nice try. But I'll stick with tennis."

"Then what can I do for you, Detective?"

"Tell me what you know about a guy named Oscar Yewell."

"I don't know anyone by that name," Lenny said. "Who is he?"

"The last time we spoke, you mentioned a guy named Oscar. You said he was a good hunter who lives for the kill. Were you talking about Oscar Yewell?"

"Oscar Young."

"Okay, what can you tell me about him?" Dantzler said, scribbling Oscar's name in his notepad. "What's he like?"

"I don't know anything about him other than he's deadly with a bow and arrow and he loves to hunt. It's not like we hang out together."

"How often does he come here?"

"He's been in here maybe five or six times. He's not even a member. When he shows up, he pays the daily rate."

"Where does he live?"

"Couldn't tell you, Detective."

"Do you happen to know what type vehicle he drives?"

"Different ones. I've seen him in a station wagon. One time he showed up in a Mustang. And once or twice, he drove a beat-up old truck."

"What color was the truck?"

"Red."

Dantzler said, "If you don't hang out with him, how do you know he's such a good hunter?"

"Word gets around, you know. People talk. Friends of mine who do hunt tell me Oscar is a superb hunter. Why? Are you looking at Oscar for the murder of that doctor?"

"At this stage, I'm looking at everyone."

"Well, you can scratch me off your list, Detective. I haven't killed anyone."

"That's good to know."

"You really should consider taking up archery, Detective. I have a feeling you would be good at it."

"Not gonna happen."

"Any particular reason?"

"There's no love in archery."

CHAPTER TWENTY-FOUR

Dantzler climbed out of bed while it was still dark outside, showered, dressed and headed into the kitchen. He scrambled three eggs, fried some bacon and poured a glass of orange juice. Starving, he devoured the eggs and bacon in half the time it took to cook them. As he was setting his dirty plate in the sink, his cell phone rang. He cringed. Phone calls this early in the morning normally went one of two ways—very good or very bad. Casual calls before sunrise were a rare occurrence.

He flipped his phone open, checked the caller ID and smiled. This call fell into the very good category. Laurie Dunn was the caller.

"Did I wake you?" Laurie asked.

"Just finished breakfast and was getting ready to head off to work." Dantzler went out onto the deck and sat in the wicker chair. "How does it feel being a short-timer?"

"Feels good. I can't wait to get back home. But I have to admit . . . I've enjoyed the training. I've learned a lot."

"What about Scott? How is he handling it?"

Laurie laughed. "Scott is FBI-bound. It's just a matter of time."

"Are they recruiting him?"

"I think it's the other way around. He wants to join the Bureau."

"If that's what he wants, then he has my blessing. And I have no doubt he would be an excellent agent."

"I agree."

"Have they made a pitch for you?"

"Yeah, they're working me pretty hard."

"You giving it any thought?"

"Not really. When they bring it up, I spout the standard line. You know, maybe sometime down the road I might consider it."

"You would make a great FBI agent," Dantzler said. "And God knows they would love to have you."

"Yeah, yeah, yeah. But enough about me. Tell me how the Rafe Wiseman case is progressing."

"We took a step forward yesterday," Dantzler said. "Whether it's a big step or a small one, I don't know. We're fairly certain that Carly Shelton was meant to die in the blast. She wasn't at the clinic by accident. We've also come up with the name of a guy who is definitely worth a close look. He's a superb archer, and he drives a beat-up old truck like the one spotted at the clinic a few minutes before the explosion. Those two details are more than enough to make him a serious person of interest."

"What's the guy's name?"

"Oscar Young."

Laurie was silent for a moment, then said, "I don't recognize the name. Does he have a criminal record?"

"Don't know. I'll have Eric checked that out first thing this morning."

"What do you have planned for Scott and me when we get back to work?"

"Just pitch in and help wherever you're needed."

"I do have one request," Laurie said. "No, make that one demand."

"What?"

"I'll be home around noon on Sunday. I don't care where the investigation stands, or how busy you are, you will set aside two hours for Laurie time. That's an order."

"I'm sure I can make that happen."

"You *will* make that happen."

* * *

Eric came into the War Room with a blank sheet of paper in one hand and an exasperated look on his face. "Oscar Young has no criminal record," he said, pulling back a chair and sitting. "Not even a speeding ticket."

"Have you looked to see if he has a juvie record?" Dantzler said.

"That's next on my agenda."

Milt and Jake came into the War Room. Jake took a seat next to Eric, Milt went to the coffee pot.

"Whose juvie record are you interested in?" Jake said.

"Oscar Young," Dantzler answered.

"I know Oscar," Jake said. "And I'm not surprised that you are interested in him?"

"Why do you say that?"

"He's a couple years younger than me, but I used to see him around when we were teenagers. He was a thug, a bully. And he was dumber than a rock. I'm pretty sure he didn't graduate high school. I'd be surprised if he did."

"Wait a minute," Milt said, sitting next to Jake. "Is he one of Rufus Young's kids?"

Jake nodded, said, "I think so, yeah."

"Well, if Oscar is a thug, it just proves once again that the apple doesn't fall far from the tree," Milt said. "Rufus surely was. And he was dumber than a rock. If you want to know about Rufus Young, give Charlie Bolton a call. He can tell you plenty."

"It's Oscar, not Rufus, that I'm interested in," Dantzler pointed out.

"Talk to Charlie. Maybe he'll tell you something about Rufus that helps you with Oscar. Rufus was a criminal, and if the son has his father's genes . . . well, you know the rest."

"What did Rufus do?"

"Something to do with stealing cars and selling them down South," Milt said. "I'm not clear on the details. Ask Charlie. He'll fill you in."

Dantzler picked up his phone and punched in Charlie Bolton's number. Charlie answered after the first ring. "Are you ever going to let me retire in peace?" he said.

"Are you at home or at the lake?"

"Neither. Fact is, I'm downtown. About five minutes from your office."

"Would you be so kind as to grace us with your presence?"

"Why is my presence needed?"

Dantzler said, "I'm seeking information, knowledge."

"Go to a library."

"Get up here, Charlie. I need your help."

"I don't move as fast as I once did, so give me fifteen minutes."

"Take all the time you need. There's no great hurry."

"That's bullshit and we both know it. If you weren't racing the clock, you wouldn't need me."

* * *

When Charlie Bolton walked into the War Room, all four detectives immediately stood up. Protocol demands that you rise when royalty arrives, and if anyone was considered royalty, it was Charlie Bolton. To remain seated would be viewed as a sign of disrespect.

Despite a head of snow-white hair and sun-baked skin, Charlie looked fifteen years younger than his actual age of eighty-one. He was a legend within the law enforcement community, highly respected for his tenacity, his professionalism and for the hundreds of cases he closed successfully. Charlie had also served as mentor and rabbi for virtually every detective on the force, including Dantzler.

He was considered a god, and when one of the gods elects to pay a visit to the mortals, you act accordingly.

Charlie nodded at Dantzler, shook hands with Milt and Eric, then went to Jake and put a hand on his shoulder. "This must be Jake Thomas," he said. "I've heard nothing but great things about you. It's nice to finally meet you."

"Same here, sir," Jake said.

"Call me Charlie, son. Sir makes me sound so damn old." Charlie pointed at the coffee pot. "Has that swill gotten any better since I retired?"

"It ain't Starbucks," Milt said.

"Might as well have a cup while I'm here," Charlie said.

Jake said, "I'll get it for you."

"A detective with good manners and respect for his elders. That makes him a real outcast in this motley group." Charlie waited until Jake handed him the coffee cup, then said, "Okay, Jack. Why am I here?"

"Rufus Young. Milt tells me you're familiar with him."

"You could say that. Why? What's that low-life asshole done that has him on your radar?"

"Actually, it's his son we're interested in. But like Milt said . . . the more we know about the father, the more we might know about the son."

Charlie said, "This all goes back to the late eighties and early nineties. Rufus was part of a small gang that stole high-priced cars and sold them down South. We also suspected that he was dealing drugs. And who knows what other mischief he was into? As hard as we tried, we never could pin anything on him or his gang. I questioned Rufus on multiple occasions. Never came up with enough evidence to charge him. He's one of the guilty bastards who got away scot-free."

"If he was so dumb, how did he manage to skate?"

"Ah, good question," Charlie said. "He skated because he wasn't the leader. A guy named Buddy Raymond was. He was the brains *and* the muscle. Really sharp, really tough, really ruthless. The first time I interviewed him, I knew within ten seconds that he wasn't going to tell me anything. I could see it in his eyes. He wasn't the type who would ever break under pressure."

Eric turned his laptop around so Charlie could see it. "There is no record of any criminal activity by either Rufus Young or Neil 'Buddy' Raymond junior," Eric said. "That means they are either very smart or very lucky."

Charlie said, "They are both bad dudes, so I would never say they have gone straight. But . . . they both have enough money now that they don't need to work outside the law."

"How did they get their money?" Dantzler asked.

"The Young family owned hundreds of acres of prime land out on Old Ironworks Pike. Back in the mid-nineties, the University of Kentucky bought most of it. Rufus came away from that little transaction with millions of dollars in his pocket. More than enough to feed his family, and he has, what, ten or eleven kids. With that kind of cash, what's the point of risking arrest?"

"And Buddy Raymond? What's his story?"

"He owns The Long Branch Saloon. It's in the Woodhill Center. He bought it from his old man about twenty years ago." Charlie finished his coffee and tossed the cup into the trash. "What's got you so interested in Rufus's kid?"

"He's very good with a bow and arrow," Dantzler said. "That's what killed Rafe Wiseman."

"That's an excellent lead, no question about it. I've solved plenty of cases with worse leads than that." Charlie stood. So did the other four detectives. "What about your other case, Jack? The one involving the kid in Versailles?"

"How did you know about that?" Dantzler said.

"Hasn't it become clear to you by now that I know everything? When you break wind, Jack, I hear about it before the stink reaches your nose."

"I yield to your omniscience, Charlie," Dantzler said, bowing. "As for the investigation, it's on a ventilator, about three seconds from dead."

"Did you ever consider the possibility that you're just tilting at windmills? That maybe it really was a suicide?"

"Cyanide?"

Charlie shrugged. "Rare, I'll grant you that much."

"Rare? How about never?"

"Who caught the case over there?"

"Amos Garland."

"That's a bad break. Amos wasn't much of a detective before he got lost in the bottle. I shudder to think how incompetent he is now." Charlie went to the door. "It's been nice seeing you three guys again.

And it's been especially nice to meet you Jake. Listen to what these guys say and you'll do fine. Do you know why I say that?"

"Because you taught them everything they know," Jake said.

Charlie looked at Dantzler but pointed toward Jake. "Sharp kid," he said.

* * *

For the past two days, Paul Shelton moved like a man trapped at the bottom of the ocean. The water was dark and heavy, and each step he took required maximum effort on his part. He had never experienced anything like this—worried, depressed, scared. Those were emotions and feelings that had always been alien to him. Now they rode his shoulders like a thousand-pound boulder.

Sitting at his desk, he picked up the single sheet of paper and read it again, perhaps hoping the words would change. Or disappear completely. But they didn't change or disappear. They were real, and they stabbed him in the heart like a knife.

I WILL BE IN TOUCH

Who will be in touch? This was the question that haunted him. Not the *why*. He already knew the answer to that question.

Picking up his glass of bourbon, he went from his office to the living room. Plopping down on the sofa, he took a drink, closed his eyes and let his mind wander. The direction his thoughts took came as no surprise.

Who will be in touch?

Who was the note's author? There were three obvious choices, but he was quick to scratch them from the list of possibilities. Why? For the simple reason that they were in this mess just as much as he was. If he went down, they would go down with him. When the prison door slammed shut on him, it would slam shut on them as well. None of the three were willing to take that risk, regardless of the money. Fear of being incarcerated guaranteed their silence.

He knew there was another possibility, one he didn't want to consider. What if she was the *who*? What if she didn't truly love him and was only after his money? Maybe she had played him like a violin all this time, simply waiting until the right moment to make her move. Maybe he was the classic love-blind fool. Maybe he was the world's biggest chump.

No, it's not her, he decided. The woman loves me the way I love her. She did not send the note.

His cell phone buzzed, startling him. He flipped it open and saw UNKNOWN on the caller ID. He felt a thousand butterflies take flight in the pit of his stomach. His hands were trembling and he was nauseous. This was the moment he dreaded.

Who will be in touch?

"Paul Shelton," he said, hesitantly.

"Did you receive my note?" the caller said.

"Who is this?"

"The one person who knows everything you did and why you did it."

"I don't know what you're talking about."

"Denial is not a path you want to follow. That will only lead to an unsatisfactory conclusion. You don't want that."

"What do you want?" Shelton asked.

"Two million dollars."

"Are you insane? I don't have that kind of money."

"Then I suggest that you begin liquidating some assets, because the next time you hear my voice, if you don't have the money, I'll contact the police."

"And tell them what? I didn't do anything."

"No games. Two million dollars—have the money ready by the time I contact you."

"What if I don't pay?"

"You go to prison."

"I suppose it'll only be a matter of time before you call and demand more money. Isn't that how blackmail works?"

"This is a one-time deal. I'm not greedy. I can live on two million bucks."

Shelton said, "I'll need time to come up with that much cash."

"You have until my next phone call."

"When will that be?"

"Don't know. Could be in a week, could be tomorrow. The clock is ticking."

Shelton started to protest, to say he needed more than a week, but the caller's line went dead. He hit the Redial button, only to learn that the call could not be traced. Closing his phone, he stood and went back into his office.

Two million dollars? Okay, he thought, that's a lot of money, but not an insurmountable hurdle. Not for a man whose net worth exceeded thirty million dollars. Yes, putting it all together would require him to sell some stocks and liquidate a few other minor assets, which was no big deal. It would take some time, but he could come up with that much cash.

And he had no qualms about paying off the blackmailer. Some decisions you make, some decisions are made for you. Call it fate or providence or chance or that Eastern bullshit karma . . . it didn't really matter. There are moments in life when the situation, or a certain set of circumstances, dictate the move you make. This was one of those moments.

No other option was available to him.

I'm the man who knows everything you did and why you did it.

It was those last four words that sealed the deal.

CHAPTER TWENTY-FIVE

David Bloom stood at the bar waiting to be served a glass of orange juice and a Bloody Mary. Drinks in hand, he went to the booth where Dantzler was sitting. They were in the Tennis Center lounge area.

"Want to hear a terrific story?" Bloom said, handing the OJ to Dantzler. "It involves one of my cases."

"What about that doctor-patient privilege thing?"

"No names, just a funny story."

"If you're comfortable spilling the beans, let it rip."

"This couple comes in, been married for . . ."

"I didn't think you did marriage counseling," Dantzler said.

"Occasionally, I dabble in it. If I have the time, or am extremely bored, I'll work with married couples."

"Okay."

"This couple has been married for seventeen years. They are in their mid-forties, healthy, vibrant, totally in love with each other. No kids, but they didn't want kids, so that isn't an issue. Anyway, one day the wife decides to get herself waxed. I mean, *really* waxed. Only trouble is, she neglected to inform her husband that she was having it done. A few nights later he gets all frisky and decides he wants to do the oral thing. He makes his move, but when he gets down to prime real estate, he can't believe what he's seeing. Make that, what he's not seeing. He lets out a scream. She is totally bald down there. 'Slick as a cue ball' was how he put it. The guy is horrified, mortified, completely aghast. He asks her why she did it. She says because it's what many women are doing now. He tells her he will not have sex with a woman who looks like a five-year-old down there. And guess what? They have not had sex in four months. It's a standoff, and neither side is yielding."

"That's their loss," Dantzler said.

"Here's the best part, Jack. The guy turns to me, deadly serious, almost in tears, and poses this memorable question. 'How can I be a muff diver when there's no muff?' That's the greatest line I've heard in thirty-two years as a psychiatrist."

"I have to admit. The guy is making a good point."

"What do you think about it? What women are doing with the waxing thing?"

"Personally, I don't get it. But then, I don't get this obsession with tattoos either."

"Nowadays, *everybody* has one of those damn atrocities."

"What's the psychology behind that?"

"Has nothing to do with psychology. It's all about following the stars. Celebs and athletes cover themselves with ink, so Joe and Betty Sixpack have to emulate their idols and heroes."

Dantzler said, "Moving on to more serious matters. How is Sally Wiseman doing?"

Bloom sipped his Bloody Mary, said, "Sally is a rock. She has already given the green light to rebuild the clinic. Construction should begin within the next two weeks. She has also enlisted Sam Shapiro to head up the clinic. Sam is a retired surgeon and one of Rafe Wiseman's closest friends. Sally got really lucky when Sam agreed to run the place. He and Rafe shared many of the same sensibilities and beliefs and priorities. They were like two peas in a pod. That means the clinic's mission statement will remain virtually unchanged."

Dantzler twisted in the booth, straightened his left leg and began rubbing his knee. He had spent the past hour working out in the

Center's exercise room, and while riding the stationary bike, he felt a pop in his knee. Nothing serious, but it did hurt.

"You have any Advil or Aleve on you?" he asked.

"I don't," Bloom said, shaking his head. "Terry probably has some at the bar. Want me to see if he does?"

"Don't bother. It's nothing I can't live with." Dantzler finished off the orange juice. "Did you ever have a client named Rufus Young?"

"Not that I recall."

"What about Oscar Young?"

"Doesn't ring a bell. Why? What have they done?"

"I don't know that they've done anything. But their names have recently popped up on the radar. I need to know as much about them as I can. Especially Oscar. He interests me the most."

"To the best of my knowledge, I've never had a patient named Young," Bloom said. "Certainly not one named Rufus or Oscar. Those names I would remember."

"What about Buddy Raymond? Ever worked with anyone by that name?"

Bloom closed his eyes and thought about Dantzler's question for a few seconds. Finally, he said, "I remember meeting with a guy named Neil Raymond and his wife. I think her name was Betsy. Neil was a one-time actor, if I remember correctly. This had to be twenty or twenty-five years ago. They came in with their son. He was twelve or thirteen at the time."

"That would be Neil junior. Buddy. Why did the Raymonds come to see you?"

"I can't recall if it was court ordered or simply because they couldn't handle Buddy. Must have been the latter, because Buddy stopped seeing me after a couple visits. He couldn't have done that if he had been ordered by the court to see me. Buddy was one tough, hard-nosed cookie, I do remember that."

"How so?"

"Defiant, paid no attention to rules and regulations, no interest in school, lacking empathy or sympathy, challenged authority—pretty much all the characteristics of a budding sociopath. He was also extremely intelligent. His parents were solid people who tried to do what was best for their son. He was just way more than they could handle or cope with. They came to see me, hoping I could help. Obviously, I never had the chance to find out if I could help the kid."

"Hard to help someone who doesn't show up."

"Buddy wasn't about to listen to anything I had to say. Like I said, he stopped coming after the second visit. He was an egg that wouldn't crack. Why? Is he also on your radar?"

"I recently learned that he and Rufus Young were involved in some nefarious activities when they were teenagers. But they have no criminal record as adults, so I really don't have a reason to suspect them of anything. But Rufus is Oscar's father, and Oscar does interest me."

"Does this have anything to do with Rafe's death?" Bloom said.

Dantzler nodded, said, "I think it could. Oscar Young is reputed to excel with a bow and arrow."

"I still find it hard to believe Rafe Wiseman was killed by a bow and arrow."

"Would it have made any difference if the killer used a gun instead of a bow and arrow?"

"No, I don't suppose it would," Bloom admitted. "Dead is dead."

"You got that right. Dead *is* dead."

* * *

Milt and Jake were waiting for Dantzler when he came out of the Tennis Center. They were standing next to Milt's car, which was parked in the shade. It was two-fifty and the afternoon sun was blazing hot.

For convenience sake, Dantzler asked to meet here rather than the War Room. He had a three-thirty interview with Lucian White, and he was cutting it close. Leaving from the Tennis Center would save him considerable travel time.

Noticing Dantzler's slight limp as he came toward them, Milt said, "You okay?"

"It's nothing," Dantzler said. "Where's Eric?"

"In court, testifying."

"I forgot about that. The Prather case, right?"

Milt nodded, said, "The Prather girl killed her husband with a shotgun while he was sleeping. Then she has the gall to claim self-defense. Says the hubby beat her up on a regular basis."

"She may get off, Milt. Juries tend to sympathize with battered women."

"I'm not saying any woman should ever allow a husband, boyfriend, father or brother to beat her up," Milt said. "All I'm saying is shoot the bastard while he's awake."

Dantzler said, "I'm pressed for time, so let's get down to business. I've been thinking about the best way to put surveillance on Oscar Young. I don't want to bring him in for questioning just yet, but I would like to keep an eye on him."

"Why not bring him in?" Milt asked.

"I want to know more about him first."

"I can bird dog him," Jake said.

"No, you can't," Dantzler said. "He knows you. It has to be someone he won't recognize."

"That narrows it down to Eric or me," Milt said.

"I might have you guys do it until Laurie and Scott get back to work," Dantzler said, adding, "It would probably be safer to let Laurie handle it. Oscar might know Scott. They are about the same age."

"Whoever does it needs to know that Oscar Young is a bad guy," Jake said. "He's one of those brawlers who will die before he gives up. You don't want to turn your back on him."

"Especially if he has a bow and arrow in his hands," Dantzler said.

* * *

Oscar Young was puzzled. Not so much because his father demanded that they meet; that wasn't at all unusual. The old man always had bull-shit advice to offer or some stupid chore he wanted taken care of. But it was the location of the meeting that was strange—the Carmike 10 Cinemas on Mapleleaf Drive. Oscar knew his old man watched plenty of movies at home on one of his five huge Plasma TV screens, but he had never once seen him enter a movie theater.

Oscar was at a loss as to why the old man wanted to meet here of all places. There was no way he couldn't even begin to figure that out. But even if the meeting was for important purposes, why couldn't the location be one that wasn't going to cost him money? Rufus should have considered that before deciding on a movie theater as a meeting place.

Oscar paid for his ticket, walked through the lobby, found the movie Rufus told him to look for, then went inside the theater. It took several seconds before Oscar's eyes adjusted to the dark. Once they did, he began searching for his father. With only four people in the theater, it didn't take long to spot him. Rufus was sitting in the middle of the back row. Oscar climbed the steps and took the seat next to his father.

"Shitty movie," Rufus mumbled.

"Why did you pick it?" Oscar said.

"Because *Dumb and Dumber*, the movie about you, wasn't playing."

"Ha, ha. Very funny."

"Son, you'd be wise to lose the attitude. You're not so big that I can't still knock you on your ass. And I will. Trust me."

"Why am I here?" Oscar said.

Rufus crooked his forefinger and beckoned Oscar to come closer. Then he whispered into Oscar's ear. Hearing what his father said, Oscar whistled loud enough that two of the three moviegoers turned and looked at him.

"Are you sure?" Oscar said.

"You think I'm joking?"

"On whose orders?"

"My fucking orders, that's who."

"How soon?"

"As soon as you can get it done," Rufus said.

Oscar shrugged, said, "Shouldn't be a problem." Standing, he said, "Can I go now?"

Rufus stood and put a hand on Oscar's shoulder. "Watch your ass, boy," he said. "No mistakes. Make it perfect, just like the last one."

CHAPTER TWENTY-SIX

At first glance, Lucian White reminded Dantzler of a younger version of Brad Pitt. Lucian had the same facial structure, a similar physique, the same hair color and style, and the same mischievous grin. A handsome guy who, like Brad, probably wouldn't have any trouble getting a date.

Lucian had asked to meet in Rafferty's, which was located in Hamburg Place, less than a mile from where the Wiseman Clinic once stood. He was sitting in a booth in the bar area drinking a Sprite. Still on duty, he was dressed in his State Police uniform. He smiled and waved when he spotted Dantzler.

"It's an honor to meet you, Detective Dantzler," Lucian said. "I read about you all the time in the newspaper. You're either solving a case or winning a tennis tournament. That earns you plenty of ink."

"Don't believe any of what you read," Dantzler said, settling into the booth. "Pure propaganda."

"I've always heard that it doesn't matter what they write about you just as long as they spell your name correctly."

"In that case I'm in big trouble. I've seen Dantzler spelled a dozen different ways." When the waitress came to the booth, Dantzler ordered a Diet Pepsi. After she walked away, he said to Lucian, "Are you still on duty?"

Lucian nodded. "But it's okay. Captain Porter knows I'm meeting with you. He told me to take all the time I need. Or all the time you need would be the better way to put it."

"I know you're busy so I'll keep this short." The waitress brought the Diet Pepsi, then asked Dantzler if he wanted to order food. He declined. To Lucian, he said, "Nikki Bradford indicated that you don't believe Danny Tucker committed suicide. Is she right?"

"Man, I just don't know," Lucian said. "I don't want to believe he did. I mean, why would he do it? Things were going really good for him. He loved his wife, he was going to be a father, he was doing great on the job, he wanted to go back to school—there was no reason for him to check himself out like he did. But as a guy working in law enforcement, I'm trained to look at the evidence, the facts. And the evidence says Danny took his own life."

"What evidence are you talking about?"

"The poison, the cyanide. The fact that Danny was alone in the house. The front and back doors being locked. There's simply no evidence to counter the suicide finding."

"Tell me how and when you learned of Danny's death."

"Initially, I didn't know it was Danny."

"What do you mean?"

"I was off duty that day," Lucian said. "A buddy of mine who works for the Versailles Police Department called me. This was about eleven-fifteen. I was just outside the Fayette Mall when he called. He told me something was going on at Danny's parents' house, and that I might want to get over there. I jumped back in my car and got there as fast as I could. When I arrived, there were two police cruisers, Amos Garland's Camry, the coroner's vehicle and Keith Davis's State Police cruiser parked in front of the house."

"Where was Keith Davis?"

"Outside, sitting in his car."

"Did you speak to him?"

"No."

"Okay, what did you do next?"

"There was a uniformed officer standing guard by the front door. I knew he'd been given orders to keep everyone outside, so I didn't bother speaking to him. The front door was closed, but I could see broken glass on the porch. They had to break a window in order to unlock the front door. I went to the back of the house, onto the porch and looked through the kitchen window. By this time, they had covered the body, placed it on a gurney and were about to wheel it outside. Amos Garland and Malcolm Kinnison were in the kitchen, standing next to the table. I figured what the hell, if the body is being removed, I might as well go inside. But the back door was locked. I went back around to the front just as they were coming out of the house with the body. I was convinced that the deceased was one of Danny's parents. Probably his father, judging by the size of the body. Malcolm Kinnison came outside and I asked him who had died. When he told me it was Danny, I just about fell over. I couldn't believe it."

"Nikki Bradford said you and Danny were very close."

"If you've met Nikki, you know she tends to exaggerate things. Yes, Danny and I were close, but we didn't pal around all that much. We spent most of our time together at work, although we did go out for drinks on a few occasions, mostly prior to Danny getting hitched. When Danny left the Sheriff's Department and joined the State Police, he kind of latched onto me as someone who could show him the ropes. I became his mentor, his go-to guy when he had questions or problems. Not that he had many questions or problems. Danny was an outstanding trooper. He was professional, dedicated and serious about doing good work."

"Any enemies that you know of? Any serious issues, like gambling?"

"No. Once Danny got married, his carousing days were over."

"Other women?"

"Heavens no."

"Was the marriage a good one?" Dantzler said.

"I can't tell you what went on behind closed doors. But I can tell you that Danny was madly in love with Anna. His eyes lit up when he talked about her. Have you spoken with Anna yet?"

"We haven't been able to locate her."

"Ask Keith. He'll know where she is."

"Keith Davis?"

"Yes."

"Why would Keith Davis know her whereabouts?"

"Keith and Anna are brother and sister."

This bit of information hit Dantzler like a slap in the face. He leaned back, his thoughts traveling at warp speed. He didn't know what this meant, but he knew it was important.

But what he heard next hit him with the force of a hard sucker punch to the gut.

"If you think about it, Anna has no real reason to stay around here," Lucian pointed out. "Her husband is dead, her place of employment burned to the ground, and her boss was murdered. Given all that, why should she stick around?"

"Wait a minute," Dantzler said, trying to piece it all together. "Are you referring to the Wiseman Clinic?"

"Yes. The one that blew up a couple of weeks ago."

"Anna Tucker worked at the Wiseman Clinic? Is that what you're telling me?"

"Yes. She went to work there shortly after getting married."

"How come I'm just hearing about this?" Dantzler's question was more rhetorical than directed at Lucian. "I spoke with Keith Davis. I asked him if he knew Danny's wife and all he said was yes. He didn't bother to mention that Anna was his sister."

"I'm not surprised. Keith isn't one of the more forthcoming individuals you're likely to meet."

"Nikki Bradford told me Anna came from Alabama."

"That's true. She and Keith grew up in Birmingham."

"And yet they both end up in Lexington," Dantzler said. "How'd that happen?"

"Keith came to the University of Kentucky on a football scholarship. He was big-time, said to have NFL-type talent. Started at linebacker as a true freshman. Midway through the season, he sustained a serious knee injury. I'm pretty sure he tore his ACL. Anyway, he rehabs, comes back as a sophomore, only to tear up his other knee. Those two devastating injuries ended his dreams of playing pro ball. No NFL team was about to shell out big bucks to a guy with damaged wheels. He went on to play his final two seasons at UK, but he was never the same. After graduating, he joined the State Police."

"And Anna? What's her story?"

"I can only assume she came to visit while Keith was in school. She must've liked the area, because she eventually moved here. She met Danny, they got married, then she went to work at the clinic."

"At work, she went by the name Anna Davis."

"Anna kept her maiden name after she got married. No one ever referred to her as Anna Tucker."

"When I spoke to the manager of the Racquet Club, she said the Tucker's still rented the apartment. That no movers had taken their things away."

Lucian shrugged. "I don't know. Maybe she's with her family in Birmingham."

"I should have talked to you two weeks ago." Dantzler dug into his pocket, took out some bills and peeled off five ones. "Did you eat? If you did, I'll pay."

Lucian shook his head. "Just had this drink."

Dantzler stood and extended his hand. "Thanks for talking to me, Lucian. You've been really helpful."

"Do you think Danny committed suicide or was murdered?" Lucian said, shaking Dantzler's hand.

"Murdered."

* * *

Leaving Rafferty's, Dantzler headed straight home. He needed to be alone, needed time to think, time to process the information Lucian had provided. And there was much to think about, much to process. He felt as if he had been handed a giant jigsaw puzzle with the pieces lying scattered about, each one waiting to be put in its proper place.

Sitting on his deck, watching the evening shadows close in, he was as angry as he was perplexed. Angry at himself for doing a lousy job investigating the two cases he was working, two cases he now believed were somehow linked together. He didn't know why they were linked, or how. But he did know who linked them.

Anna Davis Tucker.

In some way, he knew, she was the key to solving the puzzle.

More than anything, though, he was pissed at himself for not putting forth a greater effort to interview her. That should have been a priority from day one. Had he tracked her down and spoken to her, many of his questions might have been answered. At the very least, he would have discovered that the Wiseman Clinic's Anna Davis was also the wife of Danny Tucker.

That little bit of information would have been nice to know.

He had done a poor job, and there was no one to blame but himself. The fault was all his. If this had been a tennis match, he would have been crushed.

But something else was gnawing at him, something other than the anger he felt boiling inside him. It was something important, maybe even crucial, but he couldn't quite put a finger on it. He thought hard about it—it was close—but he couldn't locate it. What he was seeking remained just out of reach.

And then it hit him with the suddenness of a revelation.

Something Keith Davis said.

According to Keith, the back door to the Tucker house was unlocked. This contradicted the account given by Amos Garland and Lucian White. Amos said both the front and back doors were locked when he arrived. Lucian said the back door was locked. He also pointed out seeing the broken glass, which confirmed Amos's story about having to break a window in order to unlock the front door.

What Dantzler was looking at now was a contradiction, and in his experience, contradictions typically fell into one of two camps—an honest mistake or an outright lie.

This contradiction begged the question: Into which camp did Keith Davis's story belong?

Dantzler vowed to get an answer first thing in the morning.

CHAPTER TWENTY-SEVEN

B y the time Dantzler arrived in his office the next morning, his self-loathing was holding steady. Rarely did personal failure stare him in the eyes, but this time it did. He had failed; simple as that. Failed to use his manpower in a proper manner, failed to fully utilize his resources, failed to press more relentlessly forward on the two investigations confronting him. Although he was not given to second-guessing his actions, he now found himself doing exactly that.

Milt, the veteran in the group, quickly came to Dantzler's rescue.

"Stop beating yourself up over this," Milt said. "We're all equally responsible for not pressing harder to locate Anna Davis. It just means we have to dig in and find her."

"Let me get this straight," Eric said. "Anna Davis and Keith Davis are related?"

"Not just related," Dantzler pointed out. "They are brother and sister."

Eric said, "What you're saying is, Anna Davis was married to the guy who was found dead by her brother, she worked at the clinic that was blown up and her boss at the clinic was murdered. Does that sum it up?"

"Succinctly."

"Man, there's some connective tissue involved in that scenario," Eric said, shaking his head.

"Yeah, Anna Davis." Dantzler leaned forward and opened a folder. "We need to track her down and interview her. Anna Davis is now a top priority. She's originally from Birmingham. Maybe she's gone back home, so that's where we'll start looking. There are probably hundreds of folks named Davis in the Birmingham area, but her father is the minister of a big church down there. Milt, call a few churches, see if anyone can provide you with his name. If so, give him a call. Jake, I want you to check with DMV, see if you can get a permanent address for Oscar Young. Surely, he's old enough that he isn't still living at home. Eric, when you've finished with your court appearance, come back and help Milt."

"Where will you be?" Milt asked.

"Talking to Keith Davis," Dantzler answered.

"No, you're not." Captain Bird was standing in the doorway. "Keith Davis is not available for an interview."

"Why not? Has Woody Porter put him off-limits?"

"Keith Davis is dead."

"What?" Dantzler said. "When? How?"

"Woody said Keith died sometime last night or early this morning. He didn't show up for his shift, so Woody sent another Trooper to Keith's apartment. He found the body."

"Don't tell me . . . he was killed by a bow and arrow."

"Don't know. Woody did say it appears as though foul play was involved."

"Damn, I guess this means Amos Garland is the lead investigator," Dantzler said.

"No," Bird said. "You are. Keith lived in the Brandywine Apartments on Trent Boulevard. That makes it our case. Arnie Edwards has been alerted and is already en route to the scene."

"Has the crime scene been secured?"

"Yes. Six uniformed officers are already in place."

Dantzler thought about this new information for a few moments, then said, "Okay, change of plans. Jake, you take over the search for

Anna Davis. Phone Woody Porter and find out who he contacted about Keith's death. Then give that person a call. Maybe we can get to Anna that way. Milt and I are going to Keith Davis's apartment. Eric, how long do you expect to be tied up in court?"

"No more than an hour, tops."

"Good. When you're done, come on out to the Brandywine Apartments."

As Jake stepped outside to make a call, Eric said, "I hate to keep beating the same bush, but what about Paul Shelton? Are we forgetting about him?"

"No, Eric, you're absolutely right," Dantzler said. "We need to know his whereabouts last night and early this morning. After you've testified, go pay him a visit. Hear what he has to say and how he says it. He'll have an alibi—you can count on that—but read his actions, his body language and his expressions. Judge whether or not you think he knows more than he's telling you. Once you're done with him, head out to Trent Boulevard."

"I hope that bastard is good for all this," Milt said. "I would love nothing better than seeing his ass behind bars for life."

Jake came back into the room and said, "Captain Porter talked to Ezekiel Davis, Keith's father. I got Mr. Davis's phone number and gave him a call. According to him, he has not spoken to Anna since Danny's funeral, nor does he know her whereabouts. Mr. Davis did agree to meet with us while he's in town."

"We may do that at some point," Dantzler said. "But the Davis we need to talk to is Anna."

Eric said, "Anna's husband and brother both died under mysterious circumstances. Maybe we need to consider the possibility that she's also dead."

"You may be right, Eric," Dantzler said. "But our immediate concern now is Keith Davis. We need to find out what happened to him."

* * *

Paul Shelton did have a rock-solid alibi but not one he cared to share with law enforcement. At the time Keith Davis died, Shelton was placing an old army duffel bag behind a Dumpster located in a movie theater parking lot. Inside the bag was two million dollars in cash.

Shelton received the phone call around nine that evening. He was at home, sitting in his den, drinking a scotch and soda. When his cell phone buzzed, he knew without any doubt that this was the call he had been expecting.

"Hello," Shelton said, trying to keep his voice cool and steady. "Been waiting to hear from you."

"You have the cash?"

"I do."

"All two million?"

"That's what you asked for, isn't it?"

"What's the money in?"

"An old army duffel bag."

"Excellent." Following a brief pause, the man said, "At exactly two o'clock this morning, drive to the Woodhill Cinema. Go around to the parking area at the rear of the building. You'll see a big Dumpster there. Place the bag behind the Dumpster, then get in your car and drive away. Eyes will be on you the whole time, so don't do anything stupid. If you do, or if the money isn't there, I call the police and tell them about your recent escapades. Any questions?"

"Just one," Shelton said. "What makes you so sure I did anything?"

"Because you're willing to cough up two million bucks, that's what makes me so sure."

"Who's your source?"

"No more conversation. Deliver the money and you'll never hear from me again."

"Can I count on that?"

"The only thing you can count on is spending the rest of your life in a prison cell if you screw this up."

At precisely two o'clock, Shelton pulled in behind the Woodhill Cinema building, climbed out of his car, opened the back door and removed the duffel bag. Getting it out proved to be a struggle; two million dollars in cash isn't light. Securing the duffel bag by its strap, he finally managed to wrestle it out of the car and sling it over his shoulder. After taking one final look around to make sure no one was in sight, he placed the bag behind the Dumpster. Mission accomplished, he got back in his car and drove away, two million dollars poorer.

Fifteen minutes after Shelton departed a man stepped out of the shadows and walked quickly toward the Dumpster. He was dressed in all black, wore black leather gloves and a black ski mask. He doubted that there were cameras in this location, but it was a risk not worth taking. Better to be safe than sorry. No one can recognize a face that can't be seen. Bending down, he easily picked up the duffel bag, turned and headed for his car.

Five minutes later, Buddy Raymond drove away, two million dollars richer.

CHAPTER TWENTY-EIGHT

When Dantzler and Milt arrived at Keith Davis's apartment, Arnie Edwards, the M.E., was attempting to get close to the body without stepping in blood. This was no easy task; Keith Davis was laying face down, his entire body circled by a river of dark red blood. Edwards, wearing plastic booties, finally gave up. Carefully placing one foot close to the body, he knelt down, turned the body over and began examining the wounds.

"I see at least five stab wounds," he said, adding, "although with this much blood on his body, there may be some cuts that I can't see. I won't know for sure until later. Based on what I do see, I can say with some degree of certainty that a very large knife caused these wounds. Something like a hunting knife, or maybe a military knife. One with a long, thick blade."

"That's a helluva lot of blood loss," Dantzler said.

"One of the wounds was a direct hit to the heart," Edwards said. "It pumped out a massive amount of blood before the victim expired. Then plenty more leaked out."

"Keith Davis was an ex-football player. He was also a trained state trooper. Big, strong, able to defend himself. That means his attacker had to be exceptionally tough, or he pulled off a surprise attack."

"Your second scenario is more likely the correct one," Edwards said, pointing at a kitchen chair. "The victim was sitting there when the first blow was struck. His attacker was standing behind him. I'll venture a guess that the first strike was the one that hit the victim's heart. Then the attacker probably kept the victim sitting upright while stabbing him repeatedly in the chest area. When the slaughter was finished, he let go and the victim tumbled face down on the floor. None of what I'm telling you is etched in stone, Detective. I may be completely wrong about everything, but I doubt it. I won't know for sure until I do the autopsy."

"You think like a detective, Doc," Dantzler said. "I like that. It makes my job easier."

"I'll take my job over yours anytime, Detective Dantzler. The people I deal with never give me any lip."

"Do you have a time of death?" Dantzler asked.

"Between midnight and three a.m."

Dantzler eased past the body and went into the bedroom. Coming back into the living room, he said, "Was the TV on or off when you got here?"

"Off."

"Keith is wearing boxers and a T-shirt. His bed is unmade, which means he either got out of bed when the killer knocked on the door, or he hadn't made it up from the previous night. Either way, if TOD is between midnight and three, Keith must have known the killer. There's no sign of forced entry, so Keith let him come in. He had to know the guy."

"And your killer is definitely male," Edwards said. "No way a female inflicted these wounds."

"You know the drill, Doc. Give me details as soon as you can." Dantzler went outside, located Milt, who was speaking with one of the uniformed officers, and said, "Who found the body?"

Milt pointed to a man in his late twenties who was dressed in shorts, a T-shirt and sandals. "His name is Roger Simmons," Milt said. "He's also with the State Police. He was off today. When Keith failed to show up for work this morning, Woody Porter phoned Roger and asked him to check on Keith."

Dantzler caught Roger's eye and waved him over. "You okay?" Dantzler said. "You look a little green around the gills."

"Nah, I'm fine," Roger said. "I've seen much worse than this when investigating automobile accidents. But . . . seeing a friend dead like this is not easy to process."

"What time did you discover Keith's body?" Dantzler said, taking out his notepad.

"Captain Porter phoned me at a little past nine. Keith wasn't at work, and he wasn't answering his phone. Captain Porter knew I also live in the Brandywine Apartments, so he told me to check on Keith, just to make sure everything was okay. I got to Keith's place at about nine-thirty."

"Where do you live?"

Roger pointed to his left. "Two buildings down," he said. "Took me about a minute to get here."

"Was the front door locked or unlocked?"

"Unlocked."

"So you went inside, right?"

Roger nodded. "I took one look at Keith and knew he was dead. You can't lose that much blood and keep on breathing. I called Captain Porter on my cell phone and let him know what I found. He told me to stay put, that he would call you guys. Two police cruisers showed up in a matter of minutes."

"When you were inside, did you touch anything? Maybe turn off the TV?"

"The only thing I touched was the doorknob. As for the TV, it was off."

"Do you know if Keith was having problems or issues with anyone?" Dantzler said.

"Keith wasn't the friendliest guy I know, but I can't say he was having problems with anyone. At least none that I'm aware of. He certainly wasn't having any issues with me."

Milt and one of the uniformed officers ducked under the yellow crime scene tape and came toward Dantzler and Roger Simmons. A young female, perhaps still in her teens, was walking between Milt and the officer. She wore the look of a prisoner being escorted to the gas chamber.

Milt said, "Detective Dantzler, this is Kelsey Goodall. She has something you might want to hear."

"Okay, Kelsey, what have you got for me?"

Kelsey groaned, then said, "Oh, man, if I tell you, I'm going to get in big-time trouble."

"Who will you get in trouble with?" Dantzler said.

"My parents. Who else?"

"Why?"

"Well, I have this stupid curfew."

"And you broke curfew, right?"

"Great," Kelsey said. "You get that I'll be admitting guilt if I tell you what I saw. And that will get me in deep trouble."

"Kelsey, you'll be in a whole different kind of deep trouble if you *don't* tell me what you saw."

Kelsey weighed her options, then finally said, "I'm supposed to be home by eleven, which I was. But Sidney, my BFF, sent me a text, saying let's get together up by the pool. Sidney usually has the best weed. She gets it from her brother. Anyway, I have this window in my bedroom that I can open. We live on the ground floor, so sneaking out is no problem. When I got outside, I saw this truck driving away from in front of the apartment where the dead guy lives. The truck was going really fast."

"I know it was dark, but could you make out the color of the truck?" Dantzler said.

"Yeah, it went right under that light," Kelsey said, pointing to a corner street light. "The truck was red."

"Was the truck new or old?"

"Older than my grandfather's balls," she said, giggling at her own joke. "It was really beat up. Loud, too."

"Could you tell if the driver was male or female?"

"Definitely a guy."

"Would you recognize him if you saw him again?"

"No way. It was dark and he was going too fast."

"Now this is extremely important, Kelsey. What time did you see the truck driving away?"

"Man, my parents are going to kill me," she said, the smile now long gone. "They'll have me on lock-down for months."

"Give me the time, Kelsey."

"It was one-ten when I saw the truck. Okay, there. Now are you happy?"

"Why are you so certain that it was one-ten?"

"Duh. Because I looked at my watch."

Dantzler said, "I can't bail you out for violating curfew, Kelsey. That's on you. But I will let your parents know that you've been extremely helpful in my investigation. You've provided me with some very valuable information."

"Yeah, well, I've got some breaking news for you, sir," Kelsey said. "Nothing you say is going to save my ass. I'm toast."

Dantzler gave Kelsey a sympathetic pat on the shoulder, stepped away and took out his cell phone. As he was about to make a call, he saw Eric coming toward him.

"You're already done with court?" Dantzler asked. "That didn't take long."

"Five questions asked and answered," Eric replied. "I wasn't on the stand more than ten minutes. What do you need me to do here?"

Dantzler punched in a number and held up a finger, indicating for Eric to hold on. "Jake, did you get an address for Oscar Young?" Dantzler said. "Yeah, give it to me. Great, I've got it. Yes, go see if Oscar is home. If he is, make sure he stays there. Eric and I are on our way."

"Why the sudden urgency to meet with Oscar Young?" Eric said.

"Because he drives a beat-up old red truck like the one that keeps showing up at our crime scenes. I want to check it out, see if one and one makes two." To Milt, Dantzler said, "Wrap things up here, Milt. When you're satisfied that everything has been taken care of, meet us back in the War Room."

CHAPTER TWENTY-NINE

According to the latest DMV records, Oscar Young lived on Winthrop Drive. Upon further investigation, Jake learned the residence was a house owned by Rufus Young. Rufus purchased the house in 1998 for just under two-hundred grand.

Jake traveled on Man o' War until he saw the Winthrop Drive sign. Making a right, he drove no more than a hundred feet before spotting Oscar's red truck. It was parked in the driveway next to the Ranch-style structure. The battered old truck looked as out of place in this nice middle-class neighborhood as a mule in the Kentucky Derby.

As Jake pulled up and parked behind the truck he saw Oscar coming out the front door. Jake got out of his car and headed toward the house. Oscar locked the door and had started down the steps when he saw Jake. A look of recognition crossed his face.

"Hey, I know you, don't I?" Oscar said, pointing. "Jake somebody. You were in the army. Fought in the war, right?"

"Marines. And that was a long time ago," Jake said, holding up his badge. "I'm with the police now."

"Went from the good guys to the bad guys," Oscar said. "What do the police want with me?"

"In a few minutes a detective named Jack Dantzler is going to show up. He needs to ask you some questions."

"Questions about what, exactly?"

"You'll find out when he asks them."

Oscar shook his head, said, "Well, he'll have to ask them some other time, 'cause I have to leave."

"I don't see how that's going to happen, Oscar."

"Why not?"

"Because I've got you blocked in, that's why. And I'm not moving my vehicle."

"Hey, I ain't done nothing wrong, so you have no right to order me around like this."

"It's not an order, Oscar. It's a statement of fact. You're staying here until Detective Dantzler shows up."

"What does he want to talk to me about?" Oscar said, moving down the steps and onto the sidewalk. "I haven't committed any crimes."

"Then you shouldn't have a problem answering his questions."

"Questions about what?"

Jake pointed toward Oscar's truck. "A red truck like yours was spotted at two crime scenes. Detective Dantzler wants to know if it was your truck that was seen by the witnesses."

"What kind of crimes are you talking about?"

"Detective Dantzler is with Homicide," Jake said. "You take it from there."

"Homicide? You mean, like, murder?"

"That's a good call on your part, Oscar. Yeah, murder."

Fight or flight is arguably man's most primal instinct, dating back millions of years. When threatened, do you stand and fight, or do you run for cover? It's a decision our oldest ancestors had to make, and one we are still faced with today.

Hearing the word murder triggered Oscar's fight or flight instincts. Within seconds, an internal war was raging. Run or stay put? Those were his choices. The voices in his head were loud, fueled by fear and uncertainty. Yet, despite his inner turmoil, he understood with tremendous clarity that his next course of action would have a lasting impact on his life. Right or wrong, he had to do something. Staying put was out of the question. Fight or flight—time to decide.

In that instant Oscar made two choices, both ill-advised. First, he opted to fight, and, second, he picked the wrong opponent.

Oscar started the confrontation by throwing a wide roundhouse right, a punch Jake saw coming from a mile away. Jake leaned to his right, causing the punch to hit him harmlessly on his left shoulder. Still leaning over, Jake slammed his right fist hard into Oscar's groin. Oscar let out a loud groan and reflexively doubled over at the waist. Jake's next move was to drive his right knee up hard, hitting Oscar squarely on the nose. Oscar groaned again, and his nose began to drip blood. Jake finished it with a solid right to the jaw that sent Oscar flying backward onto the grass, out cold.

At that moment Dantzler and Eric exited their vehicle and were racing toward the scene. Both men were grinning from ear to ear.

"Nice punch, Jake," Eric said. "But why not just shoot the idiot? I would have."

"I didn't want to deal with the paperwork," Jake said.

"Good point." Eric knelt next to Oscar, rolled him over, pulled his arms behind him and put on the handcuffs. "Wake up, Rocky. Time to head downtown."

Oscar's eyes rolled back in his head and he began to wretch.

Eric stood and moved back several steps. "Get rid of it out here," he ordered. "You puke in my car and I will shoot you, paperwork be damned."

Oscar wretched two more times, producing nothing but tears, snot and saliva. Finished, he wiped his nose on his sleeve, looked at Dantzler and said, "I'm gonna sue Jake for police brutality. I'll have his badge and every penny he has."

"Yeah, well, good luck with that, Oscar," Dantzler said. "Take him downtown, Jake. Have him printed, then lock him up. Call Dr. Hatfield. Ask him if he has time to drop by and take a look at Oscar. I'm pretty sure his nose is broken."

"Come on, asshole," Jake said, leading Oscar toward the car.

"Take these cuffs off and give me another shot at you," Oscar demanded.

"Oscar, you would shit your pants if I took those cuffs off right now. I took it easy on you. Trust me, it could have been a lot worse."

Oscar had no comeback for that.

When Jake and Oscar were gone, Eric said to Dantzler, "We search the house first, or the truck?"

"Neither. We aren't taking any unnecessary chances. Get in touch with Judge Black. Get warrants for Oscar's house, garage and truck. We're not going in until we have the warrants in hand."

"Under these circumstances, do we really need warrants?"

"Probably not. But if Oscar ever goes on trial, I don't want to provide some slick defense attorney with any possible ammunition that might get him acquitted."

"When are you going to interview Oscar?" Eric said.

"We'll let him simmer behind bars for a night. That'll give him plenty of time to think about things. The more stupid guys like Oscar think, the better it is for us."

Eric laughed, said, "Taking on Jake was definitely a stupid move."

* * *

Transferring two million dollars in cash from a duffel bag to three large suitcases took Buddy Raymond almost two hours to complete. A time-consuming chore, but at the rate of moving a million bucks per hour, he wasn't about to complain. Hell, if it had taken him five hours he wouldn't have complained. For this kind of money, any amount of effort was worth it.

When the three suitcases were filled and stacked against his office wall, he sat at his desk, popped open a bottle of Budweiser, leaned back and thought about things. He especially thought about the money, what he would do with it and when. Regarding the money, he had to be patient and disciplined. And he would be. He would not spend a penny of the two million for three years. This was a promise he made, one he would keep.

Having fanned through many of the stacks—all consisting of one-hundred dollars bills—he knew the bills were not in any sequential order. This meant the money likely couldn't be traced. But Buddy didn't believe in taking unnecessary risks, so he would hold onto the money for that three-year time period. To be more precise, he wouldn't be the one holding onto the money. It would be safely taken care of by someone else in a location far removed from Lexington. After an acquaintance pulled off a big score several years ago, he put the money in a Cayman Island bank account. Buddy figured it would be a smart move to follow the same procedure. He would keep the money at his house for the time being. It would be safe there while he finalized his plans for the trip to the Cayman Islands.

His immediate concern was getting rid of the duffel bag. The best way, of course, would be to simply burn it. But it was now a little past midnight, so setting it on fire was not possible. Instead, he decided to drive around town until he found a Dumpster in a secluded area, then deposit the bag there. The bag, even if discovered by law enforcement, could in no way be linked to him. He had never handled it without wearing gloves, and the name stenciled on it was Dalton. Paul Shelton probably purchased it from an Army Surplus store, and the bag had once belonged to a GI named Dalton. Still, Buddy wasn't going to take any chances. He would get rid of the duffel bag in a location a safe distance from his house or The Long Branch Saloon.

Buddy found the perfect place behind Kroger's in Tates Creek Center. There were three Dumpsters that had all recently been emptied. Buddy tossed the duffel bag into the middle Dumpster, then looked around, found several large cardboard boxes and threw them on top of the bag. By this time tomorrow, the Dumpster would be crammed full, the bag safely buried under a ton of garbage.

As Buddy was driving away his cell phone buzzed. Seeing Rufus Young's name on the caller ID, Buddy thought about letting it go to voice mail. He was in no mood to hear Rufus complain or bitch about what was going on in his miserable life. Rufus's constant whining got on Buddy's last nerve. But, Buddy reasoned, if Rufus was calling at this hour of the night, it might be something important. Better to answer than to be left wondering what was on Rufus's mind.

"What do you want, Rufus?" Buddy snapped.

"Some seriously bad shit is happening," Rufus replied, almost in a whisper. "We need to talk."

"Define seriously bad shit."

"Oscar has been arrested. The cops have him."

"Why was he arrested?" Buddy asked. "And when?"

"Sometime this afternoon. Why? I don't know. Randy Trent pulled up at the house just as Oscar was being put in the police cruiser. They had him handcuffed and everything. This is bad, Buddy. What are we gonna do?"

"Where are you?"

"Shillito Park, sitting in the dark," Rufus said. "I've never been this scared in my life, Buddy."

"Are there many people in the park?"

"Just me, the squirrels and rabbits."

"Where are you in the park?" Buddy said.

"Sitting on a picnic table, the second or third one you'll see if you come in from the Reynolds Road entrance. I'm on the right."

"Stay put, stay out of sight, and wait for me. I'll be there in ten minutes."

When Buddy turned off Reynolds Road he cut his headlights, preferring to drive in the dark. It was risky—the road through the park was narrow and curvy—but if he could find Rufus without being seen, that was to his advantage. A vehicle can't be identified if no one sees it. The odds of that happening were in his favor. With headlights off, and driving a dark blue Audi, he was virtually invisible in the night.

Buddy had to drive slow and look deep into the darkness, but he eventually spotted Rufus sitting on one of the picnic tables. Rufus was dressed in dark clothes, and he had driven to the park in his black Mercedes, making him difficult to locate. Of course, being nearly impossible to see was the reason for wearing dark clothes and driving a dark vehicle. Occasionally, Buddy thought, Rufus somehow manages to do the smart thing.

"I sure hope Oscar has the good sense to keep his mouth shut," Rufus said, as Buddy approached him. "He needs to clam up tighter than my wife's snatch."

"I think we can rule out that possibility," Buddy said. "Oscar will talk faster than an auctioneer."

"Then we're going to prison," Rufus said, his eyes filling with tears.

"Unless we get out of town, hell, out of the country, before they find us."

"Where are we going to go, Rufus?"

"Hell, I don't know. One of those countries that won't hand us over to the cops. Some damn island country."

"All beaches and sand and surf. Is that it, Rufus?"

"I don't know. But it's for damn sure we can't stay here."

"You plan on taking your family with you?"

"Can't do that right now. But I'll leave them plenty of money, though. More than enough to get by until I can send for them."

"Your plan stinks, Rufus."

"What are we gonna do, Buddy? You tell me."

"I'm going to take care of it."

Rufus hung his head and said, "Man, I sure hope so."

Those were the last words he ever spoke.

Rufus felt a sharp prick on his neck just below his left ear. Initially, the pain wasn't bad—it was like getting a shot from the doctor—but within a fraction of a second, that changed. Suddenly, the pain became intense. And, Rufus realized, whatever was causing the pain was now slowly being pulled from left to right. As this was happening, as the skin below his chin was being opened up, he could feel the cool night air being sucked into his lungs with each desperate gasp. Warm blood gushed from the wound. It took him a second to realize what was happening—his throat was being slashed from ear to ear. Fear and panic and disbelief overwhelmed him. He couldn't believe what was happening.

He was being murdered by his best friend.

Rufus tried to talk, tried to ask Buddy why he was doing this, but no words came out. The best he could produce was a sick, gurgling sound. With both hands clutched tight against his throat, he came off the table, took three steps and collapsed on the ground. Hands now splayed out in front of him, the blood cascaded from the massive wound. In less than a minute Rufus Young was dead.

Buddy had always known this course of action was a distinct possibility. Rufus was a good outlaw, even at times a good friend. But Rufus was also just dumb enough to be a major liability, and in Buddy's world, liabilities had to be eliminated. In Buddy's view, only the strong *and* the intelligent survive.

What Rufus failed to realize was that Buddy could not be connected to any of the recent string of murders. The first two, the Shelton woman and the clinic doctor . . . those murders were strictly on Rufus and Oscar. They were paid a hefty sum to commit them. Buddy's hands were clean. As for Keith Davis, it was Rufus who gave Oscar the order to do the killing. And now Rufus, the only person who could connect Buddy to that murder, was dead. And poor, dumb Oscar had no clue that it was Buddy who whispered the order to Rufus. The only thing Oscar could tell the authorities was that Buddy purchased three pre-paid cell phones. And who gives a shit about cell phones?

In the darkness, with Rufus Young's body on the ground in front of him, Buddy Raymond smiled. He was two million dollars richer, and even more important, he was in the clear. None of this could fall back on him.

After dragging Rufus's body and hiding it behind a row of bushes, Buddy jogged back to his car. He climbed in, started the motor and slowly drove away. Keeping his headlights off until he got to Reynolds Road, he made a right turn and headed home. Once he was on Nicholasville Road, he glanced in his rearview mirror and grinned. He had once again proved the veracity of a long-held belief.

Only the strong and the intelligent survive.

CHAPTER THIRTY

Oscar Young sat alone in the small interview room, doing his best to act cool, brave and disinterested. His act wasn't working. He looked like a frightened eighth-grader sitting outside the principal's office, dreading the punishment that would soon be meted out. Oscar's attempt at bravado couldn't disguise the reality that he was scared to death.

Although Oscar's nose had not been broken during his scuffle with Jake, there were tell-tale signs that a struggle had taken place, and that Oscar came out on the losing end. Both of his eyes were black, his left cheek was swollen and there was a deep purple bruise on his chin. The back of his head had also been bruised when he hit the ground.

Oscar looked up when Dantzler and Milt entered the room. Dantzler sat in the chair across from Oscar and placed a folder on the table. Milt stationed himself directly behind Oscar and leaned against the wall. Oscar shifted in his chair, looked at Milt, then turned back toward Dantzler.

"I take it that he's the bad cop," Oscar said to Dantzler. "And you're, what, the good cop?"

Dantzler didn't respond.

Milt leaned down and whispered in Oscar's ear. "Get this straight from the start, Oscar. We ask the questions, you answer the questions. Exactly like it's done on *Jeopardy*."

"I don't know nothin' about *Jeopardy*," Oscar said.

"I'm not surprised," Milt said, leaning back against the wall.

Dantzler said, "Oscar, we know quite a bit about your recent activities. You . . ."

"You don't know squat about me, dickhead."

Dantzler nodded, said, "If you think we've been sitting around twiddling our thumbs while you've been our guest here, you would be dead wrong. We've done a complete and thorough search of your house, your garage and your truck. And I have to say, we've found some very interesting items."

"I don't have interesting items," Oscar replied.

"Oh, I beg to differ with you, Oscar. You have plenty of interesting items."

"Such as?"

"Such as a compound bow that experts tell me is top-of-the-line quality. How's that for starters?"

"Shit, that's no big deal. Thousands of people own a compound bow."

"I'm sure you're right about that. But along with the bow, we also found fourteen arrows that perfectly match the one used to murder Dr. Rafael Wiseman. That makes them extremely interesting items."

"So I have a bow and some arrows? So what? That don't mean shit, dickhead."

Dantzler leaned forward, said, "Call me dickhead one more time, Oscar, and this is what will happen. Milt and I leave, Jake Thomas comes in. I really don't think you want that. So be nice, answer my questions in a polite manner and we'll get along just fine."

"I ain't afraid of Jake Thomas," Oscar said. "Send his ass in here."

"Did you really say that?" Milt said. "Are you really that stupid? After what he did to you, I can't believe you'd ever want any part of Jake."

"If that's what you want, Oscar, I can make it happen," Dantzler said. "Jake is just down the hall. I can have him here is ten seconds."

"Which is about seven seconds longer than it will take him to teach you another lesson," Milt said, laughing.

"Want me to get him, Oscar?" Dantzler asked.

"Well . . ."

"I didn't think so," Dantzler said. "So let's continue with our little chat. In addition to the bow and arrows, we found a Damascus Bowie hunting knife in your garage. Has about a seven-inch blade. A truly scary-looking weapon. It also has blood on it. I'm going to make you a wager, Oscar. Tests will confirm the blood came from Keith Davis. You willing to make that wager?"

Before Oscar could respond there was a knock on the door. Dantzler stood up, stepped outside and listened as Captain Bird whispered something in his ear. Bird delivered his message in a matter of seconds. When Bird was finished, Dantzler nodded, came back into the room and returned to his seat.

"Bullshit time is over, Oscar," Dantzler said. "Now we're going to get serious. Your responses from this point forward can work for you or against you. If what you tell me is true, and I can prove it, then I will put in a good word for you with the district attorney. If you lie or impede my investigation in any way, I'll hang you out to dry. Do you understand what I'm telling you?"

"District attorney?" Oscar said. "What's he got to do with anything?"

"You need to understand, Oscar. You are in deep shit."

"Why? I ain't done nothin' wrong. I keep tellin' you that. Why won't you believe me?"

"Oscar, we know it was your truck that witnesses saw at two crime scenes. We have your bow and arrows, the very weapon that killed Dr. Wiseman. We have the knife with blood on it, blood that in all likelihood came from Keith Davis. Add that all up and it's overwhelming evidence. You know, Oscar, with four murders to your credit, you almost rank as a serial killer."

Confusion registered on Oscar's face. Making a fist with his right hand, he began counting on his fingers, stopping when three fingers were raised. He looked at Dantzler and shook his head.

"Four?" he asked, bewildered. "Who's the fourth one?"

"Danny Tucker," Dantzler answered.

"Whoa, hold on a minute," Oscar screamed. "I didn't have nothin' to do with killing Danny Tucker. No way I'm taking the rap for that one. Okay, I'll cop to the other three. But I did not kill Danny Tucker. You can't pin that one on me."

"Slow down a minute, Oscar," Dantzler said. "Are you now telling us that you killed Carly Shelton, Rafael Wiseman and Keith Davis?"

Oscar nodded.

"I need a yes or no, Oscar."

"Yes."

"Did you also bomb the Wiseman Clinic?"

"Yes."

Dantzler said, "Telling the truth is good, Oscar. Now what I need from you are details. Start at the beginning with the bombing. Why did you do it, and on whose orders?"

"I don't know the guy's name. Some rich asshole who wore expensive threads and said he didn't believe in God. I told him he'd better believe in God or he would be doomed to eternal hell."

"Where did you meet this non-believer?"

"Shillito Park."

"Just the two of you?"

"No, the old man was there."

"Rufus Young? Your father?"

"Yeah. The old man was the one who knew the guy. He set up the meeting."

"Were you paid?" Dantzler said.

"Fifty grand."

"Was Rufus involved in all three of these murders?"

"Of course."

Another knock on the door interrupted the investigation. This time Jake was the intruder. He opened the door and handed Dantzler a sheet of paper. On the paper were close-up head shots of six men. Dantzler thanked Jake, closed the door and sat down, not letting Oscar see the photos.

"This Shillito Park guy, what orders did he give you and Rufus?" Dantzler said.

"Blow up the clinic and make sure his wife was inside when the blast went off."

"You drove to Carly's house and said what, exactly?"

"That I had just driven by the clinic and there seemed to be something going on there. I said it sounded like an alarm was going off. She must've bought my story, 'cause she booked out of there right after I did."

Dantzler said, "When did you set the bomb?"

"Earlier that night. I had already poured gasoline all around the building. In fact, I did that for three straight nights. I soaked the place."

"Where were you when the bomb went off?"

"Home, asleep. My job was done."

"Let's talk about Dr. Wiseman," Dantzler said. "Did the Shillito Park guy also order that hit?"

"Yep, he did. He paid us twenty-five grand for that one and twenty-five grand for the clinic thing. Like I told you, fifty grand in all."

"Why use a bow and arrow?"

"Two reasons. It's silent, and I'm damn good with one."

"How did you know Dr. Wiseman would be outside that early in the morning?"

"The Shillito Park dude said the doctor walked his dog every morning. I got there before sunrise, found a good spot and waited. He came outside and I let him have it. Simple as that. It was much easier than killing a deer, that much I can tell you."

"Did the Shillito Park guy also order you to kill Keith Davis?" Dantzler asked.

Oscar shook his head, said, "That order came from the old man."

"Who gave it to Rufus?"

"I don't know. Hell, I don't even know *why* he wanted me to do it. He never said. Just told me to get it done."

Dantzler turned the sheet of paper over and said, "Look at these photos. Tell me if you recognize anyone."

Without hesitating, Oscar pointed to a photo of Paul Shelton that Jake had pulled from Shelton's business company website.

"That's him," Oscar said. "That's the dude."

"This man, Paul Shelton, is the person who paid you and your father fifty thousand dollars to burn down the Wiseman Clinic, and to kill Carly Shelton and Dr. Rafael Wiseman. Is that accurate?"

"Right as rain," Oscar said, almost gleefully.

"But to the best of your knowledge, this man, Paul Shelton, had nothing to do with the death of Keith Davis? Is that also accurate?"

"I don't know if he did or he didn't. All I can say for sure is that it was my old man who gave me the order."

"Which you did, using the hunting knife, right?"

"Right."

"You're doing really good, Oscar," Dantzler said. "You're being truthful and forthcoming. I appreciate your cooperation. But that being said, I'm having trouble believing that you didn't have anything to do with Danny Tucker's death. That's difficult for me to swallow."

Then Oscar said something that made perfect sense.

"Look, I've already copped to three murders," he said. "Why would I lie about a fourth one, if I had committed it? Three or four—what difference will it make? I'm fucked either way."

"Okay, Oscar, I believe you," Dantzler said. "Now . . . one final question. What role, if any, did Buddy Raymond play in all this?"

"Buddy? He didn't have nothin' to do with any of this. Why are you askin' about Buddy?"

"Because he and your father have been friends since they were kids. They used to be involved in some enterprises that weren't necessarily legal. Given their past history together, I can't help but wonder if Buddy was involved."

"Nah, Buddy ain't involved.'

Dantzler leaned back and rubbed his eyes with his hands. What he was about to say next was never easy, not even when saying it to a three-time murderer. After several seconds, he said, "Oscar, I know the last couple of days have been pretty shitty for you. Unfortunately, what I'm about to tell you isn't going to make you feel any better."

"What now?"

"Your father is dead, Oscar. His body was found in Shillito Park earlier this morning. I'm very sorry for your loss."

"How did he die?"

"It looks like a homicide. His throat had been cut."

"That bastard did it." Oscar pointed again at the photo of Paul Shelton. "He's the one. Go lock his sorry ass up."

"We will," Dantzler said, standing. "And again, Oscar. I'm very sorry for your loss."

"Maybe he got the better end of the deal," Oscar said. "At least he won't be spending the rest of his life in a crummy jail cell."

* * *

Back in the War Room, Milt poured a cup of coffee and leaned against the wall. "I can't believe that poor kid didn't ask for an attorney," he said. "All that time, all those questions, and he never once uttered the word lawyer. He dug himself a deep grave."

"We were with him for almost three hours," Dantzler said. "If he'd wanted an attorney, all he had to do was ask."

Jake said, "Should you have suggested that he might want a lawyer present?"

"No way," Dantzler answered. "It's his responsibility to seek legal representation, not mine. If he chooses to go it alone, then I'm certainly not going to make the call for him."

"You know his defense attorney is going to see it in a different light," Milt said. "He'll argue that the kid should have been advised to seek counsel."

"This will never go to trial, Milt. With the evidence we have, no attorney is about to let Oscar walk into a courtroom and face a jury. But even if the case does go to trial, I'm not worried. We read Oscar his rights, and we interviewed him. We asked, he answered. It's all on tape. We did everything by the book."

"You seem a little glum," Milt said. "You should be dancing the jig. We just closed three murder cases. Four, if you count Rufus Young's death."

"That's the one that troubles me, Milt. Eric says Rufus's throat was cut from ear to ear. He says it's a deep, savage cut. Do you really see Paul Shelton committing an up-close-and-personal murder like that? I can't. I can see him paying someone else to do it, but no way do I see him as the doer."

"You think Oscar was lying?" Jake said.

"No, Oscar was telling the truth. He genuinely believes his father was murdered by Paul Shelton. I'm just not convinced Shelton did it."

Milt said, "When are we going to bring Paul Shelton in?"

Dantzler looked at his watch. "It's eleven," he said. "Shelton should be in his office. We go get him now."

"Shelton will ask for his attorney," Milt said. "I believe his name is Jay Matthewson."

"I don't care if he asks for Jesus Christ, he's coming in with us," Dantzler said.

"Cuffs on or off?" Jake asked.

"On. And I want his hands behind his back. No way I'm letting that bastard use a coat to cover his hands. If anyone sees him, I want them to know he's wearing bracelets. He's involved in two murders. He gets no breaks from me."

"Who's going?" Milt said.

"The two of us," Dantzler said. "Jake, you hang around downstairs. When a suspect like Paul Shelton is arrested, word can spread more rapidly than a virus. In case a crowd gathers on the street, make sure we have a clear path to the door."

"We'll part it wider than the Red Sea," Jake said.

"Now why couldn't I come up with a line like that?" Milt said, tapping Jake on the shoulder. "You're almost too good to be true, kid."

"Come on, Milt, let's go," Dantzler said. "This is one arrest I'm going to enjoy making."

CHAPTER THIRTY-ONE

Paul Shelton's receptionist was a tall, beautiful, statuesque black woman with cocoa eyes and a thousand-watt smile. She flashed the smile the instant Dantzler and Milt entered the office. It disappeared just as quickly, the second Dantzler flashed his gold shield and asked to see her boss.

"I'm afraid Mr. Shelton is tied up at the moment," she said. "He and Mr. Daniels are in a meeting with one of our most-important clients."

"Well, here's the thing, Miss . . ." Dantzler looked at her nameplate. "Jefferson. That meeting is about to break up. Is Shelton's office in the back?"

"Yes, sir," she said. "Do you want me to buzz him, let him know you are here?"

"Don't bother," Dantzler said. "He and I are old friends. I'd much rather surprise him."

"Yes, sir. As you wish."

Shelton was sitting behind his desk, conversing with a heavy-set man Dantzler presumed to be the important client. Jonathan Daniels, Shelton's partner, was standing off to the client's left. All three men turned toward the door when Dantzler and Milt entered.

"You're interrupting an important meeting, Detective," Shelton blurted out. "Can't this wait . . .?"

"Stand up," Dantzler ordered.

Milt moved quickly behind the desk, pulled Shelton's arms behind him and put the handcuffs on.

"Paul Shelton, you are under arrest for the murders of Carly Shelton and Dr. Rafael Wiseman," Dantzler said, as a preamble to reciting the Miranda Warning.

Shelton's reaction was predictable. He appeared annoyed, as though the king was being hassled by lowly peons. The first words out of his mouth were also predictable.

"Jonathan, call Jay and tell him to get his ass down to police headquarters," he said. "Tell him to get there fast. I will not spend more time in that shithole than necessary."

"I wouldn't make any immediate plans if I were you," Milt said, yanking Shelton toward the door. "I'm fairly certain you'll be with us for a while."

"Don't count on it," Shelton said.

* * *

Dantzler's prediction came true. In the hour it took to arrest Paul Shelton and drive him to police headquarters, a host of interested bystanders had gathered on the sidewalk. Dantzler estimated the number to be between twenty-five and thirty, but with the vast majority either talking on their cell phones or texting, it was only a matter of time until the size of the crowd doubled, maybe even tripled. Word was spreading with high-tech speed that a prominent Lexington businessman had been arrested. That was more than enough to intrigue the curious.

Jake and Bruce Rawlinson were in charge of handling the on-lookers. They had managed to divide the crowd into two groups, the smaller group facing east, the larger group, the one Jake was handling, facing west. Between the two groups was an open lane that led straight from the street to the police building.

Dantzler parked his car directly in front of the building. Milt got out on the passenger's side, then opened the backdoor and helped Paul Shelton get out. Dantzler and Milt flanked Shelton on both sides and began leading him toward the building.

"Seems like you're a popular guy," Milt said. "It's a shame no TV cameras are covering the big event. Bet you would look good on the evening news."

Shelton sneered, or maybe it was a smirk, but he didn't respond.

As Dantzler, Milt and Shelton neared the building, Jake noticed an individual weaving through the crowd. The person was wearing sneakers, jeans and a gray hooded sweatshirt. The hood was up, and dark sunglasses covered the person's eyes. Sensing something odd in the individual's behavior, Jake felt his pulse begin to quicken. His military instincts kicked into high gear. He'd seen enough suspicious individuals during his time in Iraq to know when something bad was about to happen. This was one of those times. The hood and sunglasses were enough to cause concern, but it was those hands hidden in the individual's sweatshirt that sent Jake's internal warning system into high alert.

Jake began moving to his right at the same moment he saw the individual's right hand come into view. What he saw justified his concerns and verified his worst fears. In the individual's hand was a dark blue pistol, which Jake instantly recognized as a .45.

"Gun," Jake screamed, as he lunged to his right, slamming the full weight of his body against the individual. The force of Jake's blow sent them both crashing to the pavement. But Jake's move, quick as it was, had been a split-second late. Before being taken down, the individual managed to get off a single shot, the bullet hitting Paul Shelton in his upper chest.

Pandemonium ensued. On-lookers scattered, some screaming, some falling to the ground, others running for cover. Milt dropped to his knees, his hands pressing hard on Shelton's chest, doing his best to stop the bleeding. Rawlinson was on the phone, calling for an ambulance.

Jake had the shooter pinned down, his left hand on top of the pistol. He ordered the shooter to release the weapon, which the shooter did. When the gun was clear of the shooter's hand, Dantzler kicked it away, bent down and helped Jake to his feet. Then Jake leaned over, pulled the shooter up, pushed the hood back and removed the sunglasses.

The shooter was female.

Dantzler moved closer to her, nodded, and said, "Anna Davis?"

"Yes."

CHAPTER THIRTY-TWO

T he next hour could best be described as organized chaos. Milt and Rawlinson continued to work on Shelton, doing everything possible to stem the blood flowing from his wound, until the ambulance arrived. When Shelton was laid on the stretcher, his glazed eyes were open and his skin was the color of gray metal. Jake escorted Anna Davis to the War Room, Eric took charge of the weapon—a .45—handing it off to the ballistics experts, and Dant-zler met with Captain Bird, filling him in on what had transpired and how he wanted to proceed.

With so much happening, it would be more than an hour before Dantzler could begin his interview with Anna. Milt, who wanted to be in on the interview, calling it his "last hurrah," had to rush home to change shirts. The one he had been wearing was drenched with Paul Shelton's blood. Also, Dantzler asked a doctor to stop by the War Room and take a look at Anna. He was concerned that she might have been injured when Jake tackled her. After examining her for thirty minutes, the doctor told Dantzler that Anna and her unborn baby were fine.

When the doctor left, and a few minutes before Milt got back to headquarters, Dantzler went into the War Room and asked Anna if she was comfortable and if she needed anything. He fully expected her to ask for an attorney but she didn't. All she wanted was something to drink, so he gave her a bottle of water.

"Is Paul dead?" she said, as Dantzler was leaving the room.

Dantzler nodded, said, "He expired in the ambulance on the way to the hospital."

"So sad," was all Anna said.

Anna Davis was one of those attractive women that most men would rank squarely between above average and stunning. Her features, taken individually, were nothing out of the ordinary. However, when taken as a whole, they somehow worked, transforming her into a beautiful woman. She had dark hair, hazel eyes, unblemished skin, and even with the baby bump plainly visible, it was obvious she had a splendid figure. She also had a warm, wonderful smile, a disarming smile. When Dantzler took her the water, and she hit him with that smile, he had to remind himself that the attractive woman sitting at the table was nothing less than a cold-blooded assassin.

There were times when Dantzler was convinced that if everything he *didn't* know was turned into rocks and stones, God would have enough material to create another mountain. This was one of those times. Yes, he knew plenty, but there were still a number of questions to be answered, blanks to be filled in. Hopefully, and with only a minimum of prodding, Anna Davis could answer his questions. She could help him bring down the mountain.

Anna sat at the table, arms straight out, fingers interlaced. She still had on the jeans, a blue T-shirt and sneakers, the sweatshirt having been removed when the doctor examined her. Two reminders of her encounter with Jake Thomas were evident—a bruise on her right cheek and an abrasion below her right elbow.

Anna looked up when Dantzler and Milt came into the room. Dantzler sat in the chair directly across from her, while Milt, rather than station himself behind her, took the chair next to Dantzler.

Anna smiled, and Dantzler had to fight the urge to give her a sympathetic pat on the shoulder, or maybe even a hug, once again reminding himself that she was a murder suspect and nothing more.

"For the record, would you state your full name," Dantzler said, beginning the long-awaited interview.

"Anna Marie Davis," she answered.

"Were you married to Danny Tucker?" Milt said.

"Yes, I was."

Dantzler said, "You've been something of a phantom, Anna. We've been trying to get in touch with you for almost three weeks. Where have you been keeping yourself?"

"In a loft on Angliana Avenue."

"Have you been hiding from someone?"

"Hiding? No."

Dantzler opened the folder he carried into the room, then said, "I know most of the details of what has been happening, but there are still some questions I need answered. I suspect you are the one person who can give me those answers."

"I will tell you everything I know," Anna said. "And I will be honest and truthful. However, before we get started, there are two things you need to understand. First, I had absolutely nothing whatsoever to do with any of these murders, and, second, I did not know about the murders until after they had occurred. My knowledge came after the fact."

Dantzler was skeptical, saying, "I'm not sure I believe that, Anna. But in fairness to you, I will wait until I hear all the details before I render a judgment on the truthfulness of those statements."

"But I have no reason to lie," Anna said.

"Great," Dantzler said. Then: "We have much ground to cover, Anna, so what I want to do is take the deaths in chronological order, beginning with the murder of your husband, Danny Tucker. And it was murder, wasn't it?"

Anna nodded and said, "This will sound insane, but all of this happened because of an overheard phone conversation. I was talking to Paul—it was late one afternoon in the clinic—and that's when I told him I was pregnant, and that the baby was his. I had no idea Dr. Wiseman was . . ."

"Hold up for a second," Dantzler said. "You and Paul Shelton were having an affair?"

"Oh, no, Detective, it was more than an affair," Anna corrected. "We are deeply in love. We've made plans to eventually get married."

"But those darnn spouses can be a pesky nuisance, can't they?" Milt said.

Dantzler said, "Go on with your story, Anna."

"Dr. Wiseman was standing at the copier while I was talking to Paul," Anna continued. "The following day Dr. Wiseman called me into his office and informed me that he heard the conversation. I could tell he was very upset that it was Paul rather than Danny who was the father. Dr. Wiseman was a highly moral, highly principled man. He told me that if I decided to terminate the pregnancy, he would perform the procedure, and that no one at the clinic would ever know. I told Dr. Wiseman that I needed time to think about it, which was a lie. I was thrilled to be having a baby, and doubly thrilled that Paul was the father."

"What happened next?" Dantzler asked.

"I talked to Paul and told him that I would start divorce proceedings," Anna answered. "I also told him that he should do the same thing, that if we were going to be together, we had to get divorces. But Paul told me to hold off until he had time to figure out some things. Three days later, Danny was dead."

"Paul Shelton murdered Danny? Is that what you're telling me?"

"No, Paul didn't do it himself. He paid someone else to do it."

"Who?"

"My brother."

"Your brother, Keith Davis, murdered Danny Tucker? Is that what you're saying?" Dantzler shook his head, then said, "How did you feel about that? Your brother killing your husband?"

"I was sad, of course," Anna said. "I didn't think it was necessary. Danny was a terrific guy, I liked him a lot, but I never loved him. I never should have married Danny. Therefore, I would have had no qualms about getting a divorce. Truth is, I wanted a divorce. So I didn't see any reason for Paul to have Danny killed."

"How did Keith manage to get the poison in Danny's coffee?" Dantzler said.

"Keith knew the Tuckers had a programmable coffeemaker. You

know the kind, where you put the coffee in the night before, set the time, and then in the morning the coffee is ready. Keith went to visit Danny the night before it happened. He knew about the coffeemaker, and he also knew Danny drank two cups of coffee every morning. At some point, Danny went out of the kitchen, leaving Keith alone. Keith put the poison in with the coffee. The next morning, when the coffee began to brew, the poison went right into the pot. Danny drank it and he died."

Dantzler scribbled some notes on a piece of paper, then said, "Did Keith ever actually tell you he poisoned Danny?"

"Yes, he did."

"Okay, let's move on to the clinic bombing and the death of Carly Shelton. We know Paul Shelton paid to have that done."

"Then you know more than I do," Anna said.

Milt said, "You're asking us to believe that you didn't know Paul Shelton blew up the Wiseman clinic and murdered Carly? You're stretching credibility with that one."

"I *suspected* that Paul ordered it, but I didn't know for sure. You see, I haven't seen or spoken to Paul since the day after Danny's funeral. I've been staying at the loft on Angliana, which Paul's company owns. But there has been no communication between us. None. That was Paul's idea. He said we needed to stay apart until things cleared up."

Anna took a sip of water, then continued. "I did not leave the apartment at any time before today. Not once. If I needed anything, I would contact Keith, and he would bring it to me."

"What did you think when you first heard about Carly Shelton?" Milt asked.

"Well, I pretty much knew Paul had it done," Anna said. "I mean, who else could it have been, right? And once again, I thought it was a mistake. There was no reason to have her killed. I begged Paul to get a divorce, but he said he couldn't, that if he did, Carly would take every penny he had. I told Paul I didn't care, I loved him, not his bank account. Besides, Paul makes serious money. Even if Carly took it all, Paul could easily have been back on solid financial footing in five years. But . . . he chose to go another route."

"Yeah, I'd say you're right about that," Milt said.

"Who did Paul pay to do destroy the clinic and kill Carly?" Anna said. "I know it couldn't have been Keith. He never would have agreed to do that."

"Are you familiar with Rufus Young or Oscar Young?" Dantzler asked.

Anna shook her head, said, "Never heard of either one."

Dantzler said, "Paul paid the Youngs twenty-five thousand for the clinic/Carly thing, and another twenty-five grand to kill Dr. Wiseman."

"When I heard about what happened to Dr. Wiseman—and I only learned about it from watching the TV news—I knew for sure Paul had it done. He didn't just hate Dr. Wiseman, he loathed him. But Paul didn't hate Dr. Wiseman for the reasons he normally gave, that Dr. Wiseman was a baby-killer and murderer. No, his hatred of Dr. Wiseman stemmed from jealousy, pure and simple. You see, Carly worshipped Dr. Wiseman. She had him up high on a pedestal, like he was a god or something. Well, Paul felt that if anyone was going to be on Carly's pedestal, it should be him. Paul has a high sense of self-worth—some might even call it arrogance—and in his mind, that top spot should be reserved for him and him alone. I also believe that deep in his suspicious heart, he suspected that Carly was having an affair with Dr. Wiseman, which, of course, was nonsense. Dr. Wiseman would never cheat on his wife."

"I appreciate you providing these details," Dantzler said. "You've been helpful and enlightening. And I do believe that you've basically been honest with us. However, there are a couple of facts you've given that don't ring true. Concerning them, I think you're lying."

"I have not lied to you," Anna protested. "Everything I've told you is the truth."

"No, it hasn't all been the truth." Dantzler looked at the piece of paper he had previously scribbled notes on. "How did Keith know about the Tucker's coffeemaker? And how did he know Danny always drank two cups of coffee every morning? How could Keith have possibly known those two things?"

"Maybe Keith had been to the Tucker's house before," Anna said. "Or Paul could have told him."

"That's bullshit, Anna, and we all know it. There is only one person who could have provided Keith with those details, and you are that person. Not Keith, not Paul . . . you, Anna. So, yes, I'll buy your story that you didn't have prior knowledge about the clinic bombing and the deaths of Carly Shelton and Dr. Rafael Wiseman. But both logic and the facts tell me that you were complicit in the death of Danny Tucker."

"You are dead wrong," Anna pleaded. "I am totally innocent."

"You'll need a damn good lawyer, then, if you expect a jury to believe you," Milt said.

Dantzler said, "Okay, Anna, now for the million-dollar question: If you loved Paul Shelton so much, if you planned to marry him and have his baby, why did you kill him?"

"Because he murdered my brother," Anna said without hesitation. "I loved Paul, but Keith is blood. He's my big brother, my best friend, my defender. As much as I loved Paul, I couldn't let him get away with what he did to Keith."

Dantzler and Milt exchanged glances, then Dantzler said, "You really believe Paul Shelton murdered your brother?"

"Of course."

"Why do you believe Paul killed Keith?" Milt said.

"To ensure silence," Anna answered. "Paul couldn't risk the chance that Keith might at some point slip up and tell someone what had happened. Knowing how Paul thinks, I'm also sure he was concerned that Keith might come back and demand money for silence. You know, blackmail Paul. That's why Paul felt the need to eliminate Keith. Get rid of the threat."

"Well, I've got some big news for you, Anna," Dantzler said. "Paul Shelton did not kill your brother, Keith Davis. He had no hand in it at all."

"Sure, he did," Anna said, trying to convince herself more than the detectives. "Who else could it have been?"

"Do you know how your brother was killed?"

"No, I've heard no details, other than he died in his apartment."

"Keith was stabbed repeatedly in his chest," Dantzler said. "It was an especially brutal killing. Do you really think Paul Shelton could take a knife and repeatedly plunge it into another man's chest? Remember, we're talking about a guy who pays others to do his dirty deeds. Do you think he's suddenly capable of turning into Norman Bates?"

"If Paul didn't kill Keith, who did?"

"Oscar Young, on orders from his father, Rufus. We suspect someone else may have been involved, but we don't know who that person might be, or if, indeed, there was another person. What we do know for sure is that it wasn't Paul Shelton."

"Paul didn't kill Keith?" Anna whispered, tears beginning to leak from her eyes. "Are you absolutely sure?"

"Yes. We have the knife Oscar used in the attack. The knife has Oscar's prints and Keith's blood on it. Oscar's pick-up truck was seen leaving the Brandywine Apartments. To top it off, Oscar confessed to the crime. We've cleared the book on this one."

"I can't believe it."

"You killed the wrong man, Anna," Dantzler said, closing the folder, "I can't say you killed an innocent man, but I can say the man you killed was not involved in the death of Keith Davis. So, Anna, the man you gunned down was innocent of the crime he died for. How's that for irony?"

"What is going to happen to me?" Anna asked. "Am I going to prison?"

Dantzler stood, said, "Yeah, Anna, you're going to prison. You shot a man in front of fifty bystanders, which translates into fifty witnesses against you in court. Plus, you've freely confessed to the crime. I'd say that even if Jesus Christ was your attorney, he couldn't get you off the hook."

"What about my baby? What will happen to it?"

"I can't answer that," Dantzler said. "But I would guess that once it's born, Child Services will take the baby and place it in a nice home with a good family."

Anna hung her head, then said, "You must really think I'm a horrible person."

"Here's what I think, Anna," Dantzler said. "Divorce would have been the smarter option."

CHAPTER THIRTY-THREE

After Anna was taken away to await her arraignment, Milt went to check the video of Anna's interview, to make sure there were no glitches. He spent fifteen minutes completing that task, then headed to a restaurant for a late lunch.

Dantzler left the War Room and went straight to Captain Bird's office to fill him in on how the interview had gone. Bird was pacing his office, cell phone pressed against his right ear, a scowl on his face. Dantzler had seen that look enough times in the past to know something important was happening on the Bird home front. Everyone knew Bird was a terrific leader, a superb administrator, an average investigator and an exemplary husband and father. They also knew that at home, with a wife and two daughters, he ranked fourth on the totem pole. Dantzler suspected that one of Bird's three superiors was giving him a hard time about something.

Bird shrugged and motioned for Dantzler to take the chair across from the desk. A moment later, Bird said, "I need to go now. Jack is in the office. We'll discuss this later, when I get home."

"Sounds serious, Rich," Dantzler said.

"Serious? This is a disaster." Bird plopped down in his chair and ran his hands through his hair. "Kelly has just been accepted into UCLA. She plans to go there and study Film."

"That's great news, Rich. You should be excited for her. And proud."

"UCLA? The last time I checked, that's in California," Bird said. "California. She'll be out there with all those crazies, those loonies, those hippies."

"California is actually a very progressive state, Rich. Home to a lot of thoughtful, liberal-minded people."

"If you're trying to make me feel better, you're not doing a very good job." Bird leaned forward and put his elbows on the desk. "Well, on the bright side, she wants to be a director, not an actor. Thank God, she has no interest in that heart-breaking side of the business. But . . . couldn't she have chosen a school a little closer to home?"

"You've gotta let her fly, Rich. You gotta let her chase her dreams."

"Yeah, I know, I know. And I will. But . . ." Bird let the thought die. Then he smiled and said, "I spoke to Jake Thomas. He watched the interview with Anna Davis. According to him, it went well."

"Actually, it went better than I expected," Dantzler said. "She answered most of my questions. And she did it without asking for an attorney."

"Things always go more smoothly for us when one of those shysters isn't in the room," Bird said. "You cleared five murder cases with one interview, yet you don't seem all that thrilled. Why the sour look?"

"The Rufus Young murder. That's bothering me."

"Oscar says Paul Shelton did it," Bird said. "Why not let it go at that?"

Dantzler stood, walked to the door and said, "Because Paul Shelton didn't do it."

* * *

Dantzler stopped by the break room, bought a can of Diet Pepsi, then returned to his office. For the next few minutes, he leafed through the statements of the bystanders who witnessed Anna Davis shoot Paul Shelton. Those statements, which had been collected by Eric and Jake, were so similar in content that they may as well have been one long document. With one exception, the witnesses gave a straightforward account of the incident, offering no unnecessary details or personal opinions. The one exception came from a witness who wrote that "the whole scene reminded me of when Jack Ruby stepped out of the crowd and gunned down Lee Harvey Oswald."

Satisfied that the documentation was solid, Dantzler turned his thoughts to the Rufus Young murder. He fired up his computer, pulled up the notes Eric had typed in and began reading them. That didn't take long; there simply wasn't much in the way of details. And it wasn't because Eric had done a poor job investigating the case. Eric never did a poor job doing anything. But he had very little to work with. There was Rufus's body and nothing else. No murder weapon, no footprints, no tire tracks, no witnesses . . . absolutely nothing. This was one of those cases that likely wouldn't be solved unless someone confessed.

Dantzler shut down the computer, leaned back and thought about what Oscar said. And what Captain Bird was willing to go along with. That Paul Shelton killed Rufus Young. Lay the blame on Shelton, close the book and forget about it. All Dantzler had to do was sign off on it, and it would all be over and done with.

But in order to do that, Dantzler would have to get past the very question he had posed to Anna Davis: Did he really believe Paul Shelton could take a knife and repeatedly plunge it into another man's chest?

No, he didn't believe it. And for one simple reason—it never happened.

"I'm missing something here," Dantzler said, as he left his office.

* * *

As soon as Dantzler and David Bloom entered The Long Branch Saloon, Bloom pointed to the big picture behind the bar and said, "That's Neil Raymond standing between John Wayne and James Arness." Then lowering his arm, he said, "And unless I'm badly mistaken, that's Buddy Raymond sitting at the end of the bar."

There were maybe twenty customers in the place, with the male/female ratio about evenly divided. A few of the patrons were at the bar, but most were sitting at tables or in booths. Since Dantzler had never been in The Long Branch before, he had no way of knowing if business was slow tonight, or if the place was really hopping. Not that he really cared much either way.

The waitress, a tall twenty-something with bright red hair and about five million freckles, finished removing empty beer bottles from one of the tables and came over to greet Dantzler and Bloom.

"Sit anywhere you like, gentlemen," she said, smiling. "My name is Miss Kitty. I'm the bartender. Tell me what you're drinking and I'll get it for you."

"We need to have a word with the owner," Dantzler said.

"That would be Buddy Raymond." Miss Kitty cocked her head to the right. "That's Buddy sitting over there."

"Thanks," Dantzler said.

When Buddy looked up and saw Dantzler and Bloom coming in his direction, he had the look of a man trying to match a face with a long-ago memory. It took a few seconds before recognition hit him. Once it did, he pointed at Bloom and smiled.

"Hey, I know you, don't I?" Buddy said. "You're the shrink who tried to get inside my head when I was a kid. Am I right?"

"I plead guilty," Bloom said.

"You didn't learn much, did you, Doc?" Buddy said.

"You didn't stick around long enough for me to learn anything," Bloom said. "If I recall correctly, you only came to two sessions."

"I don't believe in shrinks. If you have a problem, work it out yourself. Don't go whining to someone else. That's the coward's way."

"And you're no coward, right?" Bloom said.

"You got that right." Buddy nodded at Dantzler. "Are you also a shrink?"

"Homicide detective," Dantzler said.

"The way you say that, I can't tell if you're trying to impress me or scare me," Buddy said. "Doesn't really matter, because I'm neither impressed nor scared."

"I wasn't trying to do either one," Dantzler said. "I was simply answering your question."

Buddy grinned, said, "How about a drink, fellas? On the house."

"Maybe later," Dantzler said. "But first I would like to ask you a few questions."

"About what?" Buddy said, still grinning.

"Do you have some place where we can talk?" Dantzler said. "Some place a little quieter, more private?"

"What questions do you want to ask me?"

"Do you have another place to talk, or not?"

"What if I said no, Detective?" Buddy said. "What if I said I didn't want to answer any of your questions? What would you think about that?"

"Well, Buddy, to be perfectly honest with you, I wouldn't give it much thought at all. Dr. Bloom and I would leave. Maybe have a drink before we left, maybe not."

"Yeah, and while you're walking out, you're thinking to yourself, well, he refused to answer my questions, so he must be guilty. I know how you cops think."

"You an expert on law enforcement officers, are you?"

"Okay, sure, you have questions, I'll answer them." Buddy hopped off his stool. "My office is down this hallway. Follow me."

Buddy's office was only large enough to accommodate two chairs. He took the one behind his desk, Dantzler and Bloom chose to remain standing. Buddy locked his hands behind his head, leaned back, put his feet on the table and smiled.

"Sorry for the cramped quarters," he said. "Rarely are there ever more than two people in here at the same time."

"Not a problem," Dantzler said.

"Okay, then, fire away with your questions, Detective," Buddy said.

"Did you hear what happened to your old pal, Rufus Young?" Dantzler asked.

"I heard he met with a rather grisly demise," Buddy said. "A real shame, too, him leaving behind a wife and a whole flock of kids. Who's going to take care of them now? Tragic."

"When was the last time you saw Rufus?"

"Oh, five or six days ago. He dropped in to say hello. You have to understand, Detective. We didn't see each other nearly as much as when we were younger. Back then, we spent a lot of time together. But Rufus sold some property a few years back, which made him a very wealthy man. When that happened, he moved up several notches ahead of me on the tax scale. Since then, we haven't been as close as we once were."

"Did you hear how he died?" Dantzler asked.

"Only what I read in the newspaper. His killer used a knife, if I'm not mistaken. Ouch, that had to hurt."

"Do you own any knives, Buddy?"

"Come on, Detective, I run a bar. You know I have knives here. Knives are needed to slice lemons and limes. Open boxes and crates. If you wish to see them, ask Miss Kitty. She'll gladly show them to you."

"What about at your house?"

"Yeah, I have a few knives," Buddy said. "Dull as hell, because I rarely use them. If you want to check them out, come by my house and have a look."

"No hunting knives or switchblades?"

"No, Detective, I'm not a hunter. If I want to consume meat, I'll go to McDonald's or The Chop House."

"Can you account for your whereabouts three nights ago, say, between midnight and three a.m.?" Dantzler said.

"Detective, if you own a bar, and if you are actively involved in the operation of that bar, then your world revolves around two places—the bar and your house. That's where I spend ninety-nine percent of my time. So on the morning you are asking about, I was either here or at home. The bar closes at one. I usually stick around for thirty to forty-five minutes to get some things taken care of, and then I head for my house. That's my standard routine."

"Do you have security cameras here?"

"We do. And you are more than welcome to pull the tapes and look at the video."

Dantzler said, "Do you know Paul Shelton?"

Buddy shook his head, said, "Isn't he the poor sap who was gunned down in front of police headquarters?"

"Yes."

"Sounds to me like you need to do a better job protecting your prisoners, Detective."

"I repeat—did you know Paul Shelton?"

"I know about him only from what I read in the papers and saw on TV. I never met the man."

"What about Oscar Young? Do you know him?"

"Since the day he came into this world."

What Dantzler said next was an outright lie. But in his experience, a lie could sometimes trick the truth from a guilty suspect. It was a ploy that had worked for him in the past. No reason not to try it now.

"Oscar says you killed his father, Rufus. He also says you paid him to kill Keith Davis."

Buddy smiled and shook his head, said, "Detective, we both know that's not even close to being true. Oscar didn't say any such thing, because it never happened. I did not kill anyone, or pay to have anyone killed. And let me assure you that if I had killed someone, Oscar Young would be the last person in the world to know about it. The kid's a blockhead and a dunce. So he didn't tell you anything about me. Furthermore, Detective, if he had told you, and even if you only halfway believed him, we would be having this conversation in your office, not mine. And I would be wearing handcuffs. It was a nice play on your part, but it was doomed to fail. You see, Detective. When you plant the seed of truth in a pile of manure, it will never flourish."

"Jesus, Buddy, that's the best line I've ever heard in an interview," Dantzler said. "Sounds like something straight out of the Old Testament. You should be a poet."

"Nah, that's harder than running a bar. Less profitable, too, I would imagine."

"One more thing," Dantzler said. "We recently learned that Paul Shelton sold some stocks and liquidated a few of his assets. Came to a grand total of two million dollars. You wouldn't happen to know anything about that, would you?"

"Detective, I didn't know Paul Shelton, so how could I know about his money? But I'll tell you this: If I did have two mil, I wouldn't be running a second-rate bar. I'd be sitting on the beach, drinking Wild Turkey and listening to Alan Jackson."

"So if I get all energetic and check your phone records and e-mails, I'm not going to find any communication between you and Paul Shelton, right?"

"If you're all on fire with excess energy, I say go for it. You won't find anything."

Dantzler edged toward the door, said, "Thanks for your time, Buddy."

"My pleasure, Detective. Come back anytime."

"I have a feeling we might run into each other again sometime down the road."

"I eagerly await that day," Buddy said, smiling. "You and the Doc have a drink before you leave. Hell, have as many as you can handle. Tell Miss Kitty I said they are on the house."

"Some other time," Dantzler said, as he and Bloom walked out of the office.

Outside the bar, Bloom said, "You are aware that he lied to you. In fact, I'd say ninety percent of what he said was not true. He is, as the Yiddish would say, a classic *ligner*."

"Yeah, I know. The bastard murdered Rufus Young, and I don't have a shred of evidence to prove it. He's gonna walk."

"It's like I told you, Jack. He's an egg that won't crack."

"Damn, I hate to watch a murderer go free," Dantzler said, once they were in his car. "It drives me bonkers."

"Maybe you need to see a first-class shrink," Bloom said, knowing what Dantzler's response would be.

"I would. But there's one major problem: I don't know a first-class shrink."

CHAPTER THIRTY-FOUR

It was Sean Montgomery's idea to have Milt's farewell party in McCarthy's Irish Bar. Sean was a former homicide cop who quit the force, went back to law school, and was now considered one of the top defense attorneys in town. He had, in Dantzler's words, "traded catching the bad guys for defending them." Despite having gone over to "the outlaw's side," Sean was one of Dantzler's closest friends, and one of the few people Dantzler trusted completely.

As for Dantzler, being involved in setting up Milt's party was not a top priority. With Laurie back in town after nearly a month's absence, all of his attention was focused on her. The two of them spent the weekend at his house, making up for lost time.

The night of the party would have been the ideal time for Lexington's criminal element to come out of hiding. Virtually every law enforcement officer, past and present, was on hand to celebrate Milt's retirement after almost forty years on duty. Some of the older guys had worked with Milt as far back as the mid-seventies, not long after he joined the force following his return from Vietnam.

Among those in attendance was Charlie Bolton, the legendary cop who had been on the force more than a decade *before* Milt came on board. Everyone, including Dantzler, worshipped at the altar of

Charlie Bolton. He was accorded a level of esteem given to only the chosen few.

Dantzler had taken enough time away from Laurie to give a call to Jenny Saunders and Renee Connelly, and to invite them to the party. Being prime-time revelers who never shied away from alcohol, they quickly agreed to join the fun.

An hour into the party, things turned semi-serious for a few minutes, as each person offered a tall tale, an anecdote or an outright lie that related in some way to Milt. In truth, it was more celebrity roast than anything. Milt, for his part, took it all in stride, mostly laughing, while occasionally fighting back tears. Only twice did he flip a bird to the person speaking.

When the final speaker, Captain Bird, concluded his remarks, Milt stepped up front and center, and said, "You're all a bunch of scoundrels, reprobates and rapscallions." Turning toward Laurie, Jenny and Renee, he said, "And hussies." Then: "And I'm proud to include myself among such a sorry group as this. Except for you, Charlie. We all know you're Saint Charles."

With that, a chorus of "Saint Charles, Saint Charles" rang out, causing Charlie to simply smile and nod, as if to say, "Yeah, you're right."

Peter, a native of County Waterford and one of the bar's co-owners, presented Milt with a bottle of Jameson and a McCarthy's T-shirt. Then in an act of extreme generosity, Peter announced that the next round was on the house. Jenny and Renee were the first to get their free refill.

As most of the crowd eased toward the bar, Dantzler went out the back door to the open-air patio and took a seat. With the evening darkness in full splendor, he sat there alone, his thoughts several galaxies removed from the jubilation taking place just a few feet away. All he could think about now was unfinished business.

Several minutes later, Sean Montgomery walked through the back door, a pint of Guinness in each hand. He handed one to Dantzler, then took the chair across from him.

After taking a drink, Sean said, "You look more like a man about to have a root canal than a man who's supposed to be having some fun. That's some serious look on that mug of yours."

"I have an itch that I can't figure out how to scratch," Dantzler said.

"Buddy Raymond," Sean said, taking another drink. "I know. Bloom told me all about it."

"Yeah, well, Bloom sometimes talks too much."

"Only among friends." Sean set his glass on the barrel that served as a table, then said, "Look, Jack, we both know how this will eventually play out. Buddy will tell someone, who will tell someone else, who will tell still yet another person, until somewhere down the line, one of those bozos lets the cat out of the bag and Buddy goes down for it. Or the other scenario is, Buddy commits another crime, only this time he's not so careful and meticulous, he leaves behind some incriminating evidence and you nail him. In the end, when all is said and done, you win. Just keep in mind what that oft-quoted American philosopher, Lawrence Peter Berra, famously said: 'It ain't over, till it's over.'"

"That's a pep talk worthy of Vince Lombardi, Sean. Throwing Yogi in was an especially nice touch. But in this case, I'm not so sure either of your scenarios will come to fruition. Buddy Raymond is no dummy. He's no talker, either. He'll keep what he's done to himself. Another thing: I'm convinced that somehow, someway, he got two million dollars from Paul Shelton. If I'm right, then Buddy has so much money he doesn't need to commit another crime. He's gonna beat us."

"Come on, Ace," Sean said, standing. "Let's forget about the Buddy Raymonds of the world and get back inside. We need to celebrate a great cop's career rather than obsess about a worthless scumbag."

"He may have two million dollars, Sean," Dantzler said, chuckling. "He's not exactly worthless."

"Okay, so he's got some money. That only means he's a rich scumbag."

Back inside, Dantzler got a hug from Laurie, then went over to where Charlie Bolton and Captain Bird were talking.

"Rich just informed me that Milt's not the only detective you're losing," Charlie said. "He says Scott is joining the FBI."

"Yeah, he has two more weeks with us, then he's gone," Dantzler said. "It's what he wants, so I'm happy for him."

"Taking two hits at the same time can translate into a manpower shortage," Charlie said. "I hope you don't think I'm coming out of retirement."

"Relax, Charlie, you can continue your on-going battle with the fish. We're getting Jake Thomas full-time. And trust me, Charlie, in a one-for-two swap, if the one is Jake, you don't lose a thing. He's a terrific cop."

Charlie said, "You two clowns do realize that you're gonna lose Dunn at some point. Not to the FBI; she'll go to Homeland Security or the Justice Department. But sooner or later, you'll be replacing her."

"When you retired, Charlie, we lost you," Bird said. "As great as you were, the world continued to spin. It'll keep spinning if and when Laurie decides to leave."

"Don't let him kid you, Charlie," Dantzler said, walking away. "The world doesn't spin nearly as smoothly as it did when you were around."

Dantzler saw Jenny Saunders beckon him to come over. Jenny and Renee were sitting in the booth by the front window.

"I had no idea law enforcement officials were such good partiers," Jenny said.

"Protect, Serve and Drink—it's in our DNA," Dantzler said.

"Well, I must say, Renee and I are very impressed. We need to hang out with you guys more often."

"The welcome mat is always out for you two."

Jenny said, "Did you know that the clinic is up and running? Well, for the time being it's up and running on a smaller scale. We're currently working out of a suite of offices on Perimeter Drive. But the new building is expected to be completely finished in about three weeks. Then it's back to business as usual. I can't wait."

"I spoke with Sally Wiseman yesterday," Dantzler said. "She told me things were speeding along at a good pace. That's great news. I'm sure Dr. Wiseman would be pleased."

"How is Anna holding up?" Jenny asked. "Given the future she's facing, I'm sure she's terrified."

"All I know is that she was denied bail, so she'll be locked up until her trial," Dantzler said. "I did hear that she hired Susan Bradley as her defense attorney."

"Susan is supposed to be an excellent attorney."

"She'd better be," Dantzler said, adding, "Listen, you guys stick around as long as you want. Have fun."

When Dantzler walked away, Jenny motioned for Laurie. "Detective Dunn . . ."

"Please, call me Laurie. There are no cops here tonight. Only sinners."

"Okay, Laurie, one question," Jenny said. "How serious is it between you and Detective Dantzler?"

Laurie laughed. "With him, who can ever know?"

"Well, just for the record. Renee and I have both agreed that if we ever switch teams and go over to the heterosexual side, we're going after that man."

Laurie smiled and said, "You could do a lot worse."

ACKNOWLEDGMENTS

Thanks to those friends who have stuck with me and encouraged me throughout the writing of six novels. This special group includes Julie Watson, Denny Slinker, Suzanne Slinker, Christina Young, Scott Boggs, Chris Boggs, Jimmie Nell Jenkins, Grant Sparks and my aunt Bobbie Watkins. A special thanks to my hunter-gatherer relatives Bobby Glenn Stevens, Cy Dossett and Dale Dossett for providing information and insight relating to archery, which I know nothing about. Many thanks to McCarthy's owners Roger O'Byrne, Peter Kiely and Edwyn Kiely for allowing a Scotsman to hang around and drink their Guinness. Thanks to Frank Hall, founder of Hydra Publications, for guiding my previous two novels through treacherous waters, and thanks to Tony Acree for taking the reins and continuing to run Hydra in a professional manner, And, of course, thanks to Marilyn Underwood, who reads everything first and isn't shy about letting me know when something stinks.

ABOUT THE AUTHOR

Tom Wallace is the award-winning author of seven other novels, including *The List, Gnosis, Heirs of Cain, What Matters Blood, The Poker Game, Murder by Suicide* and *The Devil's Racket*.

Tom is also the author of five sports-related books, including the highly successful *Kentucky Basketball Encyclopedia*. He earned his B.A. in journalism in 1982 from Western Kentucky University, then became sports editor for the Henderson *Gleaner*, where he was twice honored by The Kentucky Press Association for writing the best sports story in the state. After leaving the *Gleaner*, he became editor for Cawood Ledford Productions in Lexington.

He is an active member of Mystery Writers of America and The Author's Guild. Tom, a Vietnam veteran, currently lives in Lexington, Kentucky.